HER LAST WORDS

Jo Barney

Penner
PUBLISHING

Los Angeles, California

This edition published by
Penner Publishing
Post Office Box 57914
Los Angeles, California 91413

www.pennerpublishing.com

Copyright © 2011, 2013, 2015 by Jo Barney

ISBN 13: 978-1-940811-40-6
eISBN 13: 978-1-940811-39-0

Cover Designer: Christa Holland, Paper & Sage Designs

For my friends, the old ones, from years ago, lives ago. Could we ever have imagined this day, this world, in which we find ourselves wandering?

ALSO BY JO BARNEY

Never Too Late
The Runaway

1

**Early Monday Morning: Flotsam
Lucius**

"My God," Lucius says, as close to praying as he has been in years. "We're on Venus." Monoliths rise ahead of him like black specters, their crags and angles cutting through the mist, jutting towards the high, bluing sky.

The others, silent, have dropped their handholds on the rope. Lucius bends to loop it over his arm, and as he does, he sees the man in the slicker, his bag over his shoulder, kneeling, rising, waving at them.

"That guy's found something. Let's go."

He runs, slogs, really, his boots heavy with water. The women in their sneakers move faster, their arms reaching out to the dark figure and whatever lay at the foot of the rock he's leaning against. Lucius cannot tell if it is the gulls or the women crying out.

Then they drop to their knees, a huddle of sorrow. They don't look up as Lucius and the two firemen come up behind them. The mussel gatherer, his empty bag hanging from one grimy hand, a walking stick in the other, stands to one side, his eyes red and wild-looking, his sou'wester pulled down to his eyebrows. Hanks of wet, black hair drag over his eyes, drain down his cheeks like tears.

Madge Slocum lies wedged under an overhang, her face gray. Sand seeps from her mouth. A strand of seaweed wraps her out-flung hand like a bracelet, her bare feet seem ready to run, the toes spread, arched. An arm folds over her body, across a pack strapped to her waist. Several mussels have fallen from the pack and nestle at her throat.

"She came here for mussels," Lou cries. "For us." The women reach for her. They grapple with the iron until it falls, and they pull it away from her. Their fingers close her eyes, brush grit away from her lips. They remove the pack and empty it of its black shells. Joan crouches, takes a hand, massages it as if to warm it. Jackie closes the torn jacket, covers the white skin under it.

The ocean ripples as it awakens. White-edged swirls send the little birds skittering. Lucius motions to the men, and they consider how to this. Then the young one, Steve, bends and picks her up. "Over my shoulder," he says, and the others help him drape Madge across his back. He flexes his neck against the cold wet seeping over his collar, down his spine.

As they round the point, Lucius manages one last look back into the cove. Mars, not Venus, he thinks. A fucking Mars. Red now, a sliver of sun making its way through the clouds. He should come back, when things die down, when he can think of what he's looking at, not like now, when what just popped into his head is where the hell did that mussel guy go?

"Almost there," he hears someone call. He doesn't look up, just reaches for Steve's belt as he feels him go down, yanks him up, hears him groan.

"Doin' great," Lucius tells him. One of Madge's arms has slipped out of Steve's grasp, hangs down the slick back of her bearer, swings against Lucius' wrist, as if she's trying to get his attention.

2

Friday, June, 2004: Storm Warnings
Lou

On the day the four of them are to come together at
Madge's beach house, Lou pulls her car into an empty parking pad at the end of the gravel driveway. She's not surprised she is the first to arrive. Joan is driving north from
San Francisco, and Jackie is always late to everything. But
where is Madge's car?

She opens the car door, steps out into a gentle breath of
ocean air. For the past thirty miles her body has felt as if
she were wearing too many layers, heavy, moist. When she
left the cabin on the mountain that morning, the thermome-
ter needle had pointed at 36 degrees. Dropping down into
the valley, heading to the coast, the balmy air filling the car
sent a wave of queasiness through her and she had to unzip
her parka to breathe.

The nausea wasn't only about a jacket and a change of barometer. Whenever she leaves her forest, descends to the flats, pokes her way around the tangles of towns that grow like lichen along snow-fed streams and rivers, she becomes anxious, almost fearful. The clumps of people, the throb of voices, the thrusting groans of passing cars collide with the fragile sense of peace her new life has brought her.

No crowds here at this cabin, though, only four good friends. Taking a deep breath, she feels the heaviness lift. She pulls her duffle from the back seat and steps toward the small cedar-shingled house. The wild fuchsias along the path have been recently trimmed; splashes of red curl under the bushes like snips of velvet. Madge has been busy getting the place ready for their old lady slumber party, this one almost fifty years after they first met at the dorm cookie shine.

Did any one of them ever believe a day would come when they spent their time together remembering instead of dreaming? Lou's hand brushes against a gathering of lantern blossoms and she wonders how they'd do on the mountain. She must remember to take a cutting or two when she leaves for home.

Then the blue door opens and a smiling Madge steps out, holding out her arms to her. "Lou?" she calls. Lou steps into her friend's hug. They and the duffle bump through the door and into the hallway. Over Madge's shoulder Lou gets a glimpse of green shimmer at the end of the room, the Pacific, not so pacific at the moment, white froth lapping at the sand under the cabin.

They make their way through the open kitchen. A jagged row of yellow Post-its flutter on cabinet doors like resting butterflies.

"What's all this?" Lou asks. "Another decorating fad I've missed?"

Madge waves a dismissing hand and moves on. "I'm cooking dinner," she says as if that explains everything. "Come sit down. Don't worry about your bag. I want to hear how your garden's growing."

They talk. Madge's hair is short and brown, and she pats at the wayward tendrils over her ears just as she did years ago. She nods at Lou's description of her mountain house's newest additions, two wild rhododendrons nestled against the wall of logs and the stone chimney and she hesitates when Lou asks her about her writing. "Going fine," she says.

But Lou sees that something's not fine with Madge. As they talk, her bright gaze lands on Lou for a moment then casts about as if she has lost something, a gesture catches in mid-sway, thoughts break in half.

"Are you all right?"

Madge doesn't answer. Instead she checks her watch, rises, and goes into the kitchen. She runs a finger down a yellow note. "Good," she says. "Glass of wine?"

She is opening the bottle when the blue door swings open and Jackie swoops into the house. "Hey, let it begin," she calls. "I'm here!"

Lou looks up and she wonders for an instant at the sense of relief she feels as she moves into Jackie's swirl of arms and bags and hugs her. Behind her Madge repeats softly, "Jackie," and then louder, "Welcome! How was the drive?"

Jackie, still tall at sixty-six, looks as if she is about to pull off her sweats and run a marathon. Instead she drops the two suitcases she's carrying and reaches for Madge. "Same as usual, RV's and trucks and me on a two-lane road to your little village. How can you stand it?"

"Don't drive much anymore." Madge pokes a finger into the black curls bouncing above her as they touch cheeks. "God, I'm still envious of your hair, even in my old age."

"I've always liked yours too."

"No, you didn't. The first time I cut it you said I looked like a boy."

"I've always liked boys, also." Jackie grins at Lou and adds, "And if mine were silver like yours, I'd save a fortune at Ardella's salon."

Lou can't remember the last time she went to a beauty parlor. Or whatever they're called these days. When it needs it, Susan cuts her white hair near the compost pile and the birds make nests of the trimmings.

The three of them move to the window and look out across the ocean. Everyone who enters this beach house does this, following a worn path in the carpet, eyes searching the horizon. Especially on a cloud-clear day like today.

"Japan, maybe?" Lou murmurs.

Madge apparently is still thinking about hair. "I haven't had the courage to find out what color mine really is. I've had to look young and vital on my book covers. My agent has hinted at even more drastic alterations." She faces her two friends and pulls at the skin under her ears. "What do you think?"

They go to the old sofa, set down their glasses.

"Better wait to ask Joan. She's the one with the new neck," Lou answers. A bit harsh, she scolds herself. When will she learn to burst the bubble of jealousy that pops to the surface whenever she hears Joan's name? Should have outgrown it forty or fifty years ago.

Madge must think so too. She points a finger at the room the two women will be sharing. "Want to unpack?" A sticky note with their names on it wavers on the door.

After Lou and Jackie line up their suitcases next to the bed, they go back to the living room. Lou pushes into a corner of the sofa, her legs tucked under her, Madge settles into the opposite corner, and Jackie falls into one of the large armchairs at the side of the stone fireplace.

Lou has always admired this room, its large windows with the ocean churning behind them, the knotty pine walls aged to a warm orange, several blue seascapes at either side of the couch, in fall-back positions in case fog blocks out the real thing outside. She could easily go to sleep right now, her eyelids heavy in the midst of a sip of merlot and the soft laughter in the story Jackie is telling Madge.

Except she sees that Madge is fiddling with her hair again, smiling vague twitches, nodding every so often to keep Jackie going.

Madge is not Madge, the friend Lou's known for almost fifty years, the Madge who would listen so carefully she could repeat what you said years later, with whom your secrets were safe and your faults accepted. That familiar woman is somewhere else. This Madge's gaze wavers, her easy flow of words are now spurts of escaping thoughts. Her lips, once loose and ready for whatever came next, are tight, as if she is afraid of what will leak out if she isn't careful.

Jackie doesn't seem to notice as she goes on in her usual scattered way about roads and her decision to keep her hair dark except at the temples and her daughter's recent visit and her hope for a low tide and finding a Japanese glass float in the morning.

Then, headscarf around her neck, her blondeness unruffled despite her two-day drive, Joan breezes through the open door. She still looks good, Lou observes. Not just the new neck. She glows as always with her California tan and her perfect lips and her smooth yellow hair. And she's held up a lot better than the rest of the foursome, boobs and waistband still in the right places. Lou takes a last sip at her wine and stands to greet California girl. *Time to grow up,* she tells herself. *Time to let it go. If not now, when?*

They open another bottle, this time from Joan's cellar. A half hour later, Madge looks at her watch, goes to the kitchen and slides a casserole, lasagna Lou guesses, into the oven. She watches as Madge squints through the reading part of her glasses at several notes lined up on the cabinet.

"Any munchies?" Joan has joined Madge behind the island in the kitchen. "I haven't eaten a thing since breakfast and I need food if I'm going to drink more wine, which I am." She pushes aside cartons and bags and pulls out a package of cheese. "What happened to the idea of eating out most nights? You have enough stuff here to feed us for a week." She is reaching for a knife when she sees a list held by a magnet to the side of the refrigerator. "Menus? Damn, I'm cooking enchiladas on Monday? Appropriate since I'm the only one from California. Maybe the recipe is on the can."

"It is." Madge is standing next to Joan; her lips mouth words as she reads from a label. "Right here."

Joan stops slicing into the block of cheese and looks at Madge. "Can I help?" she asks. In the living room Lou hears the answer, a whisper floating over the muffled groans of the sinking tide outside.

"Yes, you can, but later."

Lou feels her jaw tighten and sends her gaze out over the quiet sea. What will it take for her to accept Joan's perfection—and even more painful, her closeness to Madge?

It has always been that way, Madge and Joan, hasn't it? She straightens her back, tells herself to stop slogging like a lost soul along this trail to nowhere. She glances at the two women in the kitchen, at Jackie by her side. *No. I'm wrong.* Madge is good friend to all three of the women in this room. She has brought them together this weekend and other weekends in the past. Because of her, after all these years they still think of themselves as sisters, like they did in the smoking room of the Gamma Psi house

From the kitchen, Madge turns to Lou and Jackie and calls, "Let's go down to the beach. The tide is out. Dinner will be ready in an hour."

The four of them walk down to the water's edge, follow meandering curves of wavelets to the south, the sand firm under their feet. Seagulls sail overhead searching for what the tide has left behind, and the women also search, for luminescent agates, prizes to be tucked into pockets and lined up on sunny windowsills in their other lives. The world is green, blue, and then pink with sunset, the ocean almost silent as it calms, readies itself for its return journey to the rocky arms that reach out for it.

The casserole is indeed lasagna, from Costco, Madge confesses, and smelling of herbs and cheese and tomatoes. By the end of the meal, Lou can see that they all know something's wrong with Madge, even Jackie who has stopped talking and is shooting anxious frowns at her and Joan.

After dinner, they clear the table and take thimbles of brandy to the couch and chairs facing the warmth of the fireplace.

"Kind of like the solarium." Madge's voice, wistful, young, surprises Lou. *Solarium.* Until today, Lou hasn't thought of that midnight room in a long time. Madge sets her glass on the chest that serves as a coffee table. Her hand is shaking, a drop of brandy spills onto her finger and she licks it off. "Only we don't smoke anymore."

For a moment, no one speaks. Perhaps, Lou thinks, that old room is lost in a fog of years. No, she can still smell it, hear its voices. The others can also. Jackie sits straighter, opens her mouth, for once doesn't speak. Joan's blue eyes narrow with remembering.

Then the question fills the quiet room, brushing against lips, raising the hairs on Lou's arms. Joan places her drink next to Madge's and asks it. "What's going on, Madge?"

Madge breathes deeply, her lips trembling.

3

Saturday Morning: Cloud Cover
Jackie

Unlike last night, the room warm with talk and wine, the
cabin this morning is cold. Jackie glances at the fireplace,
sees one thin curl of smoke rising from the remains of papers
crumpled at the edges of the burned logs and wonders if she
should start a fire. As she bends to lay out the kindling, Lou
passes by, whispers, "Don't. Let Madge's pages burn." Jackie feels a hand on her arm. "Let's go for a walk, the way
Madge planned." Lou's eyes are red, puffy with tears, and
will be for a long time, Jackie thinks. Must be a relief, to be

able to cry when you need to. Jackie yells at these sad moments, usually, dry grit rattling her head, body, thoughts. She leaves the smoldering papers and follows Lou out the door.

Ten steps down the path she hears Joan call at them to wait. In a moment, she catches up, her mouth set in its determined way. "We need to look for the walking stick, like Madge said. And we need to breathe in the morning air to get ready for this day."

They are at the front of the dune when Lou stops. "Why aren't you crying? Either of you? She's gone. We all heard her walk away from us this morning." Lou takes a Kleenex out of her pocket, wipes it across her cheeks. "You, especially, Joan. Maybe her best friend."

Jackie doesn't want to defend her tearlessness. She is trying to figure it out herself, but she especially doesn't like Lou's comment about best friend. Madge doesn't have best friends, not that Jackie has ever noticed, not like Joan and even Lou sometimes, leaving her out of their secrets—back in college and even now. Especially Joan. "I don't cry easy," she says. "Doesn't mean I'm not sad. And I'm still confused. I didn't want to do this, you remember." She isn't sure Lou is listening, and Joan moves on ahead of the other two and calls, "We need to look for the damn walking stick. I will cry later." They don't talk, just scan the wet beach in front of them until Lou points, runs to the stick partly buried in the swoosh of a sandy wave.

Once they get back to the cabin, they place the stick on the mantel and of coffee in front of the fire. Jackie whisks the old ashes into the blaze she's building. Then they wipe tears from cheeks, Lou's, of course, and Joan, and even Jackie, as if the others' sadness is contagious. They sit without speaking, unable to look at each other, until Lou says, "I'm empty," and reaches down to capture the tissues under her feet.

"I'm taking a shower. Then we'll have to..." Joan sinks back into her chair her eyes shut. "Damn. I need a little more time."

Jackie sniffs back the snot that won't stop running. "What I don't get," she manages to say after a moment, gurgling a little, "is why she involved us."

Lou's not empty yet, still blowing, sighing. *Where does all that fluid come from?* Jackie wonders. Some mechanism in the body that is dormant until the finger of fate pushes its button? She herself feels sad but now a backwash of anger inside her is also rising. She needs a drink to force it to retreat, to keep unwelcome thoughts at bay. About death. Not just about her own death, but the nearly completed death of a man she loved and still loves, a man beyond decisions. She stands up, picks up her coffee cup, heads to the kitchen.

Joan, watching her, says "Not yet, Jackie. We have work to do."

"Shit, Joan. Who made you Mistress of the Universe?" but Jackie knows Joan has always been Mistress. Maybe that's part of her anger. She's gotten into this mess mostly because she didn't want to disappoint a friend, and that friend is not here. She's not sure where she stands with the two women in this room. And she's not going to take Joan's bossiness any more. She reaches for the kitchen phone, dials a number written on a list of emergency contacts Madge taped next to it.

Saturday Noon: Slack Water
Lucius

The sheriff is not pleased. It is Saturday, finally spring, a month past flood season, the golf course has dried out, and he has a tee time in forty minutes. Liz, the teenaged girl who answers the off-hours phones for the office, a local who is pretty good at the job except for her pronouns which are indigenous to this slip of Pacific coastline, calls to say a message has just come in. "Something about a cane left on the beach. Some woman missing. The lady was kind of excited and I couldn't understand her. Me and my mom thought you should know?"

Lucius Baker took the job of sheriff in Greensprings as a soft landing after his flight from twenty-five years on a city police force and three disappointing marriages. The town, just a few miles inland from the ocean, has a population of three thousand people and at least twice as many cows standing motionless most of each day in the midst of vast green meadows, their noses pointed into the wind.

So far, in the year he's been at this job, Lucius has chased a number of rampant Holsteins down county roads, waded across flooded fields to rescue cats and goats from the roofs of outhouses, calmed fist fights in each of the two taverns on Main Street, and once he investigated a series of obscene phone calls thought to be coming from a beach house down the road. The cabin turned out to have neither electricity nor a phone. That file still lies on a corner of his desk, but since the calls have stopped, he isn't spending any more time on it, concentrating instead on his golf game at the local public golf course, formerly a pasture. Still a pasture, really, cow pies moldering under the rough green grass from which he should be teeing off at this moment.

He looks at his watch and dials the number.

5

Saturday Noon: Riprap
Joan

When the phone rings, Joan waves a hand at the others.
"Let me talk." She licks her lips, a nervous trait familiar to
the women stilling their own lips, and with a voice she manages to twang with tension, Joan tells the sheriff that when
the three friends woke up this morning, a fourth friend,
Madge Slocum, was gone. "On a walk, we thought, so we
went out to meet her on the beach. That's when we found
it, the walking stick, the one Madge uses going up and down

the road and to poke in the sand, lying there just above the tide line."

Joan looks at the other two to see how she is doing. Jackie is hunched in a wicker chair, drinking something clear, concentrating on slits of ice cubes threatening to inhibit her next swallow. Lou is walking around the kitchen plucking yellow sticky notes off the stove, the refrigerator, the microwave, and wadding them in her jeans pocket.

"We kept walking and reached the end of the bay and we didn't find her." So far, so good. Joan listens, uh-huhs a goodbye, hangs up the phone.

They decided last night that Joan would be their spokeswoman. Jackie, in a fit of anxiety, mislaid that decision in the tearful hours of the morning and took it upon herself to make the first call to the sheriff after which Joan told her to never pick up the phone again. Perhaps this second phone call has repaired the damage.

"He's coming by," Joan says. "After his golf game and dinner. He figures she just might be taking a time out from us."

"Shit." Jackie rouses herself and stands wobbling and slightly cross-eyed. Jiggling the ice cubes in her empty glass, she says, "I'm going to have trouble with this, Joan. It's against my belief system."

"Your belief system isn't your problem, friend. Go drink some coffee and get ready. We're in this together." Joan calms her voice, no need to get angry, adds, "Remember?"

She goes to the big window, looks out at the blueness spreading out to the horizon. A small dune rises in front of the cabin, its flowing grasses cushioning the rumble of the sea lying in a broad glistening streak beyond them. She will not give in to the sadness that is washing over her, sinking deep like a cold wave on sand. She sits down, opens a magazine, and forces herself to bring back a better day. Joan can still hear that sweet man's voice. For the few hours they were together, he never lifted his eyes from hers. Or so it seems now. She turns a page, then another.

From the kitchen Jackie yells over the clatter of ice cubes. "How long do we have to wait?"

"Patience is a virtue." She must have caught it from him, this urge to use adages to sum up things. When he did it, she laughed. No one is laughing now, though, in this anxious room. She watches as Lou wipes her eyes on the neck of her sweatshirt as she crunches yellow slips of paper. She reads out loud, "5:30, turn on the oven," and looks at Joan, and Joan nods.

Saturday Late Afternoon: Downdrift
Jackie

Slumped back against the sofa cushions, Jackie thinks about
the walk down the beach yesterday afternoon, when Madge
was with them, all of them grinning, an aura of warm sisterhood swirling around them. That's when she was sure she
would be able to let it out, tell the others what happened
and no one would say I told you so. They would marvel at
her finding the truth, finally. She's been looking for the
truth for a long time. That, of course, was before Madge
read her story last night, asked them to help, before Jackie

understood that her own story wasn't why they had come to the beach house, was not even very important.

She grimaces as she rubs the lumps of knuckles that used to be capable of gripping ski poles and parts of bodies when she was in college. It still pisses her off, this falling apart. In her head she's still the girl who got only one sympathy vote from the committee when she tried out for rally squad, she being about ten inches taller than all of the other girls, as tall as some the basketball players who needed to be cheered at and probably as good a guard as a couple of them, and who went on to become a champion snow ski bum.

Every weekend the Gamma Psi's housemother squinted at the forged note from Jackie's parents, put it her pocket, and sent her off to the mountain in a borrowed VW. She returned Sunday nights, sometimes with a trophy, always sucking breath mints as she sidled past Mrs. Troutman. Similar mints hide in a few pockets and purses today. For a good reason, Jackie tells herself, willing her knees to straighten, hold her upright. Right now, she needs to focus. She had agreed, finally, hadn't she? And the menu on the fridge says she is in charge of dinner.

"Madge said stir fry tonight," she calls out as she opens the refrigerator door. "I can handle that." Chopping the greens and marinating the sliced chicken, concentrating on keeping her fingers away from the serrated blade, quiets the vodka, scatters the anger, and she decides it's time to open some wine. Joan and Lou agree when she raises the bottle towards them.

A half hour later, their chopsticks poke into bowls of rice and bok choi, and the Gallo Sauvignon (not Jackie's choice but what did the mountain girl who brought it, know about wine?) edges closer to the bottom of the bottle. "So what now?" Jackie can't help saying out loud as she pushes her bowl away. She's still having a little trouble tracking.

"Like I said, Lucius will ask us to repeat what I've told him." Joan's fingers scoop up the last of her rice as Jackie watches in disbelief. California Girl wouldn't be doing that if she weren't annoyed at Jackie's tracking problem. Patience is a virtue, she would like to remind Joan.

"Lucius?" Lou's skinny elbows rest on the table and prop up her head up as if it is too heavy for her neck. Jackie has felt that sensation herself, sometimes from alcohol, sometimes from worry. Lou's heavy head would be in the second category.

"The sheriff. He asked me to call him by his first name. It's a small town thing, I suppose. He'll say he can't do anything until it's been twenty-four hours and she'll be officially missing." Joan sends her arched-eyebrow look at Jackie who is pouring the last inch of wine. "We need to not drink anymore," she says, as she licks a finger.

7

Saturday Early Evening: Lagoon
Lou

Lou forces her lips to move. "What, just think about it, what if Madge just left her walking stick, left it on the beach, and went somewhere, a B&B or somewhere. She could have. She wasn't really out of it, you know." Lou hopes there might be a smattering of truth in this idea, but a sudden wash of reality dampens the thought. Madge's goodbye had become gray ashes in this morning's warm fireplace.

"No," she says, as she picks up their dishes. "I suppose she did it, don't you think? Madge always did what she said she was going to do. She was good that way."

She glances around the kitchen. She's gotten them all, the Post-its Madge had pressed onto the cabinet and refrigerator doors to help herself get through yesterday. Tossing them into the fire will be like a ritual, a way of sending a part of Madge into the universe, along with, perhaps, a bit of the ache lodged deep inside herself, near her heart.

Joan has moved to the window again, looking for Japan, perhaps, and Lou wonders if she is feeling the same ache. Joan is opaque when it comes to revealing her feelings. She's doesn't share them, and she doesn't invite sharing from others. Her only response to the news of Lou's divorce five years ago was to tell her that her own divorce resulted in the solid earth heaving, new ground revealed, new growth promoted. At the time, her words didn't seem comforting. Perhaps now they are.

Jackie, back on the sofa, "I let the fire go down." She raises her glass to Lou, says, "While you're up, maybe?"

Lou makes her way through the huddle of fat armchairs to the fireplace, finds the same box of matches Madge must have used this morning. She reaches into her pockets, and in a moment, the Post-it wads flare up. She adds kindling and bark to keep the flames alive. A fire, even though the heat goes up the chimney to the seagulls hovering above, warms a person.

It's the same on the mountain, under the Doug firs. She and Susan always keep a fire going at dinnertime, even in the summer when the garden glows in purples and greens and yellows and they have worked themselves into a sweat beating back the wild stuff that lives miles beneath the fir needle turf. "It may be trying to tell us something, this soil," Lou said once. "Like, why fight nature?"

"Indeed," Susan had answered.

8

Saturday Evening: Undercurrent
Lucius

Through the open door, Lucius smells burning oak and
something Chinese. The kitchen, visible above a narrow divider wall, is to the left of the entry. Dishes are stacked in
the sink; an empty wine bottle stands alone on the counter.
They have just finished dinner, he guesses, maybe even saving a plate of leftovers for their missing friend. Two women
sit on a sofa at the ocean side of the house, under windows
looking down on the surf. The blonde who meets him at the
door points to an armchair in front of the stone fireplace.

"I'm Joan Costas. Please sit down." Her voice reminds him of warm cream. A thin, silver-haired woman on the sofa raises her head at him and then looks down at the hands folded in her lap. The woman sitting next to her pushes a wayward strand of black curly hair from her forehead and smiles a small hello.

Joan chooses a chair on the other side of the fire. "Is this too warm?" Without waiting for an answer, she gestures towards the others. "Lou Hanley." The thin woman looks in his direction. "And Jackie Clayton." The tentative smile dissolves. Something, fear, maybe, widens the Clayton woman's eyes, pulls her mouth into a straight line. "Hello, Sheriff," she says, the s's and f's slumping against each other.

Each looks to be in her sixties somewhere. The blond, white, and in Jackie's case, black, hair can't disguise the age of the rest of their bodies, their hands and necks freckled and dried by a sun worshipped fifty years earlier.

Lucius has become aware of such changes in himself lately when he squints into his shaving mirror. The brownish spot on his temple has widened, the hair over his ears is crosshatched with white. At fifty-nine, the ravages of time are setting in, around the eyes, especially.

He's maybe a decade younger than these women, but they still look pretty good, the blonde, Joan, especially. She probably has had some work done, of course, but who hasn't these days? Not Lou, her thin legs now crisscrossed in front of her, bare feet up on the cushions, her face, furrowed the way thin women's faces get after a while.

Then the one named Jackie, tall, his height if you count her wavy mane of hair, stands up and crosses the room. "I can't do this, Joan. This is too awful." She wiggles goodbye-fingers at him as she bumps through a doorway that Lucius guesses leads to the bedrooms.

Joan is silent until a door shuts somewhere. "Jackie's taking Madge's disappearance very hard, as we all are, and she's had a bit too much wine at dinner. She'll be all right as soon as Madge comes back. So will we all." She looks at Lou who is staring at her folded hands.

"Is this a habit of Madge's? Taking off?" Lucius would like to ask the same question about Jackie.

"No. That's not Madge. We have to believe she'll be back soon, don't we?" Lou nods, and Lucius wonders if the woman ever speaks.

"This is all we know at this point." Joan lifts a long walking stick from the mantel and hands it to him. "We found this on the beach. It's hers." The stick, carved and notched, its handle dark with oil, a scruffy leather thong dangling from one end, the other end blunted by uncounted plunges into sand and rock, has seen long use.

He rubs his fingers along the etched wood, across the notches marking its travels. "This is a very personal thing, this stick. Years old, I imagine." He directs his question to the silent Lou. "If she's gone off somewhere, would she leave it on the beach for just anyone to find?"

Lou uncurls, loosens her hands. "No. Madge wouldn't. It was at the tide line below the house." She points to a stretch of sea grass at the edge of the dune in front of the cabin. "In the wet sand."

"And no note, like where she was going or anything?"

Lou turns back to him, her eyes dark, unblinking. She shakes her head. "No."

"We haven't really looked." Joan places the stick back above the fireplace. "We keep thinking she'll show up. But we panicked a little when we realized she hadn't been here since early morning, and then we found the walking stick." She sits down in the chair next to him. "That's when we decided to call you."

"Her family?"

"We haven't contacted anyone yet. Her sons live on the East Coast. The man she lives with is traveling. Madge is a writer, spends most of her time in front of her computer in the city or here. This is her house, you know."

No, Lucius doesn't know and it doesn't make any difference, except that it probably means that the missing woman knows her way in the green hills that cup the village and isn't lost. He glances down at the notes Liz has given him. Madge Slocum. "What kind of books does she write?"

"Fiction. About women's lives, mostly, love, children, getting old. Her last book was reviewed by The New York

Times and sold quite well. She's working on another..." Joan pauses, runs the tip of her tongue over her upper lip... "I'm not sure what it's about."

The oak log has dissolved into graying coals. Lucius gets up, pulls the baseball cap from his pocket. "Well, we can't do anything until tomorrow. How about a picture?"

Lou hands him a book from the pile on the end table. Madge Slocum's photo fills the back cover. Dark hair, pale skin, wide eyes and a generous mouth that seems to be saying, "Life is Good." She looks about forty-five but so do most authors on their book covers, Lucius has noticed in the past. Even the males who write the thrillers he's addicted to. "I'll take the jacket. Probably won't need it, but just in case." As Joan follows him to the door, he asks her how they all know each other. He can't think of four friends he'd want to spend a lot of time with, stuck in a small house like this one. Women are different. After three wives he knows this for a fact.

Joan's milky voice seems to smile at his question, at him. "We went to college together, then went our separate ways, our families grew up, and when our husbands died or we divorced them, we got back together, every few years, to compare stories. This year it was Madge who sent the invitations to come here to her beach house. She seemed very excited to see us." As Lucius steps over the doorstep, she touches his arm, says, "That's why this is so upsetting."

He is surprised by the woman's gesture—intimate, unexpected. He wants to ease her mind. "Just keep a plate warm for her for when she shows up tonight."

9

Saturday Evening: Squall
Joan

"Jackie! Come out here!" Joan shrieks in a way she knows
Lucius could not have imagined possible after that little scene. By the time Jackie, already in her flannel pajamas, shuffles into the living room and sinks to a chair, Joan has
pulled herself together. "You can't do this again, Jackie. We
need to present a united front. The sheriff is important to
us. Do we have to drain the wine bottles?" At this threat,
Jackie shakes her head and says no, and both Lou and Joan

are relieved. At least Joan is. A few glasses of wine might be the only way they get through the next several days.

Lou holds out a corkscrew tied to a loop of yarn. "This will be a little hard to sleep on," she says, "but this is apparently my role here, sommelier." She slips the ungainly necklace over her head.

"There are always screw tops," Jackie says, but without conviction.

"And there are always screw ups. Don't even think of it." Joan's eyes burn with fatigue. Except for a couple of hours in the middle, she's been up since yesterday morning. Madge had needed to talk last night—a ramble through sixty years which Joan encouraged with throaty sounds and touches on a still shoulder. Madge confessed a short-lived affair with a poet long-dead, her anger at a husband who didn't trust her enough to tell her the truth, the fear that every book she'd written had been wrapped in. Joan listened. And she wondered what she would do with these secrets. Now, as she turns towards the bedroom she shared with Madge, she thinks about her friend's last words, and she realizes they were a precious goodbye gift, not to be shared yet, if ever.

However, old ladies don't do well without sleep. Not that she is an old lady yet, really. One has to lose a lot of herself to be an old lady. Joan can visualize one final thrust at winning before the losing starts happening. Arthritis in a thumb doesn't count. Nor does having to go through part of the alphabet to remember a word like—those little green things one puts on salmon, damn. She rubs her eyelids. A. B. C. Capers, of course. The caper brain cell destroyed by who knows what, white wine, probably. Not like Madge, though.

She undoes the top button of her jeans, takes a relieved breath. "Tomorrow we read Madge's stories about us. Right now, we're going to bed." She doesn't care if she sounds bitchy. She is, for good reason. "By the way, Roger called. While you were taking a nap this afternoon."

"Roger? My God! What did you say?" Lou still holds her wine opener bobble, its pointed screw shaking at Joan.

"Careful." Joan brushes past Lou to her bedroom. "That she was out on the beach and that I wasn't sure when she'd be back."

"And?"

"That I'd tell her he called. He's staying at his mother's, and I took the telephone number in case it's not on Madge's cell." Joan aims a reassuring pat at Lou's arm. "He asked how she was and I said fine." Sitting on the bed, she pulls her legs out of her pants. At some point she'll have to admit they are too tight, give in to baggy stretch waists like everyone else.

"He should know, Joan." Lou's thin fingers clutch at the old quilt folded over the footboard, a defense against the evening cool. "He, of all people."

"He, of all people, should not know. Madge was clear about that. For his own good." Joan wants to add that this isn't the time for more tears. She'd like to give Lou a good shake, knock some backbone into her.

"And when she doesn't call?" Lou loosens her hold on the quilt, steps back, blinks her eyes dry.

Skinny as a broom, always has been, quiet and at times surprising tough. Fearless, it seemed, when she left her marriage. Maybe Lou'll be okay with all this once she gets a grip on her sadness. We all need to get a grip, Joan tells herself, or at least a few hours' sleep.

She takes a moment to pull her nightgown over her head. "He called again, left a message because I took the phone off the hook. We'll get in touch with him again tomorrow." She moves to the mirror over the bureau, inspects the gray pouches under her eyes. "God, I'm ten years older than yesterday." Lou takes the hint and leaves, closing the door behind her.

10

Saturday Evening: Breakwater
Lou

Too empty to question her new role as her sister's keeper, Lou wraps the corkscrew in toilet paper to keep it from stabbing her in the middle of the night, and settles on her left side, the side the orthopedist claimed opened the body best. She breathes the way Susan has taught her: count of five in, hold a count of seven, count of eight out. One concentrates on the count, the filling, the emptying, and one's mind benumbs. The hip hadn't been broken, only a sciatic nerve inflamed and healed, but the habit of counting her breaths is now a ritual and usually brings a sweet void and sleep, unless an anxiety storm sweeps through, creating havoc.

Like right now. She shouldn't have napped this afternoon; now she can't even make her eyelids move toward each other. Jackie's soft snoring on the pillow next to hers, little puffs at the end of each rumble, isn't helping. This afternoon her bedmate had stayed awake, drinking herself into an out-of-body state of denial. At the moment, Lou would welcome Jackie's alcoholic coma.

The pillow lumps under her head, her neck aches, her thoughts swirl until she sits up, turns on the light, reaches for the book on the table next to her. But even Annie Proulx doesn't stop the swirling. She switches off the light, lies back and sinks into a sea of ancient memories, the four of them, blowing smoke rings, French-inhaling, rolling eyes at each other, talking dirty at 2:00 a.m. in a darkened sorority solarium.

11

1955: Hinterland
Madge

Madge has just that day cut her hair short, really short this time. The back of her head, in fact, looks like a boy's, Lou has informed her. Bristly. Ten or so girls, young women, if they are talking sisterhood language, lounge on the floor and furniture in the solarium, once the original homeowner's glassed addition to his large faux colonial house meant for the growing of exotic plants. No greenery has lived in this space for twenty years, filled instead with old spring-shot chairs and a couch shoved helter-skelter amid ashtrays and forgotten books. The house holds thirty Gamma Psi's, most of whom have taken up cigarettes as prerequisites to college life. These days the solarium's only blooms are flames at the end of matches.

Madge feels eyes squinting at her through the gray air, assessing the new do. She looks back with a brave squint of her own. "I wanted something easy." She runs a hand over the top of her head. Her neck really does feel like a boy's, alien.

"It'll grow out. Mine did," Jackie says as she flips a bang into the dark halo of hair curling around her face. "Don't worry."

Madge doesn't want to be the object of pity, especially from a girl whose unruly hair she's envious of, grown in or not. She lights a cigarette and drags noisily, on purpose. "I like it."

A set of fingers pats at first, then begins to massage her scalp. "Just needs to be softened up a little." Joan speaks with her usual certainty, her own blond hair contained in its perfect pageboy. Approval from Joan about hair, about a lot of things, means something, and Madge relaxes under the strokes of those confident fingertips.

Joan is from California, and this weekend she knocked everyone out with her sexy blond hairdo as Sweetheart of Sigma Chi, not to mention her tulle and crinoline strapless and her popular escort, Tim Costas, captain of the basketball team. At Lee University, being from California is like being royalty on tour, college just a rest stop on the way to someplace spectacular. Joan and the three other California girls in the house are from San Mateo. How they found their ways to a Podunk private school in the middle of backwoods Oregon is not a mystery.

Twenty years before, the University spawned a graduate from California who soon made millions building warships. He credited his college for this success despite the fact that he had majored in literature. In gratitude, he offered scholarships so that other Californians would have the same opportunity, but without the war, of course.

Most people do not know about the alumnus since recipients of the money are asked to not reveal its source, lest he be bombarded by requests from poor non-Californian would-be Lee students.

Then last spring Madge mentioned in the solarium that she might not be able continue on for her junior year unless luck intervened. Her father had been laid off and her mother, in desperation, had started working on the pear line at a cannery, the only job that met her homely resume. College tuition wasn't on her parents' list of necessities. She tried to joke about it. "I'm pretty sure that Miss Kilpatrick, the floor manager at Lerner's, will be thrilled to have me back full time," she said. "I hold the record for the fewest balanced cash register tapes ever recorded in the history of the children's department."

HER LAST WORDS

Sally Olson was listening. Even though she was from the Peninsula, Sally was not on a California scholarship, since it was her father who administered the fund for the Big Alumnus and, out of ethical considerations, he had not tossed his daughter's name into the Adansky Corporation scholarship bag. Sally, however, provided her father with occasional reports on the subsidized students, especially those who might need small reminders of who was paying the bill.

Over the weekend, she called and informed him that Madge was as close to being a Californian as an Oregonian could get, and she needed a leg up. Sally's family owned ten horses and a ranch behind Stanford, which accounted for the horsy allusion. A few days later, after a series of tearful goodbyes to her Gamma Psi sisters, perhaps her best friends ever, Madge received a letter informing her that she was among the very few northerners to ever receive an Adansky scholarship.

That still meant, of course, brown-nosing Miss Kilpatrick at Lerner's but just for the summer, pretending she could add, and begging her parents for extra items like the $85.00 formal she really needed for the Homecoming dance. She did both and she hated it.

And that's why, when she came back to school this fall, she cut off her hair. She would become a new person. Independent. She would do the shit work, she'd already signed up for the dishwasher job in the Gamma Psi kitchen, but she'd do it on her own terms. And no more begging willing

but unable parents. No more Yes ma'ams into the iron bod-
ice of a shop tyrant.

An hour after she left the beauty salon, she changed her
major from education to psychology, and then over coffee
and a cigarette, alone at Sam's Cafe, she decided not to hold
out any more on her current steady, Ralph, not that she'd
go all the way. Who wanted to get pregnant like Lily last
semester, a nightmare for the sorority, her parents, and obviously, for Lily?

However, tonight, under the calming strokes of Joan's
massaging fingers, the former Madge still lurks. That Madge
is worried about money, feels stupid about Hemingway,
knows that she talks too much to be a psychologist, and,
worst of all, still nurtures an impossible dream of becoming
a writer of stories that others will read and find a speck of
truth within.

She exhales, turns off that kind of thinking, and tunes in
to the solarium's swirl of smoke and voices.

Liz Wyndam, a year older and decades more mature, a
drama major, is drawing ovals in the air, the tip of her
French cigarette glowing at the end of each swing of her
arm. "It's so over-valued," she intones in her Barbara
Stanwyck mode. Her cigarette swoops. "The penis," she
says. She drags on the brown stub and mashes it into the
pile of butts in the ashtray in front of her. "A carrot works
as well." Liz leans back into the legs of the girl sitting in the

chair behind her and waggles her eyebrows. "Of course, you all know this, right?"

No. Madge is pretty sure that most of the giggling girls in the Gamma Psi solarium this night, despite their hoots and nods in agreement, don't know. And if she does, no one is admitting it. Madge can picture it, the carrot. Actually, she can feel it. She thinks she would prefer a boy's fingers, two last night, wiggling a little. Of course, a carrot might be longer or self-managed, not like the painful poke that brought the date to a halt. She leans forward, snags a cigarette from the pack in Lou's hand, and turns to Jackie, who is always good for a laugh. "So how was skiing this weekend?"

12

1955: Hinterland II
Jackie

Jackie needs a shower. Only the smoke in the solarium ob-
scures the fact that her body is exuding an exotic scent. She
hadn't actually smoked the reefer that Billy offered her, like
only one lungful. But the car reeked of it and she reeks of it.
She doesn't mind reeking of it, and she liked Billy's smudgy
kiss that started on one side of her face, tracked its way to
her mouth, found the other ear. Doped kisses are messy but
take in a lot of territory. She answers Madge's question by
pulling up a pajama leg and rubbing her calf. The purple

lump has sloughed into a mauve and reddish lake that floods almost to her ankle, marking her, once again, as the crazy person in the house.

"God," someone gasps. "Is it worth it?

"I had a great weekend," Jackie answers. "Snow was great, the parties..." She stops. She needs to be a little discreet about alcohol despite or because of the fact that one of the senior officers of the sorority had been caught with a bottle of Chivas and a bucket of ice cubes in the basement just before Winter Break. Astonishment had run the gamut from how could she, right here in our house, to so why didn't she invite me? These comments, of course, were not voiced during the Gamma Psi special meeting where the offending sister was grounded, lucky her. Several others in past years had been kicked out of the sorority for similar offenses, but this particular girl was six weeks from graduating mid-year and was a senior scholar in sociology/psychology with a minor in French. Jackie is inclined to believe that it was the French that impressed the presiding alum.

She, herself, is not interested foreign languages, or sociology, or psychology. She is interested in skiing. And, in the other seasons, swimming and shooting arrows. She loves knowing about her body, other bodies, everything about why a muscle aches, a calf turns purple, how an arm can throw a perfect curve ball. In fact, she is in the midst of an intensive study on the throwing arm of a farm boy from Boise. They haven't actually dated yet, but she has spent a few hours in the grandstands at the baseball field during practice, taking mental notes. She also likes his thighs and his slight overbite. Tomorrow she'll walk back from the stadium about the time he will leave, wet from the shower, moving fast towards the Zeta house and dinner. Like she did today, only tomorrow she plans to catch up with him, start talking.

A soft bell signals Quiet Hours. Most of the sisters are already asleep in bunk beds on the sleeping porch above them. Jackie tosses his name out like a knuckle ball towards the whisperers huddled in the center of the room.

"Who?"

"Cute, red curly hair, kind of shy," she answers.

"Jackie! Poor guy, he doesn't stand a chance. Is he tall enough for you?"

"I don't worry about tall."

Smirks, as Jackie expects, snuffle through the musty air. She loves the excitement of crushes, the chases, the captures. She lets most of her captives loose once she has them, or parts of them, in hand, though. She can't stand the idea of being pinned to one guy forever or even for a semester.

One by one, pajama'd bodies slip out of the solarium and up the stairs to their narrow cots. Madge and Joan head toward the kitchen, the only place they are allowed to type late at night. Only Lou and Jackie still sink into the pits of pillows at the ends of the couch, feet almost touching. Lou holds out her pack of cigs, her forehead more furled than usual. Jackie shakes her head. "What's up?" she asks.

Lou snorts a deep sigh, then, "Something's wrong with me. Maybe I wasn't meant to be a woman. Look at me." She pats her chest, hands flat against rib bones.

"What does your Mom say?"

"My mother is a Christian Scientist. She prays for me."

"God, Lou, you need to see a doctor. Have you ever seen a doctor?"

"Once when I broke my arm playing wall ball at school and Mom couldn't make the bone straighten out." Lou shrugs, hugs herself. "I'm just weird. An asexual being, a human spore."

"Spore?"

"You remember. Biology."

"I must have missed that class. An eight o'clock, right?"

"I'm serious. No boobs, no monthly reminder of my precious womb, if I have one." Lou sniffs a laugh. "Even worse, no date for the house dance."

Jackie raises herself and grabs the hand that still clutches bony ribs in a hopeless sort of way. This isn't normal, being stuck at thirteen, or maybe twelve if she herself is an example. What a waste of seven years. "Tomorrow we go to the doctor. He'll have a pill or something." When Lou protests, Jackie adds, "I guarantee a boyfriend by Christmas. You'll exude womanliness. I get really horny when I get the curse."

Lou pushes up from the sofa and heads for the door. "Okay, if you think. Thanks for...you know. I haven't a clue."

"Right." No, Lou doesn't. That's what Jackie likes about her. Even though Lou is really smart, an English lit major, she really doesn't have a clue.

13

1955: Hinterland III
Lou

Ten minutes later, Lou, rolled up in the patchwork quilt her grandmother made, sorts out the night noises of the sleeping porch. Someone is weeping softly. A nose whistles. The girl in the bunk above her tosses with a dream that rocks the metal structure against the wall. Various gasps and purrs swim in the gentle wind that blows through open windows and across smooth unconscious foreheads. It isn't just the absence of a monthly flow of blood. She isn't sure a pill can cure what stirs inside her on sleepless nights like this one.

JO BARNEY

She doesn't have a name for it; perhaps it doesn't have a name. Perhaps it is hers alone, this stirring.

1955: Hinterland IV
Joan

In the late spring, the rhododendrons banking the sorority house walls glow their blessing the evening Tim and Joan decide. Later in the solarium, Joan wonders if it seems like bragging to hold out her ringed hand, wait for fingers to reach out for hers, and to expect cries of excitement and envy, not shock.

Her sisters shouldn't be surprised. After all, she and Tim have spent the usual amount of evenings grappling amongst the bushes in front of the house, as well as in other campus cubbyholes. He is a year older and has been accepted to med school, although he'll have to make up a couple of prerequisites before he can start next January. And she'll be a senior in the fall, graduating a semester early.

"In December," she tells them, "in California. You're all invited." She herself does not quite believe it, but she and Tim decided they can't hold out much longer, and because she is a Catholic now, who knows how soon they'll get pregnant once they finally do it. Not that she'll mind getting pregnant. Their babies will be tall, good-looking basketball players just like Tim. She hopes that at some point she'll have a girl to keep her company in the kitchen. But if they can wait, she'll have a little time before all that begins to be a teacher and save up some money for a house and a television and the other things they'll need while Tim builds his practice.

Joan, researching in her thorough way for her new life, has ordered Van de Velde's Ideal Marriage from Book-of-the-Month and she agrees, when the others find out about it, to read aloud whenever she finds something interesting, which is pretty much every page. The smoking room percolates with midnight seminars.

Lou has trouble accepting the clitoris and she uses her compact mirror to confirm its existence. Madge needs the part about other possible orifices read twice, as she closes her eyes and tries to imagine. Jackie nods at most everything and adds tidbits of information that she has picked up elsewhere, like how a friend of hers got pregnant through her underpants. Joan takes note of this comment, and she skims the index of the book in her lap looking for "heavy petting."

Once the new school year begins in the fall and her wedding is only months away, Joan realizes that she is leading her friends to their own womanhoods. They watch as she makes lists, listen as she argues with her mother long-distance about fruit punch or wine, and discusses the font for the invitations with her printer. They commiserate as she worries over the costs and are relieved when her mother produces a small cache of dollars. "The money for her funeral," Joan tells them. "We'll have plenty of time to pay her back." They nod, narrow-eyed, as she raises her shoulders and deflects the usual solarium questions: "How is Tim? What are you guys doing this weekend?"

Actually, it seems like a betrayal to Tim to talk about their relationship since she is experiencing a few problems with it. They're spending a lot of time together looking for a place to live and working out the money part of being married, and that's mostly what she shares with her sisters, but not the fact that Tim and she also spend a lot of time in a sweaty frenzies in the car that often involve begging on Tim's part, followed by a couple of cooling beers and a resentful kiss at the Gamma Psi door.

"Soon, honey, only a month or so," she promises, as she pulls down the skirt lodged under her armpits or fastens at least one hook of her bra. Van de Velde has prepared her for several of Tim's requests to which she eventually complies, in order to ease the tension between them. However, she isn't happy with his handling of himself when he gets really frustrated, like the time he did it in front of her, drunk and unzipped. She'll be glad when they are married and not having to worry any more.

15

1956: Hinterland V
Madge

The last month of their senior year, Madge misses Joan a lot. The solarium isn't the same without her, especially since Jackie has been confined to the guest room with a cast on her leg after she leapt out of a second story window and limped her way to a clandestine beer party, where she passed out, not from the alcohol, but from pain.

"Why do you suppose she did it?" Bleary-eyed from reading for an exam one late night, Madge and Lou are taking a break over cups of hours-old tar-coffee from the kitchen. "I just don't get it. Let's find out." Stocking-footed, they sneak down the hall leading to Jackie's isolation ward.

"Quien sabe, amigas?" Jackie looks up from a Sports Illustrated magazine, grins and moves over to give them room on the bed. Other than her one phrase of Spanish, she offers no explanation for her breakout.

Madge tries to do it for her. "You know, Jackie, you follow your own star or male, whichever comes first. A free spirit. When you set your mind on something, you do it. You ski like a maniac. It's a wonder you haven't broken every bone in your body."

"And," Lou pats her thrust-out chest, "you just about saved my life when you dragged me to that doctor." She turns to Madge. "Have you noticed? Still kind of small but growing, I think."

"Impressive." Madge licks a finger, rubs a wisp of hair defying the hairspray helmet she had applied that morning in an effort to look like Audrey Hepburn. "I'm not a free spirit. I still have the same haircut I got last year, when I thought a shaved neckline would make me courageous." She gives up, lets the escapee go its way, grins at Jackie. "I'd love to jump out of a window without thinking."

"Well, you are, sort of. Have you and Jerry set a date?"

"Doesn't feel like a leap, just a step over a curb into the road of life. He got the scholarship, you know. Graduate school. I'll teach until he gets out."

"Then?" Lou has settled back against the footboard, her feet at Jackie's shoulder.

"The usual. Maybe I'll try writing in between babies. Mr. Richards, my writing teacher, says I might have a knack for it. I'm not sure I should believe him since he also confessed to one hundred-and-twenty rejection letters this year. By the way, Joan thinks she's pregnant."

Lou sits up abruptly, thumping a knee against Jackie's cast. "They've only been married for four months. How did that happen?"

Jackie rolls her eyes. "The usual way, probably."

"Damn! I'm so behind. Despite the ripening mammaries, I've had one date all this year, and I asked him to the house dance."

Madge tries to take it back. "Maybe not. Could be a false alarm."

Lou pulls her pack of Pall Malls out of her pajama pocket as she heads to the solarium. "Nope. Joan does not have false alarms. This will be our first child. Start knitting."

16

Saturday Evening: Eddy
Lucius

It isn't that Lucius doesn't like women. He does. He's just a little suspicious of them, and he has to admit he's been careless in his choices of the women he's married. He lowers himself into the desk chair left him by the previous sheriff, which is okay once he fits a pillow at the small of his back, lays his cap on the corner of the desk, and fusses until he's comfortable. These beach women fit right into this suspicious outlook he's developed over the years.

"What about the lady who disappeared?" Liz's question yelled from the reception area disrupts the train of thought that has arrived on schedule this evening, like most evenings, during the quiet Greenspring hours between golf and going home to Clive Cussler.

"Her friends seem a little agitated by her taking off. Can't really do anything until tomorrow. Why don't you go home? I'll be here for a few minutes writing up my notes and then I'm out of here too."

Liz leans against the doorframe, her fleece jacket already zipped. "So no murder?"

"Not until tomorrow. Sorry to disappoint you."

"And my dad. Him and his buddies were about to get a posse organized."

"Your dad reads too many Westerns. Goodnight Liz."

The front door slams.

Those women in the beach house are hiding something. This intuition reminds him of other times he's felt this way about a woman, three women, actually. He sinks back and waits for the train carrying his wives to pull in. As usual, first wife steps down and onto the platform. Lucius greets her with the pint of whiskey he uncovers from the wastebasket under his desk. Sarah. Pretty but very, very tidy. She produced a son in a tidy way who's grown up in tidy haircuts and Sunday church suits. Sarah tried hard to tidy up Lucius too.

Her efforts were unsuccessful because Lucius couldn't be tidy in any way. Early on, he worked as a carpenter's helper with a local builder. He didn't shave on the weekends, despite the family's attendance at Sunnyside Baptist; he wore paint-spattered pants to PTA meetings and pajamas all Saturday if he chose to. His sneakers and jackets roamed the house on their own; his newspapers flew about with abandon.

After a few years of trying to change him, Sarah gave up the project, even after he went to school to become a policeman and began to clean up a few parts of his life. "I might have to be your angry housekeeper," she declared, one night as she stuffed a wad of jockey shorts into the laundry bin, "but I'm not going to be your ever-willing bedmate anymore."

It was difficult for Lucius in those days to understand the connection between those two wifely roles.

They divorced after he met Ruby. He has a glimmer of what Sarah was talking about now that he's older, and he sometimes regrets Ruby. Sarah tried, at least, and his grandson has her green eyes.

Lucius looks at the half-empty bottle and takes another swig, this one dedicated to the second woman at the train door, the remedy to Sarah. Ruby was attracted to him because by then he was a policeman and his uniform made him seem in control, not that being in control was a priority of hers. She herself was often out of control and willing to get even wilder when it came to sex, so they should have been a good match, and they were for a few years, scuffling through their apartment looking for his shoes or the TV remote or her purse or the car keys usually hiding under the unmade bed. His steady salary as a cop and his odd hours suited her just fine too.

He discovered the maxed-out Visa, with its shopping network purchases, and the naked FedEx driver who delivered them, on the same day. Ruby was partial to uniforms, it turned out. Later, in the lawyer's office, she tried to explain. Mainly, she didn't like the fact that he never listened to her, ever, not even when she was miserable with the cramps that sent her to the sofa for three days every month. Of course, she turned to QVC and its driver for solace. Who wouldn't?

"What the hell," Lucius fumbles for the glass he's hidden in his bottom drawer. He pours out the last of the bourbon and waits for the next passenger arriving on this train to nowhere. Elaine alights slowly, hesitantly, looks around until she sees him. She's wearing the green coat he likes so much. Her skin glows. Her black hair is tied back into a ponytail at her neck; her red lips grin at him.

She's so young. Too young. Too young to stay interested in a fifty-year-old, pot-bellied, shaved-headed officer of the law. Especially when meth entered the picture. After a few months of stomach-turning suspicion, then eyeball-to-eyeball, hands-clutching-shoulders pleading, Lucius turned into the cop he was. She screamed that he had also become her father, always telling her what to do. Made her sick. Made her crazy. Then one day she just disappeared. Lucius, when he thinks about Elaine, like now, can still feel the young soft fingers on his face, the young wiry body under him.

He has a right to be suspicious of women, especially women who want something from him. Lou, Jackie, and especially that arm-fondling Joan, definitely want something.

With a couple of drinks under his belt, he puts that thought aside and goes back to considering how much he had to do with the ways his marriages turned out. The quiet of this little town with its raging cows and Saturday night rumbles has given him plenty of time to wonder about that.

Enough. Lucius stands, picks up his cap and pulls it onto his head, gets his keys out to lock up as he walks out. Clive Cussler is waiting at home.

Sunday Morning: Tide Pool
Lou

The beach house deck faces the ocean, and the yellow early-morning sky is reflected on the slack waters, orange lazy wavelets, green glowing depths. It's chilly outside and will be until the sun makes its way to it, but the afghan helps. Lou's nose is cold, and she wipes it on her pajama sleeve. She doesn't bother being sneaky about it; the other two are still asleep and will be until she starts a pot of coffee. She has held off in order to be quiet for a moment, to think about the situation. She wants to call Susan, ask her advice, but she knows what her friend will say. "You've been buddies for almost fifty years, sweetie. You can't back out now."

It isn't that she wants to back out. Well, she would like to not even know about it, of course, to be in her garden on the mountain, mulching and whistling at the birds in the firs above her head. But she owes Madge. When everyone else thought Lou was crazy to walk out of a thirty-year marriage, Madge told her that she was brave. "It's chance to find out, finally, who you are." Lou had used those words as an antidote in the guilt-sick months after she had abandoned her old life. When she needed to talk, Madge listened and cheered her on, and Lou had begun to discover pieces of herself, hidden, waiting.

Lou stirs, opens the blanket and steps to the wooden rail in front of her. She inhales the misty cold, fills her chest. "Probably about time everyone else found me, too," she whispers and wonders how she'll tell them.

"Thought you'd have the coffee on by now." Jackie is pouring coffee grounds willy-nilly into the paper filter. "I need a barrel of it after last night. Was I bad? I don't remember saying anything I shouldn't have. All three of us seemed a little unhinged, probably still are. For good reason, damn." As she waits for the coffee, she reaches for a book on the counter. "Madge's? I haven't read this one. Old Ladies' Home. What's it about?"

Lou finds a mug and not waiting for the machine to finish, pours herself a cup. "It's about five old women who decide to live together in an ancient house with a front porch and five rocking chairs. They've known each other forever, through husbands, lovers, and cancer. What one can't do, one of the others can. The assisted assisting the assisted. Could be us, someday."

"So they end up peaceful and content?"

"So they discover the one thing they aren't willing to do for each other, at least the majority of them." Lou looks down the neck of her pajama top, points at a red tender spot. "The corkscrew is back in the top drawer. Watch yourself, yourself."

"You're speaking of sex? My kind of book." Jackie pours a cup of coffee and grins at Lou, who is rubbing a finger against the wound on her bony clavicle. "Perky, still, I see." She turns to go to the living room, and coffee sloshes down the front of her robe as she bumps into Joan who has come up behind her.

"God, Joan. Watch it!"

To Lou, the words seem fueled with more anger than spilled coffee would inspire.

Joan has several folders under her arm, and she doesn't react to Jackie's dabbing at herself or her bad humor. "We have Madge's latest project to finish today, just as she asked." She moves past Jackie and goes into the kitchen. Reaching for a cup, she adds, "Remember? Our stories? Her new novel, Think on These Things."

"Why does that sound familiar?"

"Jackie, we had to say it every week for four years." Joan sets the folders on the counter and opens the fridge, takes out the milk. "I can't believe you don't remember. 'Whatsoever things are true, whatsoever things are honest, whatsoever things are just, whatsoever things are pure,' and so on."

"'If there be any virtue and if there be any praise, think on these things.' Philippians 4:8," Lou finishes the verse. "I used to choke up at the sound of our voices chanting those words."

A candlelit room, thirty sisters standing in front of wooden benches, heads bowed, the concrete basement walls exuding a musty, exotic scent that used to make Lou almost sick to her stomach—chapter meetings.

Jackie shrugs. "You were probably reacting to the mumble from the back row. I never knew what came next, honest, pure, lovely, shitty, whatever, so I made up words."

Joan sends a disgusted look at Jackie, apparently not in the mood to reminisce. California girl is stressed, Lou is surprised to see, a crack or two in the façade. Even her voice is brittle, chipped. "Besides her own story that we heard Friday night, Madge began three more. About us, only our stories aren't finished. She's asking us to provide the endings. We promised we would."

"Damn." Jackie's cup sails across the drain board. "I'm sick and tired of your bitchy know-it-all-ness, Joan, the coffee soaking down the front of me, this whole impossible scene. I know I agreed to go along with it all, but this is way too weird. I'm taking a long, long walk."

Joan's arm blocks her retreat. "We have to do this, Jackie. Tonight. According to the Madge's plan. We'll have a ceremony. Candles." She pushes a folder at her. "After you've read this, take your long walk and go to the store in the village and buy candles, a lot of candles. White, for hope."

Lou clutches her cup, turns away from the wave of tension spilling into the room, says, "White is also the color of mourning." Then, in the silence that trails her words, she sees the copy of Old Ladies' Home and flips through a few pages. They'll have to lighten up or they wouldn't get through the next day or two. Maybe a laugh from Madge will help. She taps the book's cover, tries to grin.

"Madge told me she was imagining us in our ancient years, together again, not in the solarium, but in an old house. We grow restless rocking endlessly on the long front porch and decide to kidnap a delivery boy, offer him mention in our wills, and coerce him into servicing us. When the word gets out, other young men show up at our doorstep, along with the police and a few irate mothers."

She slides the book across the counter. "Madge could be very funny, you know."

"Is, Lou, is," Joan says. She is not to be diverted. Now Lou finds herself on the receiving end of orders. "You, my literary friend, will arrange the readings and songs. And snacks. I am in charge of Lucius, who will be here shortly. Our main job, though, is for each of us to read her folder, take a look at everyone else's, and be able to say "The End," by tonight." Joan suddenly breaks into her admirable smile. "Am I being too bossy?"

Jackie meets Joan's eyes with a reluctant blink. "Yes. But someone has to take charge and it isn't going to be me." She heads to the bedroom. "I will manage candles. And I'll pick up the wine while I'm at it."

Lou curls up on the sofa. She needs to go for a walk, too. The tide is out, leaving tide pools and waving sea anemones to poke at, live things, like her garden, and if she goes now, she won't have to face the sheriff again. She moves to get up, sits back down when Joan shakes her head at her, and when the knock sounds, Joan answers the door. Lucius steps in, glances around, tips his baseball cap at Lou, and then follows Joan to the fireplace chairs.

"No word?" He chooses the same chair as before.

"I was hoping you'd have heard something. She might be hurt somewhere, on the point, or in the forest. We need help, Lucius. Now." Joan leans toward the man who, according to the plan, will get them through this.

Lucius adjusts his body against an interfering pillow, leans a little himself. "We'll organize the Boy Scout search team and send them out into the woods this afternoon. Some people in town will volunteer to help. They always do when there is the promise of some excitement." He pauses. "Sorry, I didn't mean that in an unfeeling way. How are you all holding up?"

"We're worried." Joan lowers her eyelids, her mouth trembling a little. Lou feels her mouth trembling also, a collaborative show of concern that Joan is good at inspiring. "The walking stick, you know. But if she's hurt somewhere, she knows we won't abandon her. Jackie is about to go out now, walking the dunes and on the road. Lou will be out there soon, too. I'll stay here waiting for your call, keeping watch."

Joan reaches out to touch the sheriff's arm and then pulls back her hand. As she shuts the door after him, she turns and grins. "No need for overkill, is there?" Lou gives the performance a splatter of applause from her front row seat.

18

Sunday Morning: Accretion
Lou

Lou's glad she's wearing her sweatshirt. The breeze is coming up and even in the hollow behind the grass of the dune, the pages flutter and threaten to escape from the folder Madge has put them in. She turns her back to the wind, uses a shoe to hold the papers down and begins to read.

WHATSOEVER THINGS ARE PURE:
LOU'S STORY

This is the way I've imagined you. I hope

HER LAST WORDS

I've found some of your truth.
I will miss knowing how
your story ends, but I know your life will
be full love and flowers. M.

The hand that covers Lou's is crusty with dirt, its nails black, as befits the master gardener it belongs to. It doesn't matter. Her own hand is as dirty. What matters is the tattoo of her heart against her ribs. Susan laughs, gives Lou's fingers a squeeze, and pushes herself up as tall now as the old rhododendron they've been trying to yank out of the ground. Lou tugs one last time at the thick root at her feet. Perhaps she has imagined it.

"We'll have to cut it down first, and then dig it out," Susan is saying. "Don't you think?" She wipes her forehead, leaves yet another crusty gray-brown streak on her face.

Lou takes her friend's elbow. "Let's have a glass of iced tea and talk about it in the shade." The two women wash off under the hose and settle on the wooden deck chairs to sip their drinks.

"I love working with you," Susan says.

Lou takes a long swallow of tea, looks up from her glass. "Me, too." In her throat other words, risky words, clamor to be set loose. She silences them, says, "Let's hire the Samson boy to take it out. Give ourselves a break for once."

They've worked hard all spring on the garden, weeding and planting the one island of sun that appears each day within the wall of tall Douglas firs surrounding the cabin. At its perimeter, ferns, hostas, Solomon's seal, astilbe, and hydrangeas keep a solemn green watch over the sunlovers, purple penstemon, nicotinana. Foxgloves and fireweed flaunt their colors on the center berm. The rhodie, a scarlet urban misfit, rises uneasily at the edge of the porch, planted by a previous owner inspired, perhaps, by its pale pink and white cousins in the woods a few feet away. The gardeners have agreed that this showy wad of bush is a city creature, belongs next to a large brick house with ten of its sisters, not at the door of a tiny log cabin, three miles off the highway and one mile from its closest neighbor.

The hiring of the Samson boy decided, they relax into the cotton cushions at their backs, and each shuts her eyes. She can't guess what Susan is thinking, but Lou, for some reason, the rhododendron probably, is floating towards a spring more than forty years earlier.

Rhododendrons stood like fat sentinels at each side of the porch in the front of the Gamma Psi house. Rather than guard the young women inside, the shrubs provided a series of leafy love nests in which couples, urged on by the 10:00 p.m. curfew, worked furtively to satisfy their bodies' burgeoning urges. The activities in the bushes were restricted by the Fifties mores as much as the uncomfortable edges of shiplap siding. Lou was not a regular in the bushes. She, lost in a world of others' words, was barely aware that her body had urges. She spent her four years at Lee University under a pile of books, emerging only to go down to the smoking room, which the sisters called the solarium even though sunlight rarely penetrated its northern windows. Someone there was always ready to talk or lend her a cigarette.

That first year in the house, late at night, stoked on No Doze and nicotine, she sometimes recited a little of Chaucer's *Canterbury Tales* or a few verses of Burns in an unlikely Scottish burr, and her audience would applaud and laugh. She had not caused anyone to laugh before, certainly not her solemn, Bible-infused parents, certainly not her younger brother who claimed he hated her.

Lou roomed with Joan her sophomore year, a streaked-blond Californian from the Bay Area who read Hemingway and Steinbeck in high school, authors Lou's more provincial teachers considered unfit for teenagers and whom she discovered on her own a few years later. In the early smoky hours of one finals week, abandoning their stupefying Romantic Lit texts, the two of them created a patois that became the *lingua franca* for the inner sanctum of solarium friends. It involved the intense pursing of lips and touching of teeth. "I need a tis-sue!" Joan enunciated, with a perfectly contracted moue.

"Why don't you call the wait-ress?" Lou asked, cuspids tapping.

"Forsoothe, I hadn't thought of that."

"Henceforth do."

"I take umbrage," Jackie, emerging from a textbook torpor, objected.

"Soooooooo?"

Madge complained, "So, I am worried about my netherparts."

"Aren't we all?" Jackie asked.

By her third year, after a spate of Melville and her chronic dateless Saturday nights, Lou's nickname in that midnight room became Ishmael, Call Me.

Lou turns a page, remembers these silly times, warms once again with a sense of inclusion. She had not felt part of a group before, lonely without realizing it, in the midst of her books. Despite the years that have followed, I haven't changed much, she thinks, not lonely now, but choosing the simplicity of aloneness.

By her senior year, besides laughter, late nights in the solarium spawned secrets and shared angst. Mrs. T, the housemother, always retreated to her room after shooing the lovers off the front porch and locking the front door. Most of the sisters headed for their narrow beds on the sleeping porch soon after. Around midnight, Lou would shut her portable typewriter case and go to the solarium to find Joan and Madge and Jackie, maybe a couple of other nocturnal sorts, sagging on the old mohair furniture, filmy windows opened to bring some relief from the smoke. They would whisper because of the sleeping girls above them and because what they talked about was not supposed to be said out loud. Sex, mostly. They were virgins, of course. At least, no one ever contradicted that idea. By their senior years, they looked forward to summer marriages to med students, to grad students in universities thousands of miles away, to rich farmers from Idaho. They shared information about premarital examinations, diaphragms, the rhythm method. No one mentioned orgasms. Oral sex was still a raunchy joke, less so after Joan received a marriage manual from which she conducted midnight tutoring sessions.

"Smells are important," she instructed, reading from a lightly underlined paragraph. "Absolute cleanliness is a must."

"For who?" Jackie asked.

"Whom," Lou corrected. She was having trouble finding a meaningful context for this information.

"Therefore, women should wipe from the front to the back."

"Well, gaah!" Jackie exclaimed, but several others looked worried.

Joan, ever cool, said, "I think we should discuss this. Front to back, you say." Another phrase blossomed, a kind of mantra, one that popped up every once in a while, even years later, unannounced.

Lou was not shy, only reluctant, around men. Quiet philosophy majors sought her out because she herself was a seeker of truth, her sources Virginia Woolf and Thomas Hardy, Theodore Dreiser, and Maugham, but she was open to any idea that might break through the confining walls of her mother's devout Christian Scientist teachings. She preferred coffee and cigarettes at Billy's Cafe to sorority dances, and luckily, so did some of these earnest young men. If there was a whiff of sex floating through these conversations, it slipped past Lou and probably by her Nietzsche-quoting friends.

Then, in the height of the search for meaning, and despite her desperate, resurrected prayers and reading of Mary
Baker Eddy, her mother died. "Everyone dies, Louise," her
mother said, her last cogent sentence before she fell into the
sleep that swept her into her God's arms. Maybe that is the
ultimate truth, Lou thought. So where does that leave a person?

By spring, Joan was married, and everyone else except
Lou had a ring on her finger and plans for a summer wedding. Lou's major professor, Dr. Elizabeth Wilton, advised
her to go to graduate school. She had the makings of a fine
researcher and writer. Her paper on Dylan Thomas was
Master's quality. Lou was flattered, of course, but she could
not ask her bereaved and nearly blind father for any more
tuition money. Besides, she would not need a Master's once
she found a husband.

She decided, in between spates of bridesmaid gowns, to
become an airline stewardess. For no good reason, really,
except that she'd missed the deadlines for graduate school,
and she knew she'd be a really bad high school teacher. She
flew the West Coast, lived in a small apartment in L.A. with
another stewardess. Despite the exotic palm trees and con-
stant sun, she was disappointed. The men who knocked on
her door, took her to the beaches, tried to creep into her
bed, bored her. "My roommate's home," she took to saying,
closing the door quietly on hopeful grins. All she really
wanted was a conversation with a man that didn't begin
with, "My boss doesn't know shit about running a business."

She found him in the first class section of a Seattle/LA flight. "Thanks, Lou," he said when she gave him his morning juice and newspaper. He had been paying attention when the pilot introduced the attendants. When she returned a little later with his breakfast, she said, "Here are your eggs, Mr. Egan." She had read the passenger list.

By the time they landed in LA, Mark Egan had penciled her phone number on the cover of his flight magazine, and when he called, she accepted his invitation to dinner. He came in afterward, but only for a glass of Galliano. He talked marvelously, quoted Kierkegaard, Freud and Walt Whitman, sometimes in the same sentence. For the first time since college coffee dates, Lou could articulate her need to understand things to someone who had the same need. "What is all this about?" she asked, flinging a hand into the unknown, nearly spilling her liqueur.

He laughed. "On Monday, when the sun is hot, I wonder to myself a lot: 'Now is it true, or it is not, That what is which and which is what?'" Milne's goofiness sent an unaccountable moisture flowing in her nether parts.

Mark was a pilot, and looked like one, not tall, but dark thick hair and intense green eyes that made height unimportant. She liked his teeth, overlapping a little in front, insinuating a puckish sense of humor. She liked his hands that, on their second meeting, reached for her with a reassuring hesitation. When she pulled away, mindful of her boney ribcage, her small breasts, he said, "I like narrow bodies." Then he touched her in all of her narrow places. They spent their third date in the apartment, Lou, for the first time having warned her roommate to not come home till late. He deflowered her gently, a towel arranged below her, reminding her of some love scene she had read about years before. "Front to back" came to mind. She probably was thinking too much about the manual's chapter on orgasms to have one.

Their lovemaking got better as the weeks went on, no elusive fireworks for Lou, but a warm, pleasing convergence of minds and body parts that might be even better, she thought. However, Mark's ability to quote esoteric writers began to pale a little. At times, Lou wondered if he had any thoughts of his own, but not so much that she didn't look forward to his calls, his hands surveying her valleys. Only once in a while did she wish that he would sit quietly with her, read a book, languor in the Beethoven album she had been saving for such moments. When they were married, she confided to Julie, her roommate, she would have her solitude during the day, and be glad to talk with him to each evening. Except that he was a pilot and wouldn't be around every evening.

Like right then, she thought. Between their two flight schedules, she hadn't seen him for two weeks.

"Are you sure he hasn't left a message?" she asked Julie one night. She received a smug curled lip for an answer. After that, Lou didn't feel comfortable confiding her worries to a person she saw at most a few hours a week, especially after that person yawned and started pushing back her cuticles in the midst of another's misery. She longed for the late-night solarium, but those friends were sending letters addressed to

Miss with return addresses of Mr. and Mrs. Somebody Somebody. Her sisters seemed to have forgotten their first names as they disappeared into their *Good Housekeeping* lives.

Will I be like that? she wondered one call-less evening. *Mrs. Mark Egan, Pilot's Wife, waiting at the airport for his flight to come in?* She lit a Kent and inhaled deep into her toes. She wasn't doing well with the waiting part right now, that's for sure. They had only known each other three months, and already her nails were down to the nubs.

The next day, when the phone rang and it was he, she forgot these shards of worry in anticipation of his lovely hard nipples. This is the woman, she reminded herself as she turned the doorknob to let him in, who had trouble visualizing what Liz meant a year or so ago about carrots working as good.

"Well," Lou had corrected. She now knew what Liz was talking about, but a carrot didn't have warm skin, knobs of muscle, bones that rose over one and descended in such a satisfying fashion.

When he was away, Lou missed him so much she was nauseous. When he was with her, kissing her eyelids, Lou believed she knew what the poets meant by passion and that she was capable of it. Mark loved her body, her mind, and her willingness to recite *Gunga Din* as she rode him. He told her this often in the surf of pillows and sheets in which they swam like happy porpoises.

So when Lou, always irregular and scanty in her menses, told him in a moment of intimacy, that she had not had a period in several months, she was surprised at his reaction.

"Oh, God," he said. He didn't call for two weeks, time enough for her erratic flow of blood to present itself, and Lou knew he'd want to know. She didn't blame him if he were scared silly at the prospect of fatherhood. She was scared silly at the idea of motherhood. And it was really her fault that she hadn't let him know before about her little problem.

She needed to talk to him but he had not given her his number. "I'm never home anyway," he had explained and she never questioned him about it. After all, he was an international pilot, headed away in any direction most of the time.

She called United Airlines and because she was an employee, she was given his contact number. "Please tell Mark," she said to the woman at the other end of the line, "that it's all come out okay." He would get the message, she thought.

The man who loved her almost-flat chest never called again. She waited for weeks, called the contact number and hung up so many times that the woman blew up and said she'd report her. So there it was. She'd been his little secret, a willing fillip to whatever other life he lived. A mistress, if a person can be one without knowing it. Duped, for sure. Maybe he really didn't like her flat chest. Would she ever find anyone who did?

She did. A year later, she was introduced to Robert Hanley, a steady man with a sailboat on Lake Union, family connections and a businesslike view of life. No intellectual conversations, but also no complaints about his boss since he was the boss. No secrets. He had firm grip on how to proceed with life, an MBA directing him, like a leeward wind, allowing him to tack this way, then that way, to make a lot of money.

A good husband, he climbed on the roof of their new house, cleaned its gutters, scraped moss off in wads that landed on the patio. She painted bedrooms, planted her first garden, and produced three boys in seven years despite her lazy ovaries. Her father died. Not able to get to his bedside at the end, she said her goodbyes to him as she cleaned out the cupboards of the house she grew up in. She had little time to contemplate the meaning of life. She had too much life around her, needing to be corralled, taught to eat with a fork.

At some quiet moment, twenty years and four houses later, several of the boys out with their father on a lake or a soccer field, she, in her new West Seattle kitchen, thumbing through a frayed copy of *Joy of Cooking*, felt the click of the next place locking in. Often, a recipe for six had to be cut in half. Two chairs sat empty at most dinners. The tide of her motherhood was ebbing.

Soon she would be able to return to her own shoreline, walk its quiet sands.

"I don't understand," Robert said when she tried to explain this epiphany. "We own a mountain cabin, have the money to send the boys to whatever colleges they choose, we've just finished a new, and expensive, I might add, remodel on the house."

Lou interrupted. "It's not about any of that. It's about me, my separate self. I know it sounds..."

"Isn't having three sons, none of whom have ended up in jail or on the streets, a portfolio that will keep us in our old ages, enough to make a person appreciate the shoreline she's already walking?"

She gave up trying to find the words. Instead, she took to knitting, the steady movement of her needles every afternoon bringing her close to the solitude she craved. Therapy, she realized later, when she recalled those gently clicking hours, tucked like fragrant sachets between the raucous late afternoon entries, the never-satisfied appetites, of her covey of males. Her hair had begun losing its black early on; her reflection in the bathroom mirror sometimes startled her. Who is that white-haired person? she'd wonder and knit another sweater, waiting to find out.

One by one, the boys meandered off to their next lives, to women other than their mother, women Lou found quite curious for the most part. Why would Matthew like a twit like that? How on earth had Virginia brought Jeff to his knees? Well, the girl did have lovely feet, softly curving legs, and...Lou didn't want to go into this sort of dissection, her own body almost as flat and angular as it had been in college, and now, if you judged by the skin on her forearms, drying up like an autumn leaf.

Then Robert sold his business and the new owners asked him to stay on as a consultant in their home office in Los Angeles. He agreed, enticed away from their house on Puget Sound with its watery vista framed in snowcapped mountains, the home they had vowed would be forever, because he had been chosen.

"I'll set us up," he said, not noticing her inability to breathe, to protest. Three weeks later, she flew to California, where he introduced her to his new life at a party celebrating the annexation of yet another telecom, another success. Afterwards, "Do you like it?" he asked, his arm levitating across the horizon of the high-rise loft he had leased, as if he were at that moment creating it just for her.

If so, then he had chosen everything she hated: stainless steel and black leather and terrazzo entries, the sleek ambience of a space built for entertaining. The condo looked out from the twenty-third floor of a marble phallic thrust, rising in midst of everything she disliked about southern California, including the murky orange glow of an unreal sunset striping the walls.

"Is there a garden?" Lou asked. "Or a walking path? Can I get to a evergreen tree without driving fifty miles?"

After a moment, Robert said, "I'm not sure." He seemed to be trying to swallow something bitter, unexpected, as he led her to the sharp-edged sofa. "This is the main chance for me, Lou, a great job at corporate headquarters, a car and driver, a salary plumped up with stock options. At my age, this will never happen again."

She understood all this. She wondered what it had to do with her, really.

So Robert stayed in LA and Lou flew south once a month or so to clasp his elbow at company functions where it was important to have a spouse in acceptable garb. What might that garb be? Lou wondered, as she sorted through a closet of jeans and shorts and Adidas. Slinky would slide right off her body. Frilly? She'd look like a parfait. She chose, of course, not being totally out of it, a black sheath, black heels (her first in ten years), and the diamond earrings Robert presented to her in gratitude for her agreeing to show up once in a while.

When he asked again a year or so later if she would consider moving south, she answered, "No, never," the first time in their thirty years of married life that she refused him so openly, so mindful of herself.

The truth was, she loved being alone, her early morning walks around the lake, and her hours of quiet knitting and gardening, and the books that piled up beside the bed to be read long into the night, pages rustling, bed light shining onto the empty pillow next to her. She missed Robert, of course, as she sat poking at whatever she had found in the fridge for her dinner, his cheerful early-morning greeting behind the *Wall Street Journal*. She didn't miss his penis and the pain it brought whenever it entered her in recent years. Apparently, her body also was unwilling to pretend any longer.

He's changing too, she thought, as she waved him away at the airport after a weekend intended to celebrate her fifty-seventh birthday. Instead of a self-congratulatory toast to the future during their expensive evening at Cafe des Amis, however, Robert had erupted in an unusual vent of frustration. He reached for her hand, held it against the white linen. "Every day is like walking into a shredder, Lou. If it weren't for the money I'd be back here in a heartbeat."

Something about the male ego apparently allowed men to shred their lives for money, in this case, a cache intended to carry the two of them through the last leg of their trail together. The problem was, Lou thought, they stood at a Y in that trail, about to head off in two different directions.

"Maybe you'll get used to it," she said, taking her hand from his, glancing around for a waiter to fill her water glass.

A part-time job opened up in her favorite bookstore. For three days a week, she smelled books, shelved books, talked books. "Try Shreve," she told a young mother. "I really liked *The Reader*," she confided to a hesitant middle-aged browser. "Have you read Sebald?" she asked a bespectacled older man. She sat up all night to read Harry Potter. She stayed in all weekend to immerse herself in Doris Lessing. She waded into waves of words. Their coolness tingled at her temples, made her lips curve in new ways.

Her sons and their wives dropped by occasionally and told her she was looking great. "When's Dad coming back?" they asked at first and then not as often, as two years went by and Lou had convinced them that she was indeed okay. She knitted everyone, including Robert, a wool sweater for one of those Christmases. He left it in a drawer when he headed back to California after the holiday.

Their marriage sloughed away, shedding bits of itself with each phone call, every three-hour flight. Lou knew its condition was terminal before Robert did, and she forced him to face it one Thursday night when he phoned to tell her how disappointed he was that she chose to not come down to have dinner with his boss and wife. "This is important," he said.

"I choose to not be married to you," she answered. She had practiced the words but she hadn't planned for her voice to crack and break apart, for her hand to shake until she settled her elbow on the desk in order to calm the phone at her ear. "I cannot do what you want me to do. Perhaps the milk of human kindness has leaked out, left me empty and of no use to anyone."

Robert flew home, of course, gathered the sons in the living room, asked her to explain herself. The boys shifted their long bodies, glanced at their photographs on the piano, stared at their fists as the father interrogated the mother. "Why? What have I done? Can't you understand that what I am doing is for both of us? Do you know how selfish you are?"

"I've told you all I can. I don't intend to hurt anyone. The choice I've made is about me, not about you." She looked at her sons, included them in that declaration.

Finally David stood up. "You guys need a counselor or something, but not me, not us." He nodded at his brothers' silent faces, his eyes shining with tears, and Lou leaned toward him and wanted to take his hand.

She sat back, tightened her lips, girded herself. *Four men are telling me that I am wrong,* she thought, *that changing my life will disrupt theirs, that I have no right to make this choice. When, in all their changes and choices and growing up, did any one of them ever wonder if he were hurting me, ignoring my needs, leaving me behind?*

Her sons walked out. Robert remained seated in his big chair, his head in his hands. "So, now what?" he asked. "Do I stay here tonight? What are the rules?"

"No rules," Lou answered. "Stay. We probably need to talk about money." It was ironic that their last conversation that weekend centered on the division of the very stuff that had eroded their marriage. Once he understood he could not persuade her otherwise, Robert took care of the business of the separation in his business-honed way. He gave her the little log cabin on the mountain, an allowance that paid for all of her needs including the old truck she would use to haul topsoil and lumber in, a portfolio of stocks. The wedding ring remained on his finger months after Lou had removed hers.

She spent the summer on the mountain. She brought Robert's unused tools from his workbench and put them to work. She sawed new boards for the steps and porch, and sang long-forgotten camp songs as she drove the nails into aromatic cedar. She installed large rolls of pink insulation in the attic, breathing who-knows-what into her lungs, and determined that she could build a loft overlooking the front fireplace room, a cozy reading room, once she got the courage. She chinked in the spaces between rough logs and glazed windowpanes. One day she went into town and bought a table saw and, with the guidance of Jeff, learned to rip a 2 X 4 without cutting off a finger. Leaning over her youngest manchild as he guided the slab of wood through the spinning teeth, she saw that, at twenty-five, his black hair was whitening, just as hers had at the same age.

Then Matthew arrived to instruct her how to build forms for the concrete foundations of the new room she wanted to add to the back of the cabin, a room which would hold the claw-footed bathtub she rescued from the alley next to a plumbing shop. That project could take a while, she conceded, as she tried to imagine cutting a doorway through the log wall in the bedroom. One weekend all three sons drove up with a chain saw and did it for her. Afterwards, they sat around the rough wooden table in the back yard and admired their handiwork. "We probably should cover the hole before we leave, Mom," Brady said. "Unless bears don't scare you."

"Nothing scares me," she answered, "except bears," and it seemed to be true.

"Remember when Jeff was so afraid of water that he hung on to the bench during his swimming lesson screaming and wouldn't let go?"

"And the time you threw up on the Ferris wheel, and they had to stop it and let you off?"

"And the time..." Her sons. Lou could not recall ever be-fore loving them so much, could not remember when they loved her like this.

A year later, Madge held a slumber party at her beach house to celebrate the solarium foursome's sixtieth birth-days. These occasional comings together brought the friends back that early intimacy no matter how long it had been since they had seen each other. Joan admitted to having her neck tightened, Jackie to electrolysis on her chin hairs. Madge confessed to discovering that all of her parts still worked, with the help of a welder who also fixed her fence. The big news, of course, was Lou's divorce. Each of her friends in the past year had received a phone call from Rob-ert asking if she could explain Lou's decision, had she seen it coming? He had sounded miserable, maybe a little drunk. They each had answered no.

"I can't explain it either," Lou told them that first after-noon they spread a blanket on the sand and started talking. "I've never felt as strong, wrong word, as full, whole, it's a cliché, I know, as whole as I have this past year." How could she explain the exhilaration of this new life? "I wake up at dawn, go to bed whenever I feel like it, work hard and get dirty every day."

Her friends looked at her over their bi-focal sunglasses as if they were trying to visualize this life, whether they should believe her. "Let's face it," Lou said, "you all know I've al-ways been a hermit, kind of." Had her friends heard it, the waver in her voice, the click of uncertainty in those last words? She needed to change the subject. "What's happening with you, Jackie?"

"Definitely not a hermit," Jackie shrugged. "More of a nursemaid, I guess. I marry an old guy, and Joan, you marry a young one. At least you don't have to call home to see if he's burned the house down with the microwave," she said as she got up to use the cabin's phone.

They all had grandchildren by then. Everyone had photos stashed in her bags, even Lou, who brought photos of a wee little girl gifted with her grandfather's blonde curls. "That's Victoria, that's Will," naming these new persons, the new titles they themselves had acquired: Nana, Grammie, Mudgie, Gee Gee. By the end of the afternoon, they knew that at sixty they had come to a way station, a place to regroup, a time to consider their lives once more.

"We need a recognition of this moment in our lives," Madge said. "Maybe a crones' ceremony."

"Aren't crones bitchy menopausal women, like the warty witches in Macbeth?"

"Post menopausal," Jackie instructed. "Women who have lived long enough to be wise." Jackie gone through a spiritual phase a while back and had learned about crones and incantations, the result of one moonlit chant and a sexy new age-painter.

"So we are post-post menopausal," Madge said. "Very, very wise. What are we called?"

"Old." Lou couldn't resist.

That evening, they lit blue candles, read aloud from Jackie's books about potions for reviving one's liver, one's love life, one's outlook. Lou, feeling she needed to add a literary aspect to this ritual, rose, began to recite.

"Look on my Works, ye Mighty, and despair!" She pointed to the sand dunes "... boundless and bare /The Lone and level sands stretch far away."

She sat down, amazed that the words still resided somewhere inside her. "Shelley," she added, "Ozymandias."

"Depressing," Jackie said. "The poem and the fact that you can remember it."

Then they each held in her palm an object she found on the beach, a crab carapace, a sea rock, a clamshell, and predicted where she would be in five years.

"Five years hence," Lou insisted.

"Forsooth, I foretell a toothsome novel written by me, astounding the world," Madge said.

"Ergo," Joan intoned, "you'll finally be rich and famous."

"I take umbrage," Jackie said. "And I'll take a little more wine along with it."

"Call the wait-ress," Lou advised her.

"She's on the matt-ress in the pant-ry."

"God, remember?" Joan asked, her voice suddenly solemn. "How we smoked away our days wishing for a real life?"

"I've learned to be careful what I wish for," Lou said, into the murmur of the fire lighting the room. A bitter sting made her blink, look away.

"What?" Joan shifted, met Lou's eyes.

"You might get it." Lou never did this, ever, whine, except at midnight, except with these women.

Her friends waited.

"And?" Joan urged.

It seemed safe to admit now, to herself, to them. "Sometimes I am drenched in loneliness."

"Yes."

"Sometimes I wonder if I should just give in, go to LA, tough it out, be a man."

"And then?"

"Then moments of sheer joy flood in, reading Auden at dawn, watching an iris open, lying in the dewy grass near the cabin and counting satellites and shooting stars. And then I understand why I chose what I chose." Lou brushed a hand across her eyes. "Hell, where is the tis-sue?"

The tubroom was finally finished, its rough cedar boards sending waves of clean, fresh scent through the house, and Lou began planning the garden. She had planted decades of bedding plants and zinnias at their Seattle house. This land, though, was primeval: old growth firs advancing their shadows daily across the one spot of sun and its spiky rye grass on the south side, sword ferns and Oregon grape bulking up the fortlike walls at its edge. Her book had no advice on forest gardens, and after turning over one shovelful of pungent soil, she set aside her tools, knew she wasn't ready.

The small community, at the bottom of the road leading to the cabin, included a gas station, a tavern, and a multipurpose store, a large bulletin board at its entrance. One day, after searching for fresh lettuce in the bin of wilting vegetables, salads having become the centerpiece of her diet, she saw a notice. "Master gardener offering consultation on high altitude, rocky, shaded gardens. You may not believe this, but I ripened tomatoes last year. Really."

Lou gave Susan Ridge a call, invited her to coffee, asked what she charged. "Let's see what you've got first," a congenial middle-aged voice answered.

Susan was as frizzy and maroon-haired as Lou was straight and white-haired. Lou imagined that they would be a perfect do-over ad, she "Before," Susan vibrantly "After." Susan swelled in places that on Lou bones protruded, but her fingernails were black with dirt, just like Lou's.

The Master Gardener was intrigued with the possibilities of the barren, occasionally sunny spot Lou showed her. The problems, of course, were the acidic fir needles padding their footsteps, the rocks bubbling up from the dry ground, the ostentatious red rhododendron. The answer, it became apparent to Susan and then to Lou, who was both impressed and bemused by the Latin flowing from this woman's lips, the solution was to create a meadow, a mountain meadow with wildflowers, perhaps gentian, fireweed, fox glove, bears paw, a mound of wild iris to lift the spirit. Others for their color, but no zinnias. No chrysanthemums, no tight cushions of marigolds no matter how hearty they might be. A ground cover of wild strawberry and violets and buttercups. In the summer, ferns would spring up, enjoying a few moments in the sun and the watering system Susan would install.

"How about it?" she asked, and Lou answered, "Let's do it."

JO BARNEY

Perennial gardens take three years, according to gardening lore. The first year results in disappointing green knobs, the second, a promise of what will come, the third, if one's planned well, a surfeit of pleasure.

Surfeit it was, that third summer. By then Lou and Susan were friends, both of them up to their elbows in the soil and rocks of Lou's now mystic circle of light. Only the ugly red rhododendron remained, an invader in this lush landscape. And only the rest of her life.

It's your turn now, Lou. You have the words
and the courage to finish this story. Only bears
frighten you. M.

Lou gathers up the pages crumpled under her foot, shakes the sand from them, then pauses before she gets to her knees in order to stand up. The hollow she crouches in is warm. And she is warmed by Madge's words. Is she ready to face the chilling winds, her friends, let them understand what her story means? And is she willing to tell the rest of it, the secret she's held tight for forty years.

19

Sunday Morning: Turbulent Skies
Jackie

"So where's my folder?" Jackie has decided to read her story and get it over with. What the hell, it couldn't be worse than the story of this weekend. "And is there any wine left?" She opens the drawer looking for the corkscrew and remembers that Lou has put it somewhere.

Joan, brought inside from the deck by the morning's cool breeze, lifts her eyes from the manuscript in her lap and points to the papers on the trunk. "Read first, then wine."

"I can read and drink at the same time, you know." Jackie's not sure whether she's still angry or working up a panic attack. Just about when she thinks she's finally gotten her life in some sort of order, she's expected to jump out another window. Not alone, this time, but just the same.

Joan says, "Uh, uh."

"Shit." Jackie takes her folder into the bedroom and slams the door. She props up three pillows against the head-board, settles into their softness, and pulls out twenty or so pages. She reads.

WHATSOEVER THINGS ARE HONEST: JACKIE'S STORY

My friend, your complicated, wondrous life can't be captured on a few pieces of paper and certainly no one but you can finish this story. I wish I could be there to hear the ending. M.

Jackie cannot think of what to do next, or first. The thick envelope settles on the floor, its contents quivering under her hand until she lays the paper down on the table and stops trying to focus on the words. She already knows what it says. Ron called the day before and warned her. Well, not warned her as much as advised her to open her mail for once. She'd stopped looking at her mail when she realized she wasn't getting any, except catalogues and ads for new windshields. Until today, that is, when this letter-headed sheet of paper will officially inform her that her stepson Ron is divorcing her.

Fred, her husband, doesn't know that their marriage is on the rocks. Fred doesn't know anything, except the lies his son tells about her. Fred is about as senile as an eight-five-year-old can get and still sit up. Jackie reminds herself one more time that she should have suspected that smile on Ron's face at the news of their marriage ten years ago. Obviously, her husband's son had known something that she didn't.

Some weeks before the wedding, her priest friend Xavier had taken her out to coffee and asked why she was marrying an old man and Jackie answered that she liked Fred. He made her laugh. He treated her well.

"He makes you laugh? That's why you are marrying him?' Xavier broke apart a scone and gave her half.

Jackie couldn't think of a better reason. She needed to be married. She was tired of being alone, by which she meant, not exactly alone, she had lovers, but no one as cheerful and kind as Fred. Kneading her arthritic knuckles, she said, "He will take care of me." She should have knocked on wood, despite the pain, and rolled her eyes. Instead, she got up to get another scone. It didn't hurt, she added, that Fred had enough money for the both of them, a nice house, an antique silver service, and oil paintings and Persian rugs, not only in the living room but also the bedroom. These items had been chosen by Fred's deceased wife, but Jackie didn't mind. After all, she assured Xavier, she would bring things from her past life into the house, including her massage table and sheets and towels and the music system with its Wyndham Hill tapes and an assortment of oils and creams.

"That's how I met Fred," she explained. "He came to the Whole Health Clinic for a massage and exercises for his new knee, one of those silver fox guys, thick white hair, eyebrows hovering like doves over green eyes?" Jackie smiled remembering. "He wanted to dance again. He flexed his deltoids under my fingers, wiry, a wiry guy all over. I admired his body. 'Irish?' I guessed. He laughed, and said, 'Gypsy?' back at me. I rattled my earrings at him and got out the almond oil. It wasn't long before he was visiting my table three times a week."

Xavier grinned. "You're turning pink just thinking about him."

"He cheers me up. And after two months, he swung his seventy-five-year-old healed knee off the table and said it was time to start boogying again. Would I join him at the Cristal Ballroom Saturday night? Yes, I would be delighted. And later, yes, I would be delighted to marry him. Why not?"

"Why not?" Xavier repeated, looking at her over the edge of his coffee cup, smiling, she thought.

Jackie took this as a blessing from her priest so she stopped trying to explain—how she loved the elbow held out to her in that old-fashioned way as they walked into the crowded dance hall. How he had whispered, as they slow-danced, that her strong body, as tall as his, was Junoesque. She made him feel young, he said. That night as they made love for the first time she closed her eyes and could imagine him twenty years younger, his poetic moanings about moon-

light and orifices as sexy as his fingers, stroking her into a
state she had not experienced in a long time.

When he proposed, her two oldest daughters, each a
thousand miles away in different directions, told her to go
for it. Fred sounded okay, they said. As they moved into
their thirties, they had begun to experience a few blips in
their own marriages, and their voices had trembled with envy and sadness. However, her youngest daughter, Sally, an
uptight young woman, wrote from her all-white San Francisco apartment that this relationship disgusted her, some old
man on his death bed, was her mother crazy? She resurrected a couple of past involvements Jackie had confessed to in
moments of believing her daughter cared about what happened to her, relationships that curdled or blew apart at the
whiff of rings or next year, and advised her mother to cut
out the foolishness and act like a grandmother for once.

That was hard to do, Jackie wrote back, when her children and their resulting children had elected to live as far as
they could from her. Just wait, she warned Sally, you'll find
out what it's like to be fifty-five and alone. And the two of
them hadn't written or emailed until Sally called, months
later, to tell her mother she was pregnant and that she and
her partner, Billie, were ecstatic. Jackie blinked at this new
information, regrouped, and said, "I'll be happy for you and
your girlfriend, kid, if you'll be happy for me and my husband." And the deal was sealed.

Life was not all almond oil in Fred's house. After a couple of weeks of feeling spied on, Jackie blinded first-wife
Margaret's photo hovering over their bed with a silk scarf.

She couldn't remove the picture outright because Fred's son, Ron, had taken to dropping by unannounced. Under the guise of checking the plumbing or the sprinkling system, he circuited the house, commenting on furniture that had been moved, asking the whereabouts of the teapot mother brought from Germany, as if that deified it or her, and noting other items Jackie had done away with. One day he said, "You've changed the bedspread," just after she had raced him to the bedroom to un-scarf his mother, and Jackie moved in on him wanting to strangle him.

"You have no right to be in our bedroom," she snapped.

He stepped back into the hallway with a gentle smile. "We'll see," he said as he called a goodbye to his father who sat watching a different conflict on CNN and heard nothing of this one.

"You have to help me," Jackie told Fred, after Ron left and she finally got her husband's attention. "This is our house. Put your foot down."

Fred answered that he imagined that it was hard for a son to get used to his father being married. "He's just a kid. He'll get over it."

The one thing Jackie didn't like about Fred was that he never got angry, the juices required for such an effort all used up, she guessed. "A kid! He's forty with his own wife and children," she yelled, trying to whip him into a response, but Fred had begun punching the buttons on the remote by then.

After five years, Jackie was surprised she'd become taller than her husband. Then, after a couple of microwave and frying pan flameouts, she understood she could no longer trust him to cook his own lunch. Fred stopped dancing, even in their Persian-rugged living room, choosing instead to push back into his lounger and listen to his story tapes, a routine that sent her out into the back yard with a magazine until she thought to buy him earphones. It wasn't the stories that got to her, it was the speed at which Fred set his player, the voices wobbly, unintelligible prehensile growls. When she asked why, he told her he was listening slower nowadays.

He still liked sex, "playing around," he called it, but Jackie found herself doing most of the playing, and as a rule, their gropings ended with rumbles of contentment sounding deep in his sleeping throat after which she would work on her fingers on the folds of her own body.

The words "old man" popped out of her mouth the day she tried to talk about all this to Xavier. He listened in his calm way and didn't refer to their premarital conversation, except to remind her that marriage was in sickness and health, which also meant old age. He encouraged her to find new activities that would brighten her life. "Perhaps a job?" he suggested. "You liked working here at the monastery in our care center." Then he glanced at her hands.

Fred wasn't the only one changing. Jackie's body was as strong as ever, but her fingers were morphing into swollen hooks. She could barely tie her shoes. She wore nothing with buttonholes. "Arthritis, an occupational hazard," her doctor informed her. "You've worked your hands hard for forty years. They're tired." Then he added, "Good thing you're married. You'll not make a living doing therapy anymore," as he wrote out the prescription. "This might help." It hadn't, and Jackie went back to her homeopath whose brown bottles now lined up like squat warriors on the windowsill in the kitchen.

"What's all this?" Ron demanded during one of his inspection tours. He picked up a bottle. "Glucosamine? Gingko? St. Johns Wort? You're not treating Dad with any of this voodoo stuff, are you?"

And Jackie, her aching hands behind her back, answered, "It's none of your business."

That's when he let her know that it was his business. How the night before Xavier married them, his father had signed the papers that made him his father's legal guardian. "For just this reason," Ron said, waving a hand at the capsules and powders on the sill. "My father is declining under your so-called care." Then he opened the recycling bin and pointed at the wine bottles clattering inside it. "You're an alcoholic. You sedate my father with this stuff. Don't interrupt," he said, as Jackie tried to explain. "I don't think you are capable of taking care of him."

Jackie slammed the bin shut. "You sidle in here looking for a reason to get me in bad with my husband, and what you're really afraid of is that he'll die and leave me his money." Those wine bottles had been collecting there quite a while, she was pretty sure.

Ron nodded at the den door behind which Fred was snoozing, tapes rambling in his ears. "This is criminal. You have stuck him in a chair, plugged him in, mushed his brain. If I have to, I'll go to court and remove him from this house." Ron's angry face glowed pinkly, piglike, a trait he must have gotten from his mother since Jackie had never seen Fred in such a state.

She decided to tell him. "Ron, I have a pre-nup contract with your father in which he agreed that if our marriage ended by death or divorce, I will get this house and a monthly allowance to support me. Your father insisted on this. When he dies, most of his money will go to you and your family." She touched his coat sleeve to let him know she'd won. "So, see? Nothing for you to worry about."

Ron's fat cheeks wobbled at her. "No way in hell are you getting my mother's house!" He thrashed into the den. Fred reached for the pause button, but left his earphones on. He hated to interrupt a good story. "You been having a conversation?" he asked, smiling vaguely at them both.

Ron removed the phones from his father's head and asked if it was true that he had given the house to Jackie. Fred said he remembered an agreement like that; seemed like a good thing to do when he was gone. Who'd want it?

Red blotches gathered on Ron's neck, seeped into his hairline. "Dad. This is our family house. You still have mother's picture in your bedroom." Fred looked surprised at this news. "And you can't tell me she didn't trick you into signing that agreement." Ron pointed a shaking finger at Jackie.

"Like you did the guardianship, Ron?" she said, pointing back.

"Yes," Fred answered to something one of them had said, and he put the earphones back on. "I want to hear the end of this." He smiled his sweet smile. "All settled?"

Jackie hadn't told anyone, not even Xavier, about this fight. She didn't want to think about someone else being Fred's guardian. That was her job—legally, she was sure. So from then on she spent most of her days, sitting with him, rubbing his back as often as her stiff fingers allowed and feeding him the macaroni and cheese he had become addicted to. Sometimes he called her Baby, a tiny chip of memory edging up from a previous life, perhaps, but as the weeks went by, his name for her became Mother. She didn't drink wine until he went to bed, which was quite early now that he believed he was a little boy. She dressed him every morning, adjusted his headphones and set up his tape, so that if Ron came by, he would find his father clean and in his chair. She didn't mind feeding Fred, making sure he got to the toilet, helping him shower, but then he started peeing his pants and the rest of it. After one really bad weekend, Jackie had had it with sickness and health and old age and she hired a set of caretakers.

She still could not believe the way her marriage had come to a dead halt a month ago. She had gone to an exercise class, one of the few indulgences she allowed herself after Fred took his downturn. When she got home and called out her usual "Hello, honey," she was answered by a slight stir of breath, her own. Nothing else. Even the caretaker was gone.

She went into Fred's den and saw dust babies where her husband's tapes and earphones and chair had been. In their bedroom, gray outlines marked the absence of Margaret's scarfed picture and the silk rug. In the kitchen, on the island next to a dried up bowl of mac and cheese, Jackie found the court order accusing her of suspected elder abuse giving Ron as guardian the right to move his father to a more acceptable place—Ron's home. It also instructed her to not come within five hundred feet of that home until the matter was settled.

Jackie's first thought, when it all sunk in, was to wonder how Ron's exquisitely anal wife would deal with an incontinent father-in-law. Her second thought was the realization that for the first time in almost ten years, she was free. The next day, she cleaned closets, polished window panes, and cooked dinner for herself and Xavier.

She had met the priest twenty years before, as her marriage to Mitch was winding down, and she had gone back to work as a physical therapist. One of her contracts brought her to the monastery's care facility where she worked with elderly patients in various stages of rehabilitation or disintegration. Xavier was thirty-five to her forty-something and he had deep brown eyes and lovely hands which at that moment patted the shoulder of Mrs. Pierson, Jackie's next client, torqued into a wheelchair. His gold ring brushed her aged neck, a ring embossed with a cross, Jackie noticed, the only piece of the man that indicated his vocation. The rest of him wore a good-looking silk shirt and slacks.

"I feel so bad," Mrs. Pierson was saying, "and I know it is my fault. I should have never told Henry to quit snoring or go sleep on the couch."

Jackie looked at the priest.

"Mrs. Pierson's husband died on that couch fifteen years ago."

Jackie nodded. "Come on, dear, we'll take your mind off your worries with a little exercise," and she wheeled the old lady into the treatment room. Later, Xavier introduced himself and told her he admired the way she didn't deny Mrs. Pierson her feelings. "Everybody needs validation of her feelings," he said, and with that, Jackie started to tear up. He led her to the chapel and they talked, the first of many times Jackie turned to Xavier for validation and for, well, she had to admit it to herself, she was attracted to him. At first, she blamed her unhappy marriage for nudging her into this impossible crush, but even after she and Mitch were divorced, she resettled in an apartment, her girls in college, her former husband successfully boxed and stored in an only-sometimes-conscious part of her brain, she still got slightly sick to her stomach whenever she thought of the brown-eyed priest.

"Do you miss sex?" she asked several years into their friendship. By then they were intimate and honest with each other. Good friends, in fact. Jackie had accepted Xavier's invitation to a religious retreat in Montana, not really knowing what a retreat was. So far, it had meant a few titillating moments with Xavier like this one, and many quiet moments with herself, listening to chanting monks and red-winged blackbirds. At this particular moment, they lay under a tree, the only one within sight, chewing on the hard bread baked each morning by the retreat's cook, a bottle of forbidden wine smuggled in by Jackie between them.

"Of course," he answered. "I always will. But it was my choice. I can live with that decision."

"How?" Jackie asked, thinking of her own craving for both Xavier and the several other men she was seeing. How, or rather, why would one make that decision? "Are you gay?" she asked, terrified at the thought.

"I'm attracted to women. I'm attracted to you."

"And?"

"That's it. "

"And?"

"I sublimate." Seeing the look on Jackie's face, he added, "and that too."

"What?"

"Pray, of course." Xavier laughed and Jackie laughed, and she felt a flurry of hope, a prayer of a chance. Somehow, the conversation swerved to her need to be the pursuer, not the pursued, the most recent example being the painter Jackie had hired who had never quite gotten his overalls back on once he'd entered the door. "Maybe I need to feel in control," Jackie commented, not understanding that years later she would be there from necessity and that it wouldn't feel that great any more.

"I think you're afraid of being loved," Xavier said.

Jackie thought about it for a minute, answered, "But you love me and I'm not afraid."

"Yes," Xavier said, and Jackie imagined that he was praying.

After the house painter, there was the Reichian body-work person, who met her at his door in black jockey shorts. Once she settled on his mat, he pressed at every nerve in her body until she tingled with pain and pleasure and then told her to go home. "Why?" she asked, barely able to sit up.

"It's the anticipation," he answered, "that we seek."

The next time he did something with his teeth that felt like a chipmunk gnawing a nut, and she nearly exploded, and he sent her home again.

When he met her the third time, naked under a samurai's robe, white teeth glimmering, she told him to anticipate fucking himself and slammed the screen door on his foot. Anticipation was one thing, torture was another. And so it went, one strange man after another, until she took Fred as a client and then as a husband.

Jackie rereads the attorney's letter. As guardian of his father, Ron is initiating divorce proceedings in his father's name. The reason, abandonment and emotional distress. Abandonment! She reaches for the phone and manages to dial the number at the top of the letterhead. A cool, robotic voice answers and after a few sputtering moments, Jackie is connected with the signature at the bottom of the page.

"Abandonment!" she explodes. "His son took him away from this house, and has not allowed me to visit my husband or to phone. If anyone has been abandoned, it's me!'

"Mrs. Clayton. I cannot discuss this with you. I would advise you to get an attorney to help you through this." The man hangs up, and Jackie is left with an empty phone and a pain in her stomach. She leans back in her favorite mohair chair to sort things out. I have the pre-nup, she reassures herself, and for two months Ron has sent me the monthly check it promised. He's just trying to scare me.

Without a blink, her eyes cloud up, and she is crying for Fred. What, in that foggy mind of his, must he think has happened? That she's left him, dropped dead, stolen his house? Jackie blots her eyes on her collar, pours another glass of wine.

"I don't know where to get a lawyer," she tells Xavier the next day. "And I can't afford one."

She can't read the expression on her priest's face. Exasperation? Concern?

"I can lend you a little, to get you started. Ask one of your divorced friends for a name. It's not that bad, Jackie. You can do it."

Desire? Maybe? Jackie sips her latte and tries to capture the idea. As usual, Xavier is wearing civilian clothes, an open-necked sport shirt and pleatless khakis. A bit of black curl laps at his throat. At fifty, he is cragging out a little, the way runners do, the downward valleys in his cheeks giving him a solemn, thoughtful look like Abraham Lincoln. His glance sweeps into all of her empty places, and despite her depression, she smiles for the first time in a couple of days. "Thank you," she says. She resists reaching for his hand. She always moves too fast. This will have to be slow.

"You need to take a little time for yourself," Xavier is saying. "Nothing will happen for a while, once the attorneys take over. Why don't you take a week's retreat at St. Rose Ranch again? You said you liked it the first time you went."

That's true, she remembers. She had liked the silence, the long early morning walks, the conversations with the solemn men and women taking their annual breaks at the foot of mountains which lay like stone giants as far as one could see. She'd never felt safer. For a few days, she even thought she might become a Catholic, but as she read and talked, she understood that she could not be confined by someone else's idea of God. Not that she had a clue what God was, even now, at least that she could put into words. But the stony peaks, the tumbleweed drifting into the fences of the ranch, the eagle soaring above her, all informed her that She existed.

Xavier is right. Jackie agrees she needs to move off this pathetic spot. "When are you going?"

"In two weeks. I'll make reservations and we can travel together. By train?"

"No," Jackie answers, her heart tap dancing under her ribs. "I'll drive."

A day later, she hires a lawyer, Beth Newman, shows her the letter, asks her to take care of it. Jackie explains that it all seems illogical, since she has a pre-nuptial contract, provision for a monthly support, the gift of the house in case of divorce or his death.

"That's it?"

"I think so. He and his attorney met a few times a while back. I don't think anything's changed as far as I'm concerned."

"You don't?" Beth asks and Jackie understands that it has. This divorce isn't about the supposed lack of care she had given Fred, her mistakes or the trouble with the aide, Bella Blue. It's about a guardian removing an-ex wife from an old man's will.

"Shit. When the two of them came out of the den arm-in-arm, I thought my almost-new husband and his loving son had been having a little confab about marriage, maybe about sex, the opposite, of course, of the usual father/son talk before a wedding. I was so stupid."

Beth shoves a box of tissues at her and tells her not to give up. Jackie has the contract to back her up. She'll call when she knows more. Jackie leaves the office convinced that her attorney also thinks she is stupid. When she gets home, she rubs her aching hands with almond oil and remembers Fred under those hands and his little groans of pleasure. In fact, the whole Fred thing has been stupid, as her daughter Sally had warned years before. She should call Sally, ask what Madison wants for his eighth birthday, maybe talk a little.

Sally answers on the first ring. "Oh, hi," she says. She seems to be mewing. "No, nothing's wrong. I just have a cold or something. What about you? You sound horrible."

The wine is taking over. Jackie skips over the birthday. "You were right, Sally. I shouldn't have married Fred. "

"Mom, I can't do this right now."

"Goodbye, then." Jackie hangs up. No use calling her other daughters. Moira and Stephanie, caught up as usual trying to outdo each other, are in the midst of their own divorces. Xavier is teaching a course in retrograde ontology two states away. Her friends, the few she's managed to hang on to during this marriage, are struck dumb by her situation and will only say, "Poor, Jackie." She reaches for the wine bottle as the phone rings.

"Sorry, Mom. I'm not in a good place. I hurt your feelings." Then Sally's little-girl voice wails the story her gone-wrong relationship with Billie, the fight over custody of their son Madison, the other woman, the emptying of the house including the Cuisinart and the above-ground swimming pool that Madison loves so much, and the final insult of discovering that the other woman is the other man. "How could I have been so stupid?" Sally moans, and for once in her life, Jackie can identify with her youngest daughter.

"I think we all are stupid, at one time or another," she says. "Seems to go along with the fear of death." Jackie doesn't know why she said that—probably something Xavier has speculated on in one of their attempts to be philosophical. Ontology, maybe.

"I'm not afraid of death, Mom. I'm afraid of life." The silence that follows these words frightens Jackie more the sobs that preceded it.

"Come home, Sally. I'll be gone for a week, but you can relax here, get away from the phone calls, whatever, and I have a Cuisinart. You can cook for me when I get back from Montana."

"Mom, not the priest again."

"He's a friend, Sally. Maybe my one friend."

Sally will come in a few days, bring Madison if she can get him away from Billie, and in the meantime she will try to align her life forces by practicing her Qigong and meditating.

Only after they hang up does Jackie realize that she hasn't told Sally that her step brother Ron is divorcing his mother-in-law. *Probably good that I haven't*, she thinks. *You can only ask so much of Qigong.* Besides, she is going to try a little meditation herself, at St. Rose Ranch, as well as whatever else that place might offer as solace. She packs her jeans and swimsuit, has her nails done, and waits for her daughter to appear at her doorstep.

Madison stands stone-like as mother and daughter fling themselves at each other. His hooded eyes examine the doormat, his upper lip stretches across two over-sized front teeth in a vise of a pout. He closes his eyes when Jackie bends to hug him. Spiky hair pokes at her breast, her kiss lands somewhere near his shoulder.

"I'm so glad you're here," she says, squatting to try to look at him straight on. His answer comes in the narrow glance he gives her before he turns and wheels his suitcase through the door.

Sally shrugs. "He lost his Gameboy on the plane," she whispers. "I told him Portland has Gameboys too."

"Ah," Jackie answers. Gameboys are easy. Losing someone isn't, as her grandson is beginning to discover.

For two days the three of them go to movies, poke at the new electronic game, and get to know the dog and the boy who live next door. Madison smiles once or twice, and by the time Jackie drives off to pick up Xavier, she is smiling also. The trip will take two days. They'll stop somewhere in the middle at a motel. Jackie does not allow herself to think any further than that.

For the first hour or two, rolling through the Columbia Gorge, they don't say much. The yellow hills, the river that carved them, don't seem to call for words. After a while, Xavier points out the faint trail of wagon wheels above them. "Pioneers. Left their mark on the world," and Jackie says, "I would have liked to be a pioneer," and Xavier tells her she'd be a good one.

Then they talk about Sally and Madison, the chilly female attorney, and Xavier's classes on the meaning of the term *God*. Then he is silent, and Jackie sees that he is asleep, his head bobbing lightly against the car window. For the next two hundred miles she punches at the radio-seek button, trying to find a music station that sends out something other than Christian rock or seventies oldies. She finally gives up and wishes she had brought along one of Fred's tapes, anything to keep her mind occupied. The tanned, veined hand lying on its lap beside her, its ring catching odd shards of sunlight, seems to be asking to be touched. The knee, dark hairs bristling where the shorts end and the quads begin, demands to be squeezed.

Jackie blinks and tells herself to knock it off. This is what always happens. She gets swept into doing stuff she shouldn't do, stuff that always ends with her wondering if she were possessed or something. In college she'd stalked Mitch into a barbershop and he, under a shroud of white cloth, the electric razor raising the hairs on his neck, could not escape her invitation to the Gamma Ps dance. Later, under similar circumstances involving pregnancy, she'd led him into marriage. She'd sucked the toes of the bodywork guy and look where that got her. The painter had obviously met lonely housewives before but maybe not one who asked him to use a paintbrush the way she requested. She had to threaten harassment to get rid of him. And dear Fred. He didn't know what hit him the morning she swirled the almond oil over his nipples and then swirled on and on.

Passion, that was how she tried to explain it over wine to her sorority sisters, the time they gotten together to celebrate their sixtieth birthdays at Margo's beach cabin. The three of them had listened in, shaking their heads, as she called home to make sure Fred hadn't burned the house down.

"What have you gotten yourself into this time, Jackie?" They couldn't imagine what had led her into Fred's skinny arms.

"Wasn't his arms," Jackie had answered and let them suppose whatever they wished.

"Money," Madge guessed, raising a glass. "Right?"

She knew her friends didn't believe her when she denied it. How could she explain the feelings of safety and wholeness she felt with him, in his home, in his hands. "He's a nice man," she answered.

"I'd like that," Lou murmured. "Good for you," and Jackie was off the hook. She had decided not to worry about Fred for a couple of days, and when she got home, she found him in his pajamas, three days in his pajamas, his bed a smelly heap, his pajamas stiff with shit. His eyes brimmed as he told her that Ron had dropped by, got really angry, said he'd be calling her. "Mother, I'm sorry," he said.

That's when she had hired the caretakers. Mrs. Schnitzer came in at seven a.m. Bella Blue took over from four until twelve. Jackie made sure she was home every night, and most of the days, once she decided she wouldn't go crazy in this house now bristling with oxygen tanks, elevated toilets, bars on every slant and step, and a white plastic seat in the shower.

"Come sleep with me," Fred begged, and she would climb onto the narrow hospital bed and curl in on him. And her hands would hold him until he throbbed and sighed.

She and Fred and the caretakers maintained for a while, some days full of laughter, others darkly silent, Fred beyond weeping now. One night he dropped off to sleep at seven-thirty, his tape running on and on until she had pushed the machine's button to silence it, and then she and Bella Blue leaned back in the big chairs in the den glad for the chance not think about diapers and pills. Jackie had gotten to like Bella, after she got over being intimidated by the earring in her eyebrow, and Bella was describing her brother's addiction to performance art, demonstrating in the middle of the

Persian rug his facial gyrations and body jerks as a cactus, when Ron and another man came through the door, waving a flight of papers. The fact that Jackie had removed her jeans so that she could sit crisscross applesauce during the performance did not help, as he took in the scene and said, "For this I'm paying $4000 a month?" threw the Medicare papers at Jackie, and stormed out. But not before the stranger pulled out a digital camera and snapped it at her and at Bella, who stayed in character, tall and unmoving as a cactus, and was, like Jackie, a little drunk.

Three days later, Fred was disappeared, like the Argentinians Jackie'd read about in *Newsweek*. Gone with scarcely a trace.

Didn't mean I wasn't taking care of Fred, that I didn't care about him, that I don't still care for him. She turns off from Umatilla and heads into Washington, glancing, as the car sways onto the next state highway, at the gold-ringed hand lying on its tanned leg. She grips hard in the ten-to-two position on the wheel.

They stop at a motel on the outskirts of Spokane. Two rooms. And eat a silent burger at Evelyn's Roadside. It is as if Xavier knows what she has been thinking. Has entered into a prayerful state. Can no longer see her. She falls into bed exhausted and dreams little hopeful dreams.

By the time they roll into St. Rose's Ranch the next afternoon, Jackie is tired and cranky. Xavier has slept as the car wound its way through the mountains and down through the trees that got squattier as the slopes dried up and became high desert. A hundred miles of heat mirages have preceded them. Her lips are chapped from licking them. Her back aches. Passion for the gently snoring body next to her has taken a back seat to her need for water. She purposely drives over several deep potholes to wake the body up. The gravelly ranch road leads to a cluster of cabins, a large log house, and island of green, and a break from the orange sky. As the car stops, Xavier opens his eyes. "We're here already?" he says, and Jackie bites her sore lip and tries to smile.

A man, wearing jeans and a soiled T-shirt, walks towards them and holds his arms open to Xavier. "Nigel, Jackie," Xavier says, and Jackie receives a handshake and her bag is taken from her as she is led to her little wooden cabin. A gray rocking chair on the porch wavers under their footsteps. The door is not locked. Inside, alone, Jackie recognizes the brown blankets and white pillows, the small table with its reading light, the brass crucifix hanging over the kneeling bench. A rag rug at the side of the bed softens the earnest piety of the room just as it did years before on her first visit. As she had then, she comes to this place at the end of a marriage. She lies down on the rough blanket and closes her eyes. She tries to imagine what it would be like to be at peace, no churnings, no stomach-twisting memories, no needs and strivings to meet them. She allows herself to drift off.

"God, I thought you were dead." A voice yanks her out of her nap. "Get your suit on. The river is waiting for us."

For a moment, Jackie wonders if she is dead, and then the churnings and strivings return, her stomach knots up in its familiar fashion, and she knows she's not. She opens her eyes and sees Xavier at her door, a towel draped around his neck.

Each day has its schedule: mass, breakfast, chores, two hours of contemplation and silence, lunch, two hours for recreation which means swimming or a lively, disorganized game of softball, a 4:00 prayer session, then dinner and music in the chapel. Each evening ends with a quiet walk back to their cabins, Xavier touching her arm as he talks about the book he is reading or a thought he has had during the quiet time.

At first, the silent hours find Jackie lying on her bed reading one of the novels she has brought along, or massaging her hands, or trying a few yoga positions to take the kinks out of her still-sore lower back. She naps, and once she tries out the kneeler, but she is empty of prayer, her mind darting about like the hummingbird outside her door, snatching at bits of thoughts. On the third day, she finds the notepad in the bureau drawer where she has finally unloaded her suitcase. It occurs to her that she needs to corral these thoughts, get them in some sort of order. Leaning back on her pillow, the headboard creaking a little as she gets herself comfortable, she puts pen to paper and the first words that surface surprise her. "I Am A Strong Woman."

Well, I am, really, if you don't count my swollen knuckles. Her legs, only a little scaly, are as firm as they were when she played girls' basketball in college. She can still wear strappy tops without camouflaging her upper arms, thanks to the use she has put them to for forty years. Her breasts, suspended at the moment in a taupe lace bra, if not perky, are nicely rounded. She touches her neck, reluctantly fingers the ropey skin has begun to droop below her chin. She's always had a strong chin, a little like a man. Comely, Fred said. Her hair is strong too, white at the temples, a wiry black cap curling above her forehead, thicker than it had ever been as a young woman. She runs her tongue over her solid molars and winces little as she remembers her first sight of Fred's teeth in the glass next to his sink.

Is that what strong means? The pen moves again. "I was a good mother. Am," she corrects, thinking of Sally and Madison back at home. And I was a strong, uncomplaining wife to two men during the times they needed me most. She hasn't thought about Mitch for a long time, how she had supported the three of them for the two years they lived in the steel Quonset hut and he finished graduate school. She had braided hair and sewed smocks for three little girls while he struggled to find a comfortable niche in the bureaucracy of the school system he had joined and didn't have the courage to leave. She tried not to flinch when he told her he didn't love her, even as her heart burst one last time with an explosion of love for him. Of course, she figured out later that the cause of the blast was not love but anger, and she got most everything she wanted in the settlement, including their new Chevy.

Maybe strong means brave. Jackie crosses that out. I am a risk taker, she writes. Not necessarily brave. Probably stupid. Maybe Sally gets it from me, a genetic thing, she thinks, remembering their last conversation. Jackie recalls trying to stand on the seat of her two-wheeler and breaking her arm. And the night she skied under a full moon with five boys, crouching low to the ground, icy flicks of snow slamming into her face, she finally rolling to the bottom and into a ski rack, giving herself a concussion. And basking in her buddies' wide-eyed in admiration as the ambulance doors shut. And the night she accepted the dare of a drinking buddy during a moment of college senioritis and leaped from a second story window of the sorority house onto a rhododendron and into a car waiting for her at the curb. When she limped in the next morning, she was met with the secret handshake and a vow of secrecy from several of her closest sisters who thanked her for the excitement she had brought to the waning weeks of their college life.

However, the broken ankle gave her away, and she spent a few weeks in a cast grounded by the alum advisor to the first floor guest room. Much later, before Mitch left, she roofed their house, roped to the car parked on the street, the neighbors gasping below her and dodging the flying shingles.

As she gets older, though, her risks have become less physical, more emotional. During the time she was divorced, a time she now understands may have been the high point of her life, she went to clubs, the tallest woman in the room, meeting eyes for the thrill of it. She licked body parts she hadn't known existed. Was licked likewise. She stalked a man or two like the old days in college. She certainly took a risk touching Fred the way she had. This trip with Xavier is a risk. She writes that down, too.

The cowbell clangs, signaling lunch. After the dim quiet of her room, the sunlight stuns her for a moment and then she spots Xavier a few steps in front of her. He smiles, looking beatific as he always does after Silence. She can't talk to him at lunch because Fay Zanetti, an ex-nun from Idaho, slides in between them at the table. She says she is fascinated that Jackie, a person like Jackie, she means, is taking a retreat. Her questions flutter here and there and Jackie swats them off with I guesses and I'm not sure's until she gets tired of the inquisition and begins her own.

"Why did you leave the nummery?" she asks. After a moment, Fay lifts her plate and walks outside.

"Your order," Xavier says. "Why did you leave your order? Nunnery, or as you would have it nummery, is a bit out of date." His eyes crinkle at her as he adds, "Let's go for a hike."

They head out toward the gray mountains, today garnished with white poofs of irresponsible cloudlets. A lizard crosses the trail and slinks into the sagebrush. The wildflowers are nearly gone by now, the hot summer having settled in, but wisps of blue and yellow still flash at them as they walk by.

Finally! Jackie thinks.

Xavier takes her hand. "I'm worried about you. You've been through so much shit, and it's still going on, will go on." They continue up the trail, fingers entwined, Jackie's breath coming in swoops that leave her empty in between. Altitude, probably. Or anticipation.

"Despite your…" and he glances at her body as tall as his, "physicality, you are really a fragile person. I'm not sure how you keep going, this continual stress…" He stops and faces her. "Jackie, I've been praying for you, for some sort of resolution that will allow you to finally be yourself."

Jackie believes she can feel his breath on her face. She wonders if he will kiss her. She tries to inhale without gasping, to be ready. He looks at her as if he is expecting something from her.

"Thank you," she says, and lowers her eyes, waiting.

He releases her hand and lays an arm over her shoulder. They turn and try to synchronize their steps. She considers wrapping her own arm around Xavier's waist, but then the trail suddenly erupts into shale, and it is all she can do to keep herself upright as they flail through it, reaching out for handholds at the edge of the path.

"Have to go slow here," he says.

"Yes." Jackie answers, and they clutch their ways from rock to rock for the next sixty feet.

The shaley patch gives her time to collect herself. Xavier says he is praying for her, not **for** her. Talk about a slippery slopes—this was indeed a risk-taking situation.

"Do you ever take risks, Xavier?" she asks.

"I don't know. I suppose so, depending on what kind of risk you're talking about. I'm not a physical person, never have been. I've had my moments of taking risks with my thinking. I don't like what my church expects, and doesn't expect, of women. I guess that's risky. Is that what you mean?"

No, it isn't what she means. And she is beginning to feel a flare of resentment that he thinks of her as fragile. Just because she's in a mess, that makes her fragile? So does a life of tranquility and three prayer sessions a day make one invincible?

"A person can be in trouble and still be strong, Xavier," she says, and she surges ahead despite having to breathe through her mouth.

They don't talk much after that, and on the way back, she slides down the shale on her seat despite his warnings that she might not be able to stop.

That evening she walks back from vespers with Fay who confesses that an affair with a priest has unloosed them both from the fold and that she will be married to him in two weeks. This retreat is intended to reorganize her understanding of how God feels about sex. She, herself, is tired of feeling guilty about it. She wants to get on with her life.

That night Jackie opens her notebook and lists the ways she can get on with her life. The first is to forget Xavier. She can't think of a second. After twenty years of enjoying the fizz of risk her priest offers, she is beginning to see that that's all it is—fizz.

She needs something more. Jackie slips off the bed and kneels at the wooden bench. "Help me figure out what that is," she says to the pine wall in front of her. A cool blanket of quiet falls over her and she doesn't disturb it until a cramp in her left knee forces her to stand. Out on the porch, she eases herself into the old rocker and closes her eyes.

And have you figured it out, Jackie?
I so want to know that you discovered in that old rocker
the secret to your next life
and are getting on with it. You are a brave, exciting
woman,
and I have loved taking risks with you,
from the sidelines, of course.
You make me laugh and wonder at the possibilities
waiting us, if we just reach out to them. M

Sunday Morning: Choppy Seas
Jackie

"Shit." The pages are scattered all over the bed, the last one hovering on her chest. Madge always thought she knew it all, the way she'd psychoanalyze everything everyone said so that a person sometimes didn't want to say anything, but of course, Jackie always did, which got her into hot water more than once. Like, why did she talk about Xavier the last time the group got together? And the painter before that, along with the body worker. She could have kept them all a secret. No, she couldn't have. She isn't good at secrets. Hadn't few months ago she spilled the beans about her son-in-law divorcing her in an email to these friends and a couple more beans? About the retreat?

Even about the Gameboy? She flips back to the part about being strong, a risk taker. She is glad Madge saw her that way because Jackie is getting a glimmer of herself like that, too, especially when she remembers her last night in Montana. That's what she'll tell them about tonight, in the candlelight.

Time for a walk to the beach store. She'll need wine to finish her story. They all will.

Jackie zips up her parka and heads out to get the candles for whatever Lou has planned for the evening. Their four sets of footprints from Friday are gone, of course, wiped out by the tides, as is the trail the three of them left behind the next morning. A barefooted man and his dog saunter ahead of her leaving a new path to follow, wavelets already softening the edges of their steps.

The old footsteps are not so easily erased, in Jackie's memory at least. She follows the ocean-puddled trail of man and dog and finds herself walking past the access path to the store. It doesn't matter. Candles aren't important right now. Threads are, getting free of them, and she wants to keep on thinking about them for a while, about how she and Xavier have gotten unsnagged, a break that left another hole in the fabric of her life, but a mendable one.

The days in Montana had been peaceful, or as peaceful as they could be for Jackie. She read and walked and talked with Xavier and wrote in a journal she had begun to keep.

She liked the way his hand touched hers when they hiked, the way he looked at her when he said goodnight. But she began to notice that being with Xavier so much allowed her to examine their relationship, what it meant. He was a friend, of course, and she had often wished for even more, but vague dissatisfaction, annoyance, resentment, actually, was beginning to darken her view of him. It felt like the disappointment that sometimes comes at the end of a party. Or, she thought, in the last days of a marriage.

To test these feelings, she listed the things she didn't like about him, the way he always thought he had the right answer, his righteous voice when he gave it, strained, emerging from somewhere high behind his nose, the rise of his eyebrows that let her know she had just said something dumb. By the fifth day, during quiet time, she had decided that she had to stop fantasizing about him, to face the facts, to accept that he would never love her and that she probably didn't love him as she once thought she did. She wrote all this in her journal and knew it was true. Writing those words made her feel as if she was beginning to morph into a new Jackie. No longer would she anguish over a man, she wrote, even a holy one. Especially a holy one, she amended.

Pleased with herself, she had gone out onto the porch, eased herself into the old rocker, and closed her eyes. Which is why she was caught unawares when she opened them at the sound of the evening's last cowbell and found Xavier standing on the path. She threw an arm over her nightgowned chest and said, "What?"

"I shouldn't be here," he answered.

"Right," she said. Shit. Isn't this always the way, she thought. You make up your mind and then....Jackie waited, trying to breathe.

He lowered himself onto the wooden steps at her feet and dropped his head into his hands. "I'm so screwed up." He looked smaller, slumped below her like that. A little pathetic, in fact. All the men in her life had presented themselves as somehow overwhelmed. Even the painter with his tattoos and his fumed eyelids. Even Mitch, cowering under the barber's sheet. Especially Fred, savoring his last ounce of testosterone. If she were religious, she might have thought of herself as a Madonna for these guys, offering an inside track to the place where prayers were answered.

Jackie rocked forward towards her priest. She knew exactly what to say for the first time in her life. "Xavier," she would say, "I just finished figuring out that I don't love you, no matter what you are about to say. And even if I did, and even if you love me, it would be so unfair. You will always have your Catholic way of dealing with the guilt of it. Confession, penances, absolution, a retreat or two. For you, nothing will change. But I have no option except to feel ashamed or stupid, like always. And alone and regretful. I'm tired of regrets." She cleared her throat to say these words.

But Xavier's eyes lifted, met hers, flashed a warning. "I always know who I am when I'm with you." He looked out into the black trees rising at the edge of the meadow. "But not now." Jackie opened her mouth, ready, but he wasn't finished. "In seminary I had an affair, I guess you'd call it, with a fellow student that lasted a few months. It ended. I didn't see him again until last year, here. We both agreed we'd been foolish young men, water under the bridge." He closed his eyes, rubbed them. "Until last night."

That's when Jackie felt herself go into a state of some sort, as if a hand had passed over her head, blessed her, told her to go for it. She rose out of the gray rocker and bent down at his side. Her lips touched his cool forehead and she tasted the aftershave on his skin. Then she whispered, "Fuck off, Xavier. Go pray or sublimate, or whatever, somewhere else."

A minute later, alone, she lay down, drew the woolen blanket over herself, and thought of Fred and how sad she was for him.

She drove home the next day.

"You're two days early," Sally greeted her on the porch. "Anything wrong?"

"Yes," Jackie answered. "I need to see my husband."

Sally closed the door and told her to take it easy. She'd made dinner, enough for all three of them, primavera, come sit down. And when she did, Jackie saw that her daughter was swallowing more than food as she chewed and glanced at her mother.

"You look like you've just poisoned me and are waiting for me to fall face down into my spaghetti."

Madison laughed and dribbled olive oil down his super Hero T shirt.

"Later, Mom," Sally answered, and showed her son how to use a spoon to capture the strands of pasta. Jackie pushed her plate aside. *Nothing's easy, even for the new me,* she thought. She went to her bedroom to unpack.

After a while, Sally came in and sat on Jackie's bed, pushing up a pillow to lean against like she used to when she was a little girl. "It's my fault," she said. "I wasn't thinking."

Jackie stopped pulling her underwear out of the suitcase. "What?"

"I told Ron where you were."

"And?"

"He said, 'That cinches it,' and left."

The next day Jackie's attorney called, told her that Ron's divorce petition now included infidelity, along with abandonment and emotional stress. "With a priest, Jackie?" Beth asked. "An unfortunate choice. We've got a problem."

Regret is what makes one's stomach ache. She's retraced her steps and finds herself at the door of the little beach market. As she looks around for the wine, Jackie regrets just about everything in her life except the daughter who cried not only for herself but for her mother, and the grandson who, from the guest bedroom, broke that day's silence with cheers of "Okay, okay, level 89, twenty to go!"

Sunday Noon: Swells
Lucius

Lucius doesn't call before he drives into the graveled parking space at the beach house. He hears voices out on the deck and walks around the building and finds the three women lounging in the worn canvas deck chairs he had spotted on his previous trips. A cold wind flows off the ocean and the afghans the women have wrapped themselves in make them look like striped wool mummies. The fourth chair is empty.

"It's been twenty-four hours," he says, as if that is news to them. "We have officially placed Madge Slocum on the missing persons list, and I've called for emergency assistance in the search."

The mummy he identifies as Joan, by her blue eyes and the strands of blond hair escaping the scarf she wears, sits up. "Good," she says. "We're worried. We're thinking that Madge may have met someone on the beach, may have been kidnapped. She would never leave on her own, and she wouldn't stay lost in the woods, not with those Boy Scouts blowing whistles and calling for her. Something bad has happened to her."

Lou, her white hair flying into the wind now that she has unwrapped her head, turns to face him. "We're going to call her sons. They need to know. Roger, too, wherever he is in Nebraska. We'll look on her cell phone even though it won't work out here. She must have their numbers on it, don't you think?"

Lucius sees that Lou is dry-eyed and is sounding a little manic. He guesses she's operating on adrenaline now instead of tears and wonders if something has happened to bring about the change. Then he notices Jackie who has not moved since his arrival. Asleep? In the midst of a crisis?

"Sit down." Joan's freed hand points to the empty lounge. She leans towards Jackie's form and gives it a nudge. "Sheriff's here," she says. "Time to face reality." She sends a slow wink towards Lucius. "She's great at denial."

"Isn't everyone?" Jackie's muffled voice makes its way through the knitted wool. "Like why are we sitting out here freezing, as if we'll see her walking down the beach waving at us? Shit." Jackie works her way out of her cocoon and stands up. "I'm going in. Coming?"

Lucius follows her into the house and they stand in front of the fireplace, rubbing their hands. "This must be tough on you folks." If his instincts are still intact, this one, Jackie, will be the first one to crack, supposing there is something to crack about. The whole scene doesn't add up. A famous writer goes missing, and her friends haven't let anyone know? Why not?

"I'm thinking you are wondering why we've hesitated calling her sons." Joan has come in, is folding her blanket, smoothing her hair. She runs her tongue over her upper lip, shows the edges of white teeth at him, teeth not as friendly as usual. "We need to tell you something."

Lou nods, pushes a pillow out of the armchair, sits and pats the sofa next to her. Lucius takes this as an invitation and joins her. Solemn eyes meet his.

Joan clears her throat. "We think Madge may be having an affair, a secret fling, maybe, like the ones she sometimes fantasizes about in her stories."

Lucius feels his mouth open, words gathering, and glances at the women circled around him. Lou has inhaled and is holding her breath, Jackie eyes are wide and naïve, Joan's forehead wrinkles with regret and hesitancy, as if she should not be saying these words. She looks at the other two, blinks them into attending.

"Yes," Lou whispers. Jackie twirls a strand of black hair.

"And you suspect this because?"

Apparently, it's Jackie's turn to speak. "She was different than usual," she says, sifting through words to find the ones she wanted. "Giddy, I guess. A little like me when I..."

"When you're in love," Lou finishes. "When a person is in love, I mean. She could hardly get dinner on the table. She had a secret." Lou's lips purse with unusual certainty. "That's for sure."

"Very talkative. Dried out the lasagna going on about her next book." Joan shrugs. "Not like her ordinary put-together self. She hinted that she had a plan to go out, later, on the beach. 'I might be gone for a while,' she said, 'but I'll tell you all about it when I get back, maybe bring you something.' She didn't say when."

"So you weren't too worried when she didn't show up yesterday morning."

"Intrigued, mostly, until we found the walking stick, washed up in the high tide. Lover or not, she'd have that within reach if she were walking or whatever on the beach."

"You think she might have met this person, decided to leave with him?"

"Or her," Lou adds in her quiet way.

"Whoever, and that she might walk through this door any minute with a pleased look on her face?" Lucius is getting annoyed. Running after an escapee cow is one thing, chasing after a lovesick famous author is another. Women. "Yesterday morning you just got up and when you saw she was gone, you went for a walk?"

Joan gives him her blue look again. "Lucius, we're all six-ty-five or so. When one of us has an opportunity for romance, besides being a little envious, we cheer her on. I suppose we were eager to enjoy the details vicariously when she got back."

"Except she hasn't come back yet." Lou slumps against a pillow.

Lucius shifts, starts to get up. "Sorry," he says, hoping his pissedness is coming through. "This probably isn't in my job description. Maybe you all should have another glass of wine, relax, and I'll come back tomorrow to meet your truant friend."

Joan leans toward him, her hand on his arm. Even up close she's good to look at. Terrific, urgent blue eyes train on his. "Sheriff, she would never have left us hanging like this, even if she were with a lover. She believed in tying things all together, to bringing each story to a satisfying end. This is not Madge. She does not write horror stories. No call for twenty-four hours, her walking stick lying in the sand, her shrimp and lobster lying cold in the fridge waiting for the risotto."

"Risotto?" Finally something is making sense. "She's supposed to make tonight's dinner?"

"Yes. It's her turn. Jackie made last night's stir fry. Lou was on for breakfast. I have the enchiladas for tomorrow. That's the way she planned it."

"Risotto is last minute, yes? Like a lot of stirring?" Lucius knows this because of a very long evening he spent with a narrow-faced librarian a week or so or before. Her version of foreplay seemed to be stirring chicken broth and wine into rice for forty-five minutes, during which time Lucius had drunk himself into placidity. The soggy rice offered a reason to fall asleep when he should have at least tried. He should call her, maybe.

In the meantime, he knows anyone offering risotto for dinner, lobster, especially, means to be there. And she isn't. "That person must be really important to Madge, enough to abandon the meal and all."

"Not the meal, jerk. Us." Jackie has risen, and she is impressive in her tallness and lack of upper arm flab. She looks as if she might backhand him if he says another word. "Something's happened to Madge."

Joan pushes back her chair. "So that's why we're going to call her sons and try to find Roger. We think she's in trouble. She would never make us worry like this. In the meantime, we want you to make her disappearance a police matter, not a Boy Scout matter."

Because all three women have stood up, Lucius knows he's not going to be invited to the glass of wine he's been thinking about. He finds his baseball cap in his pocket, plants it on his head, and can't resist as he moves toward the door. "You've got your intuition, I've got mine. I think you'll see her in the morning." It isn't just his risotto intuition speaking now. The tide table he sees lying on the top of the kitchen divider is also chiming in.

22

Sunday Noon: Cusp
Jackie

A while ago on the path back to the beach house, the wine breaking through the paper bag she'd wrapped her arms around, Jackie had been glad she had time to be by herself, to remember how she gathered her courage, how Fred, thinking of him, and Xavier, too, had helped her decide to stay, even if she still has a few second thoughts. She always did, before taking a risk, didn't she?

Now, as the door closes on Lucius, she, a little reluctant or maybe just scared again, is also confused. "Tell me again why we created a phantom lover?"

Lou sighs. "Red herring, remember? We talked about it. In case he needs something to keep him interested until tomorrow morning."

Jackie turns and looks straight into Lou's sorrow-tinged eyes. "I don't like it when you sigh at me, when you use that tone of voice with me." She can't remember ever speaking to a friend like this. She tastes the words, finds them satisfying. She's going to enjoy talking calm and tough once in a while, instead of screeching like she's used to doing in tight situations. The words roll out from a deep part of her throat. "You remember I wasn't ready to join this project when you three first discussed it. I missed a few details."

Lou's chest rises and sinks. She's doing it again. Sighing, Jackie sees. "Sometimes I wish I had missed this whole thing. One more night. Right?" Jackie decides to sigh, too. For a moment, she's weightless. Breathing like this is about letting go, she realizes. Sighs don't mean people think you're stupid. Necessarily. Maybe they just mean the sigher is sad, or tired, or stressed. Or all three.

"I got the candles this morning," she says, pointing to the bag on the counter. "White. Tonight we finish our stories. Just like Madge wanted us to. Only we'll tell the truth," she adds. "Madge chose to make the end of her story a work of fiction. I think that her stories about us are a little untrue, too, don't you? Until we get to our endings and then we have to tell the truth. And I, for one, am ready."

Lou sighs yet another sigh. "Forsooth, whence did that feistiness arise, stalwart friend?" She grins at Jackie. "Looks good on you."

23

Sunday Afternoon: Fogbound
Joan

Joan is tapping her sheaf of papers into a neat stack and placing it on the coffee table when Lou settles into one of the fireside chairs.

"You've read yours?" Lou bends over the pile of chopped wood, arranges kindling.

"Skimmed it."

Fiction or truth? Or does it matter? It is hard to remember the truth, the memories rise up in unnatural colors, speak in unfamiliar accents, seem to be someone else's life. True, she did have an Irish silk jacket. Had Brian admired it? True, they did have an agreement to be as honest in their marriage as they had been about the past. And Madge had known about Brian's past almost as thoroughly she knew Joan's. The green bag didn't exist, of course, but the tapes did, still do, most likely hidden in corners of drawers. Madge knew the whole story, knew it a year ago, knew that Joan had been unable in that year to see beyond an outworn, useless dream to the next place. She feels Madge's hand at the small of her back, nudging her forward. Telling this story will be more difficult than anything else Madge has asked of her.

Joan pulls a parka from the rack and goes out onto the deck to read Madge's pages again and to decide how she will end the old story and begin a new one.

WHATSOEVER THINGS ARE LOVELY: JOAN'S STORY

Joan, I've valued your secrets, your willingness to share them with me.
A graceful, determined, and thoughtful woman, you will bring
this particular story to a conclusion.
A happier one awaits you just beyond the horizon.
I wish I could be there. M

Something about that spring morning, the blue sky lying still behind the still-barren tree limbs, the brisk nip on her cheeks that makes her want to grin, perhaps it is the way yellow light glances off the sidewalk and onto the bursting crocuses, but something that morning has sent her to the closets, to sort through the winter's collection of clothes, to toss and rearrange and get ready for whatever would come next.

This is why Joan finds it, the book bag, green canvas, the kind students had slung over their shoulders thirty years before. It huddles in a corner, behind her husband's gym bag, under the pile of old sweaters she had asked him to sort through and get rid of months ago, maybe years ago. She pulls it out, its weight dragging it to the floor. Books, she guesses. The bag collapses and she kneels beside it, hesitant, perhaps even fearful, to reach into the opening, touch its contents.

Brian and she had agreed when they married that honesty was the soil in which their love would thrive. By the time they met, they had lived several other lives, had loved, lost, endured and made peace with their demons. They shared those pasts, talking late into their nights, about parts of themselves they had never revealed to anyone before. She found she loved reaching into the hidden pockets of her life, his life, retrieving unexpected stones and nuggets.

"Is this what it means to finally grow up?" Joan wondered. "To be able to lay bare one's soul?" It was their wedding day. Brian laughed at her question. "Along with laying bare one's body? If so, we are very grown up." She guessed he was referring to the pouches at the corners of her lips that she had been trying to massage away and to his small paunch, visible at the moment because his skivvies dipped under it, the only evidence of his fifty-four years. They had been pleasuring each other, he rubbing the small of her back with a vanilla oil that made her wish she could lick herself, and she had been pinching his nipples with her fingertips. They fell asleep entwined and so sure of themselves.

Her first marriage had been built on a dream from the moment she had felt Tim's erection pressing at her pelvic bone as they leaned against the wall of the Gamma Psi house, his pants throbbing and then wet, leaving a stain on her skirt and her fingers sticky.

On the day the letter arrived informing them that Tim had been accepted to medical school, Joan said it was time to get married. They couldn't mess up, get pregnant, ruin it, this dream of the good life, the dream that had been hers since she was little girl.

That first year in medical school, Tim squirmed through anatomy labs that sent him home half-sick and smelling of formaldehyde, and Joan learned to teach third graders and to cook, creating lesson plans as she stirred the spaghetti sauce or sautéed onions and munched saltines to quell the strange nausea that turned out to be Joshua. Joshua was a surprise, but he probably shouldn't have been since Tim was Catholic, and to marry him, Joan had taken the lessons, became one, in name at least. The rhythm method was the only doctrine she accepted and the one Tim, it soon became apparent, didn't.

She returned to the third graders that fall, lactating sporadically at the sound of a certain pitch of child's cry wafting in from the playground. In the evenings, she spent some of the time she needed to pump milk for the next day as she paged through *The Joy of Cooking* and planned the dishes for the weekend med school parties. She basked in the other wives' reluctant praise and shared recipes on cards engraved with "From Joan's Kitchen." How do you do it all? they asked.

By the time her third son was on the way, three babies in five years, with another year of interning to go, friends teased them, asked if Tim had missed the class on contraception. He had answered yes, but he had gotten an A-plus in human sexuality, and when he had rubbed his groin against Joan's hip and grinned, she managed to grin back. "I can attest to that." Everyone thought she was funny and a great wife. So did she, herself an intern, she told herself, preparing to be the wife of a doctor.

She was shocked when Tim accepted a partnership in a small clinic in a village two hundred miles from a bookstore. "I need to be a big fish in a small pond," he said when she, the word choking her, asked why. "You'll be good at it, the Mrs. Doctor of the town. You like being queen of everything, don't you?" He didn't laugh when he said that, and neither did she. *Perhaps we are both just sick of school,* she thought, *not of each other.*

Upon their arrival in Clarkston, Joan found that the new doctor's house, "all cleaned and ready," according to the realtor who met them at the door, was a pinch-faced bungalow set on a small dry lot ringed by dead yews. In the weeks that followed, she learned that the town's movie theater was open only on Fridays and Saturdays, and the best music in town was at the Lutheran Church on Sunday mornings. Art appreciation meant crinkling up crepe paper flowers in someone's kitchen while children squabbled in the basement party room.

"When do you have time to read all of these?" Frank, her mailman, stood on her porch one sultry afternoon and shook his head as he handed her a pile of magazines: *Saturday Review, Vogue, The New Yorker*. He glanced past her, into the hallway. Two overturned tricycles and an abandoned vacuum cleaner guarded the passage, and she knew he was answering his own question.

During that first year in Clarkston, her discontent roiled in the midst of the requisite backyard barbecues that introduced the new doctor to the families of the town. Usually, the men drank too much beer and ended the evening by yanking their sulking children down the driveway, their apologetic wives waving back at Joan as she stood at the door, exhausted, more than exhausted. "That was a great feed," Tim would grin, stepping over the pile of paper plates and beer cans and taking her arm. "Let's go to bed."

At times she found herself imagining Tim's penis as a kind of bludgeon, he, a bully, using it to subdue her, get her under control. That was just when he had been drinking, she told herself. Other times the sex still reminded her of the way they could be, the way they had been at the beginning. The trouble was he was drinking a lot, demoralized, she supposed, by the unending parade of snotty children and complaining women who passed through his office. The town's older doctor, postponing his retirement, was the physician people still went to with their serious illnesses.

Tim sank into his chair at the end of the day, Jack Daniels at his elbow, the boys warned to be quiet as he watched whatever came through on the tiny TV that was their first indulgence. When he came to bed, late, depressed and sullen, he would tell her to turn off her bed light; the swish of pages kept him awake. The sound of his heavy breathing fueled night thoughts shimmering with a reddish glow behind her sleepless lids.

Her Christmas letters to her college friends spoke of small town living, boys busy and underfoot, the unreliability of a doctor's life, his being on call on the weekends, her continued membership in Book of the Month. "Have you read...?" she'd ask. "Be sure to see..." she'd advise, even though the film hadn't, wouldn't ever make it to Clarkston. Thank God for *The New Yorker*, she'd think, as she typed. "Wish we could somehow work a visit, just us girls, into our child-obsessed schedules."

And once or twice Lou and she did get together over hurried lunches when Joan's youngest son needed a specialist's attention in Seattle. And Jackie came through Clarkston on a ski trip, minus her husband, but with a couple of young Jackies in tow, one year. Madge was the communicator in the group, her regular notes and letters, carbon copied, newsy because she'd pass on news that came to her, with personal P.S.'s to each of them on the last page, and the exchanges felt a little like the midnight trading of cigarettes in the solarium. A touching of hands holding a lit match.

The boys were growing. They needed a bigger house, one with a dishwasher and two bathrooms. On moving day, exhausted from unpacking, disturbed by the discovery of termites and the smell of mold in the basement, Joan had fallen into bed and clicked off the light without picking up her book. When Tim slid under the blankets minutes later, she felt his erection rub against her hip, his hand on her breast.

"No, not tonight," she said. "I'm too tired." The words emerged as if they had been lined up, waiting, at the tip of her tongue for a long while.

Stale beer cloaked his breath. "What?"

The boys were not yet asleep in this strange house. She put her hand against his chest and whispered, "The only time you want me is when you're drunk." Once again, unbidden words, even more true. Tired had nothing to do with it.

Tim rose up, his hand on her arm, his nails cutting into her skin. "I work my ass off trying to build a practice and make money for you." His voice scraped at her ear. "For all your hoity-toity ideas, oriental rugs, copper pans, that stuff you see in your magazines, and all you can do is bitch. I'm too tired. Well, so am I, damn you." She pulled away, buried her head under her pillow, but she could still hear him. "I am sick of hearing how stupid my friends are, how ugly the town is, how bored you are." He rolled away from her to the far edge the mattress, yanked at the blankets. Cool air rushed between their bodies.

"I am sick of you, too," she murmured into her pillow. That must have been true, for the next morning her body expelled the tiny bloody fetus that had been snuggling uneasily in her uterus. She didn't tell him, saving the information, perhaps, as ammunition for the next fight.

She hadn't needed it. Their battleground was a silent, parched field, a bed sheet bounded by their silent backs. In the new house, shored up against the insects and enlivened with the antiques she found in barns and estate sales, Joan began to have gatherings, dinner parties, mostly French now that Julia Child had arrived and the children were old enough to be corralled in front of a TV with a pizza. One or two of her friends' husbands brought good wine to her table, inspired by the vineyards that were replacing prune orchards on the south-sloping hills outside of town.

Joan introduced Wallace Stegner to her neighborhood coffee klatch and she became the maven of the town's first book club. Tim's practice finally blossomed when the town's old doctor retired to his orchids. Joan became Mrs. Doctor for real, but that role didn't seem as important as it once had been.

One day, as she whipped off the sheets from their bed, Joan noticed that their marriage mattress had developed a continental divide down the middle. She didn't think much about sex any more, or the absence of it. Once in a while she would wake up to the chimes of an orgasm ringing through her body, and she would not breathe, wishing for the deep pulse to go on and on, but it never did, and her fingers could not bring it back, even when she tried to imagine the first naive convulsion that had swept through her as she leaned against the chipping paint of the sorority house.

Suddenly, their sons were teenagers. Just as suddenly, Tim began to enjoy being a father, a father of athletes who were good enough to bring him backslaps from townsfolk whose lives for six months of the year focused on sending a basketball team to State. Like Tim, his sons were tall and had good hands. There were moments when a wash of pride in her children spilled over onto the barren ground of her marriage and Joan imagined that her family would survive.

It was ironic, then that a basketball game brought an end to that hope. The team was on its way to the state tournament, and most of the town filled the bleachers cheering on their boys. The game was tight, the outcome hanging on the last sixty seconds on the clock. Tim, enflamed by a referee's call, fueled by beers drunk before the game with his coterie of sports lovers—a lawyer, a dentist, a contractor, and this particular night, the Unitarian minister—had careened down the wooden steps, leapt over the announcer's table, and smashed a fist into the face of a stripe-shirted man a foot shorter than himself.

Blood spread across the shiny maple floor, and her husband screamed words forbidden in this small town even in the heat of a game. Joan caught sight of her sons slouching like guilty penitents, elbows on thighs, eyes averted, their faces pale with embarrassment. The melee continued as Joan made her way across a wall of knees leading to the aisle, climbed the concrete stairs to the exit. She knew, walking home, that Julia Child and a book club were not enough to fill her empty places any more.

Tim did not come home that night. The next evening he didn't appear for the dinner she had not cooked. She sent the boys, who seemed to be glad to escape from whatever would happen next, out for pizza, and she went to bed. She opened her book, tried to read, but she could not see the words through the storm behind her eyes. Perhaps this was just one of those bad times, she thought. Once the boys are out of the house, she and Tim would have time to sort things out. She shouldn't rush things. She had managed this far, hadn't she? She put her book down. When she tried to bring back the images of her family, whole, the way she had once been to be able to imagine a dream life, she saw only the stricken faces of her sons, heard the crazed voice of her husband. She returned to her novel, forced herself to read word by word, until the story took over, her own story extinguished for a while.

She was startled by the sound of the front door slamming, footsteps pounding down the hall. Tim staggered across the room and made his way to the bed. He leaned over her, his face falling forward until his eyes were watery slits.

"Guess what?"

Joan couldn't look at him. She felt for her book, opened it. "What?"

The headboard shook as he leaned on it. "I found someone who loves me."

She turned a page. "Lucky you." The moment she said those careless words, the last remnant of that old dream floated away like a fleck of dust.

Tim moved out the next day, taking his skis and his leather reclining chair. He hesitated for a moment in front of the TV, but decided to leave it behind "for the boys," he said, in a fatherly way. Besides, it was only a twenty-incher.

Her sons, in turn, stopped clutching at what had been, and free-fell for a while, each getting into his own sort of trouble, graduating somehow, managing finally to leave his parents, the town, his brothers. As the last boy closed the door behind him, Joan found herself alone and ready to begin all over.

She chose San Francisco for her rebirth. She had taken *The Sunday Chronicle* for years, a nostalgic reminder of her life in San Mateo. Herb Caen still made her laugh even though he arrived on Wednesday. Despite or because of the lack of live theatre in Clarkston, she had looked forward each week to the news of the opera and play openings in the city as if she held season tickets. Just as her mother had thirty years before, she realized as she packed the few items she would keep for her new life.

Folding clothes into boxes, Joan had let her thoughts wander, and the words "season tickets" came into focus, bringing with them a vision of a young tired woman, a single mother with a child to feed, for whom going to a play in San Francisco was the stuff of dreams. Even if she could afford a cheap seat, her mother complained, she would have to pay for the bus fare, and a dress and coat to wear. San Francisco was dressy, you know, not like on the Peninsula. Despite this reality, Emily Short read reviews of the city's plays and clubs and talked to her daughter about the actors and comedians as if she knew them personally. Not being able to go to the theatres became shorthand for everything else that was lacking in her life.

They were dirt poor. Emily worked days in a commercial laundry and came home with her hair steamed and straggly and burn marks on the backs of her hands. Joan cooked their dinners and did not invite friends to her house. Neither her mother nor the house could bear the scrutiny of outsiders. Joan learned from a grandmother, during one rare complaining visit, that her father was not dead. Indeed, he had married soon after he left Emily, pregnant, disgraced. Joan supposed she had half-siblings somewhere. Emily didn't know.

The one thing Joan knew at sixteen was that she wouldn't settle for the life her mother had endured. She studied hard, worked after school, and won a scholarship to a school in Oregon where no one knew her. When she brought home the cashmere sweater and the narrow skirts she would take to college, her mother said, one more time, "I suppose you think you'll be getting season tickets."

"Yes, I will," Joan answered.

And now, finally, almost twenty-five years later, she was about to enjoy them. Amazing what a person discovers deep in the pockets of memory. Amazing, too, the ease of discarding some of those memories along with old linens and worn rugs. She finished boxing her china and called for the woman who would price the leftovers and hold the sale of her former life.

When she arrived in the City, she bought an apartment on Jones Street. Its five rooms were austere at first, a bed the one piece of furniture because she had brought only her good dishes and silver with her. She walked every part of the city, looking for the antiques and old rugs and art that would make the flat her own. And then, before the money from the sale of the Clarkston house and the divorce settlement ran out, she enrolled in grad school at San Francisco State. She would become a therapist. Teaching was no longer an option. She needed to earn enough money to support the new dream she was building.

Within five years of getting her license, she had developed a growing counseling practice of folks willing to pay her well to listen to their woes. She had also accumulated, through the opera guild, her tennis club, and reconnection with a few old acquaintances from her San Mateo days, a coterie of women to keep her company. If she were somewhat estranged from her children, well, wasn't every mother and her sons, for a while at least, while the sons worked out their own destinies?

For a time she was in love with a man who made her laugh. She'd not experienced that before in a man and she found herself tingling with delight at his knock at the door. Except that this particular tingling also involved the inhaling of a line of white powder through a rolled bill, which she did until she realized love had nothing to do with it.

After ten years, she was as firmly rooted into her San Francisco life as the tiny sequoia she had planted in the ceramic pot on her terrace the first day she had moved in. Then she met Brian Bishop.

She had known of Brian, of course, and she was flattered when she noticed him looking at her over the heads of patrons in the lobby of the opera house at the opening night of *Antigone.* She had come with a woman from her book group, a talkative, busy person who had found someone to engage in a long and detailed conversation. Joan had moved on, and she stood, leaning against a thick pillar, sipping her wine. She was wearing a pale peach shantung shirtwaist under a silk patchwork jacket and she felt quite good about her choices, especially when several pairs of jeans waggled past. Jeans with stilettos had never made any sense to her, reminding her of her days in Clarkston where jeans meant feeding chickens or wandering through Kmart.

"Who designed your jacket?" a male voice close to her asked. Startled, she turned and saw him at her side.

'I don't even know," she admitted. "I bought it in Ireland."

"May I?" and at her nod, he gently turned her collar and read the label. "I should explain. I have a shop, in Maiden Lane, perhaps you know it, Avignon?" He patted her neck, soothing the fabric back into place. "I am always on the lookout for new designers. Most of my things now are from Japan. I have several Irish lines, though, and I was sure I recognized your jacket." He grinned. "Kind of silly, I guess..."

"No, I'm flattered, Mr. Bishop." The sweet scent of his hands at her throat confused her, sideswiped her words. "I'm delighted to meet the owner of one of my favorite shops, even though I don't buy much from you. A bit spendy, you know." She could finally look at him straight on. Several years younger than she, fit, startling green eyes, and silver hair, a bit of the Irish in him, she guessed. As his hand reached for her arm, she saw that his fingernails were cut straight across, white at the tips, carefully maintained. For some reason, that pleased her.

He drove her to her home that night, thanked her for the chance to talk theatre, and shook her hand. Perhaps a woman edging in on sixty should not expect to be kissed goodnight, she speculated. Or perhaps she could have done the kissing. Who knew the rules anymore?

When her customary symphony partner called ill the next week, Joan had an excuse to call Brian and ask him to fill in. Afterwards, he bought her a drink, and they hummed the da da da dah of the Fifth and told each other of the places and times they had first fallen in love with Beethoven. Joan decided to tell the truth. "Sunday morning radio symphony," she said. "Cleaning the house so Mom could sleep." Brian's chuckle had been reassuring. At her doorstep, though, she was left unkissed once again. "This has been good," he said. "I'll call you."

He didn't. A month later, she dropped him a note and invited him to come to supper and an evening walk through Golden Gate Park. "The oleander blossoms are out," she promised. Perhaps another time, he answered; he would be out of town on a buying trip. She was out of practice, but she couldn't be mistaken about the lack of remorse in his voice as he said no, could she? Then he called to say he had two tickets to *La Boheme*. Would she like to join him? She would. She wore the patchwork jacket that night for luck, and he brought a small offering of spring tulips to her door. Their seats were excellent. The death of Mimi brought tears, as it always did, and Brian handed her his handkerchief. It smelled of something citric and earthy, and she wondered if she were falling in love. Under pale glow of the entry light, she hesitated and then asked him in for a drink. "I need to thank you for your handkerchief," she said.

He touched her chin with the tips of his fingers. "Sorry, I can't." He waited as she let herself in. Inside, she set the locks, pressed her forehead against the door and wept, quietly, so that, if for some reason, he still stood outside, he would not hear her. Perhaps he took her offer for more than a drink. Perhaps, she thought, it was.

The next day she understood that despite the very secure, hard-won port she had so carefully built for herself, moored in the safest of waters, the flashing images of his eyes, his hands, his perfect teeth, his good-natured laugh lines, were scuttling her.

She needed to take control of her ship. On a Friday night, Bartok playing, good sense prevailing, Joan, convinced that not even the youthful, silly rushes of adrenaline at the sound of his voice were worth this interior storm, with a shaking hand, her best stationery, and a glass of cabernet, wrote him. She felt they had not been honest with each other, she explained, that perhaps she had wanted more than he from their friendship and that such expectations would become terribly painful when they were not met. She thanked him for reminding her of what love might be like and instructed him to forget her as she would him. She was pleased with the reasonable tone of her words.

Brian knocked at her door two days later, a bobbing bouquet of lilies and snapdragons preceding his earnest voice. "May I explain?" he asked through the screen door, and Joan let him in and buried her nose in the blossoms, glad for a moment to calm her breathing. They sat that night at opposite ends of her sofa, the fire flickering bits of light through their wine glasses, and they talked. At the end of the evening, they both understood that they were about to step into an arrangement between two people who needed each other about as much as any two ever did.

Later, when she thought about that evening, she would remember the warm breeze of secrets that flowed between them, a connectedness that she had seldom felt with any other person. Nothing either of them said could disrupt it, even when he confessed that his first marriage had been a fraud based more on his need for his father-in-law's money than on love, even when he described the infidelities and sexual wanderings that finally forced him, in shame, to end his marriage, even when his eyes moistened and he told her he was scared to death of ever trying to really love someone like her. Joan listened and felt her heart open to him.

Then, it was her turn, the first time she put into words the truth of her subversive role in Tim's alcoholism, her condescension, her coldness, her purposeful alienation of her sons, her determined escape from her past. Brian did not turn his green gaze away from her.

Neither attempted to analyze what might have been behind the behaviors that killed their marriages. Confession seemed enough. It seemed like the beginning of love. When Brian finally reached for her, she was surprised to discover that his hand was the same size as hers, that their fingers wrapped perfectly, enclosed warm compatible palms.

The first several years of their marriage were good ones. They laughed and talked and held matching hands. They traveled and went to the symphony and theatre. Together, they renovated her flat to allow for his art, and she served lovely meals to friends alfresco under green umbrellas on the terrace or in the new dining room with its Tibetan rugs and marbled side table. Once in a while, they came close to that first evening's intimacy as one or the other dug deep in order to come to terms with parts of him or herself, and such revelations served to support the infrastructure of their marriage. Brian seemed to have put aside the shroud of guilt he had worn for years, stored it away somewhere. So had she.

She enjoyed their life, her life. She reveled in the days filled with music, laughter, bright lights, and impressive dinner partners. She looked forward to the fashion shows and fashion talk that Brian introduced to her. She loved her new neck, a concession to his still smooth cheeks and youthful gaze. She liked the fact that she could still hit a solid shot with a tennis racket and had the time and the place to do it in, since she had cut back on her practice to only a few clients. She loved the season tickets they shared to the opera, to the American Conservatory Theatre, and she thought of her mother as she ordered them each year.

If clouds appeared on the horizon, she and Brian would talk them away over a bottle of good wine. Sometimes, though, the clouds didn't disappear but instead slid behind the mountains of activities cluttering her days. When she lay unable to sleep, too much coffee too late, she would become aware of them. Why had she needed to question his itinerary for a buying trip last month? Why hadn't she, in fact, been invited? And, after he explained in his thorough way, why had she found herself looking through his Palm Pilot? For what? And why did he call unexpectedly some evenings to let her know he wouldn't be home for dinner, a client or a customer needing attention? What client? What customer? Late into the night?

When she told him of her sense of distrust and blamed herself for her insecurity, she waited to hear him reassure her that she was wrong to doubt him. That he loved her more than ever. And he listened, held her against his sweet-smelling chest, and told her just that.

Then, on that yellow spring day, she found the green bag.

As usual, Brian brings in the mail and sorts it on the dining room table. "Here's something interesting." He slides a blue envelope toward her and continues to go through the pile in front of him.

Joan recognizes the return address and reaches for the letter. "Must be from Madge. Oregon." She slips a fingernail along the flap and pulls out the note. Yes, Madge. "Another reunion. This month."

Brian looks up at her. "At the coast? The same group as last time?" He returns to his pile of letters. "Must be three years since you four got together, isn't it?"

Almost five years, actually. They, four college friends, had come together every few years once they were finished with children, other people's laundry, several first husbands, their calendars their own, finally. At the first gathering, a slumber party at Madge's big house, when they were all about fifty, all but Lou single again, they had looked around the table and had marveled at themselves. Looking good— but definitely not living the life that any one of them had predicted for herself as she scrambled for space behind the Gamma Psi bushes and caught her man.

"How could we have been so...dumb?" Jackie asked. "All I dreamed of was a ranch house with a daylight basement and someone to pay for it."

"And kids. We all wanted four kids."

"I turned down a chance at grad school because I wouldn't need a Masters to join the PTA." Lou frowned. "Come to think of it, I turned down PTA also."

"We still have time to wise up." Madge's comment led them into a familiar late-night session, minus the cigarette smoke but with the addition of clinking wine glasses, They were still able to pull up knees and feet into the cushions of her soft leather sofas, curl up in pajamas, and share recent discoveries about their bodies, the satisfying use of several openings to it, and the clever items to be found in sex stores.

"You must invest in good underwear." First rule, they agreed, inspired by Jackie's painter-revelations. "Is it front to back or back to front?" Lou asked one more time. No one could remember. For the three single women, life's blank pages existed to be written on with a free-flowing script. Lou, though, was quiet as the evening wound down, and Madge put her arm around her as they made their ways upstairs to their beds.

The next time they came together, in a B & B in Napa, the women's intimacies, inspired by mud baths and massages, swirled with sunspots and cancer and facelifts and the trouble each had opening jars.

"Damn!" Jackie had complained. "Look at me. See? I'm still having hot flashes. It's plain embarrassing when you're with someone and..."

"Serves you right, friend. Being with someone." The others laughed, and Joan realized later that this was about as close to talking about sex as they had gotten that weekend. And when it was her turn to have her friends stay at her house, a year later, she kept them running from galleries to theatres to great restaurants. Over breakfast lattes, they spoke of distant daughters-in-law and troubled grandchildren, of sons' addictions, daughters' marriage troubles— other people's seas, not their own, as if they were drifting becalmed in a midlife horse latitude.

So it was surprising that when they met at Madge's beach house to celebrate their sixtieth birthdays, Joan and Jackie had married, and Madge had found a lover. Lou, reversing the trend, had left her husband of thirty-five years. In spite of these changes, the solarium topic was not new lingerie, reawakened libidos. Late that first night, over wine, in their night clothes, the fire waning, Jackie said, "We're crones, you know. Wise women."

"And old," Lou amended. The collected response was not laughter, but a kind of knell. They acknowledged their cronehoods with blue candles and brave ideas.

As she re-reads the invitation in her hand, Joan wonders what a reunion of sixty six-year-olds will bring.

"Better mark the calendar. We're getting booked up fast for the summer." Brian turns to hang up his coat, and Joan watches his still-trim body make its way down the hall. *Maybe not so booked up*, she thinks.

Their best time to talk is just after dinner as they finish a bottle of wine and relax into the quiet of the candlelit table. This evening Joan finds it difficult to swallow and when he notices her half-eaten meal, Brian asks if she feels well. "That cold again?" he suggests, and she takes a deep breath.

"I found something of yours," she answers. "A green bag holding a pile of video cassettes." She watches his face as curiosity shifts to understanding. He blows a little gust of air from tight lips and lowers his eyes.

"I'm sorry. I didn't mean for you to find it."

"No, I don't suppose you did. It was well hidden. I looked at one of the tapes on our VCR."

He looks up at her. "That was a long time ago. Before us. I should have destroyed them. I don't know why I didn't."

"You've collected an assortment of experiences. I also played one of the small cassettes on our digital video camera. You seem to enjoy women with large areolas—a passion developed as a young child, perhaps. The rest of their bodies probably a taste acquired a little later on. You had me believing you are a restrained, thoughtful lover. You've never nuzzled me with such gusto. Too exhausted?"

"Joan, I told you before we were married, I lived a life I am not proud of. I thought you understood. These things are from another time, an insane time. I am so sorry you've had to see me like that."

"I am too. Why did you keep them?"

"Maybe I needed them to remind me how desperately lost I had been, how much I need you. Will always need you."

"But you watch them? Masturbate to them? Show them to other people?"

He shakes his head then hesitates. "Not to other people. Only sometimes when I...need them."

Then Joan understands. How stupid she has been. "You fake it with me, don't you?"

"Joan."

"You don't feel anything with me. Your gasps and little shrieks only mean you're tired of pretending and would I hurry up, please."

"Joan. Don't. "

Joan pushes her chair back, pulls the green bag from under her chair. The plastic cases rattle as it lands on the table. "We promised to be honest, to not have the kinds of secrets that eroded our lives once before. A bag slipped under a heap of old clothes in the back of a closet is not honest. It oozes shame, is a harbinger of something more to come. Like this." She reaches into the bag, takes out a small cassette, holds it out to him. "I gave you the camera that produced this tape two years ago."

Brian does not come home for dinner for a week. He sleeps in the guest room. Abject in his remorse, he has asked for a cooling off time, a time when he can make sense of his behavior, and they can begin to rebuild trust. He will see someone. Perhaps she needs to, also, to work through her anger. "You are my life," he says. They speak in harmless platitudes at the breakfast table, from behind sections of the newspaper, waiting, in limbo.

Despite her profession, Joan's solace is not in therapy, but in the hot baths she has begun to enjoy at the end of the day. This evening, the warm water lulls her into a mindlessness that deepens as she slips lower into the water and allows her ears to be filled and her hair to float gently above her. One of her hands, weightless, moves across her hips, folds comfortingly around the warm mound of flesh, fingers curled under but not moving, just holding.

A mantra, one she has not used or remembered for years, since the bad times with Tim, floats across her consciousness. "I am still I," it sings. "I am still I," and a cascade of images slide past her closed eyelids: a teenager trembling at the debate podium, eager to prove herself a scholar, a college girl living on cigarettes and black coffee as she types her way through tens of papers long after her housemates have retreated to the sleeping porch, a young woman choosing a dream instead of a man. The magazines, the book club, the candlelit dinners inserted like shock absorbers between days and years of babies and a husband, no longer her hero but a disappointed person on the verge of becoming a tyrant. Then, finally, a life, lovely and full of love. Almost as she had dreamed it.

When the water cools, she steps out of the tub and wraps herself in a towel. If I weren't married to Brian, I wouldn't have a warming rack for my towels, she thinks. She slips into bed and dims the light. I am still I, no matter what, she reminds herself.

Dawn is filtering through the blinds when she awakes to the sound of Brian showering in the guest bathroom. At first, she wonders if it were really he, and she squints at the clock on her table, 4:15. Unusual, even for their new routine. And a shower at this hour? Minutes later, she feels him look in on her, and she turns away, forcing her eyelids to remain quiet and closed.

"So, is it next week you are going off with the crones?" he asks, over his newspaper the next morning.

"Crones are post-menopausal women, entering a new wise phase of their lives," she answers. "That was at least five, ten years ago. We are post-crones. What would you call us at sixty-five?"

"Too far gone to be women of a certain age," he agrees. "How about something like solrisanal women?

She looks at him, catching his bright eyes crinkled in thought. "Why?"

"Menopausal means moon stop. The crone bit seems a little dark, like the hours of morning after the moon sets." He is trying out his clever charming self on her. "Sol, sun, risan, rise. aA new word for the time women are freed up to do whatever they want. A new sun rising for them...for you."

"Solrisanal." With no warning from her throat or her brain, tears flood onto a cheek, a corner of nose. "I believe I am being solrisanal right now." She tries to laugh as she covers her eyes with her napkin. "You and your damned bad timing." Then she is crying in earnest.

Brian moves his chair to her side. His arm on her shoulder feels oppressive, and she shakes it off. "I know, Brian," she manages to say.

He sits back and waits for her to continue. "Tell me."

"Why you were late last night. Why you slipped into the house so quietly. Why you showered in the early morning."

"Why did I do all that?" he asks.

"Don't make me say it."

"You think I was with someone last night?"

She looks at him, feels herself retreat as he leans towards her, *I am still I* a wall between his words and her body. "Yes."

He does not try to explain. "I'm sorry you believe that," he says, and he gets up from the table and disappears, his shoulders rounded, she thinks, like an old man's.

Later, as she plays the scene over in the quiet of her office, she realizes that he hasn't denied her suspicions. And before, when she found the green bag, he did not say he had stopped having his secret liaisons, much less recording them. Each time his response was an earnest statement of sorrow at having caused her pain. But that was all.

The drive over the Santa Cruz mountains, top down on the Mercedes, her hair flying from under her scarf, is a practice runaway. As long as she focuses on the narrow road ahead of her, she doesn't have to think about what she is running away from. She pulls into the parking space at the trailhead and considers not stopping, of going wherever that road takes her until she runs out of gas. Then she laughs aloud because the thought pleases her, "That is exactly what I'm doing. Going along until I run out of gas." However, a person could detour or turn onto a different path with a new destination in mind. "Or she could turn back," she says as she stoops to look more closely at the yellow wildflowers at the trail's edge. "Decide that a destination in hand is worth two in the bush."

Anyone coming along will see an older woman talking to the trees. But no one comes along, and she has the trail to herself for an hour. Then she makes her way back to the car, and not sure how it had happens, knows what turn she will take next.

So, my lovely friend, where will the next road take you?
Bon Voyage! M.

Joan closes her eyes. Madge had guessed at the mode of the runaway, and she knew, long before Joan herself understood, that once she'd tossed a dream or two by the roadside, a new destination would appear. For the first time in months, hope fills her chest, makes her lick her lips, get ready for what is coming up around the next curve.

24

Sunday Afternoon: Uprush
Joan

Joan finds the numbers she needs in the cell phone. Madge might have made it a little more complicated if she had gotten rid of the phone, but the woman couldn't think of everything, she supposes. The slow, intricate risotto was the very best thought, worthy of a novelist, as was the recipe for mussel stew that lay on top of the refrigerator. She dials the number on the land phone. A female voice answers. It is evening on the east coast and she hears the clink of dishes in the background. "Slocum's. Hello?"

Joan asks to talk with Jim, and he is silent as she tells him that his mother has been missing over twenty-four hours. "How was she when you last saw her?"

"She seemed good, happy to see us. Excited maybe, but we all were. She made dinner, sat and with us. Afterwards, she asked if we wanted to go for a long walk on the beach in the morning, but by the time we got up, she was gone. We thought we could catch up with her, but we went for a couple of miles without seeing her."

"You know about it, that she was sick?"

"She mentioned a little doctoring, not to worry. She seemed okay, in fact, very okay."

"God. She has her good days and her really bad ones. Roger has been walking her through the bad ones. Is he there?"

"Madge said he flew back to Nebraska to see his mother since she'd be with us at the beach. We had a great day together. She even showed us the unfinished first chapters of her next novel. About the four of us. She asked us how we wanted our stories to end." Joan feels her throat tighten. This part is the truth. Why does it strike like a dagger through her throat to say it? Maybe because in the past telling the truth has usually proved painful. Moreover, she needs to lie a lot for another day or so. Like now. She swallows, goes on. "We are worried, Jim. We wondered if a sneaker wave might have gotten her. We have no other explanation."

"Sneaker wave? How many of those occur? Like once a decade? You've got to be kidding. Unless I hear from you tonight, I'll be there tomorrow afternoon. Let me call my brother. He's not good with news like this. He'll go crazy if a stranger calls…"

"We're not strangers. We're your mother's friends and we're going a bit crazy ourselves. We're glad you're coming, both of you, we hope." Joan wonders if that last sounded as if she already knew what tomorrow would bring. But Madge told her, that last night, whispering last thoughts, that she wanted her boys to be near.

Children need to say goodbye, she had whispered. Everyone does, the leaver and the left behind, no matter what the situation.

Joan did not say goodbye to her mother. She had used her sons as an excuse not to go back to San Mateo when the tests came out bad. She couldn't face revisiting her mother's life-long bittersweet yearning for a better life. She understood now that the seeds of her own irrepressible need for more, always more, had been planted before she could talk, as she watched a young woman read a Sunday newspaper and weep over impossible desires. A last goodbye between an unfulfilled mother and her dream-stalked daughter might have absolved each of them of the curse of dissatisfaction. Such a conversation might have allowed the daughter to say another goodbye years later to a damaged man who entered her life carrying a bouquet of lilies and snapdragons and a dream. That goodbye is still possible. Joan moistens her lips, thinks about another man, clad in yellow and blue golf clothes, who has given her the courage to think on these things, just as the sisters used to murmur without a clue about what that really means. Whatsoever things are true... And she will visit her sons, hold her grandchildren. Soon.

The ringing of the phone disrupts her thoughts, brings her mind to the task at hand. The sheriff is on the line.

"I've been thinking about what you said, and we'll be out knocking on doors along the beach, all night if we have to. If she is with someone, we'll find her, and we'll be pissed."

"You won't be the only one, Lucius. We're worried sick and now her sons are, too. I'm still trying to find Roger, her partner. But I think I'd rather be pissed than the alternative, so please do the door-to-door thing. We'll be up waiting your call."

"You're great at this," Lou calls from the kitchen where she's shelling the lobster for the risotto. "You should be a politician or something."

Joan decides to take that comment as a compliment. Lou may be quiet, but she's got her back in all this, just like in the cop movies. And right now, she'll get Lou's back by taking over some of the forty-five minutes of stirring required by that risotto. That's what friends do.

25

Sunday Afternoon: Headland
Lucius

Lucius hikes toward the houses above the road that poke widows-walks and third-story look-outs into the fog above rooflines. Liz goes to the houses lined up against the dunes at the oceanfront. He hadn't planned on using the girl as a deputy, but he senses that people answering seldom-knocked doors, those of the few year-rounders, will not shut them in her eager face, as they are likely to do in his.

Most of the houses in the village belong to city folks and are used only on weekends, if that. Their windows are dark, driveways swathed periodically in the glow of the motion detector lights the owners have added to the eaves of their getaways. Raccoons, usually.

Lucius is not optimistic about finding Madge Slocum in the arms of a lover. He'd paged through a couple of her books in the library that morning. They weren't about sex. Well, they were sort of, he corrects himself, but they were more about...damn. Relationships.

The R word, as his second wife called it. Important for women to have them, she yelled as she walked out the door. Flipping through patches of Madge's words, he had become aware, in a painful way, of his several failures in that line. Someday he'd maybe have another chance to find out what she meant. But not right then. He closed the book with a snap and placed it back on the shelf. "We're looking for a missing woman here," he said aloud, "not *True Romance*," causing a woman bending into the bottom row in the S section to rise up and say, "I know what you mean."

For a moment he thought he should respond, but she seemed to be close to tears, the flicking eye-brows-turned-up-above-the-bridge of the nose look, the look he'd been defeated by so many times. He nodded, avoiding her wet glare, slipping by her bent body like a culprit.

Now, focusing on the wooden steps of the house in front of him, thinking of books, he considers the open tide table. One day's tides had been highlighted, the way a person might mark something he didn't want to miss in the weekend TV schedule.

Living six miles away from the ocean, he doesn't pay much attention to the tides except when his grandson comes to visit on his pre-arranged twice-a-year schedule. If it is the January weekend, they rent a boat and go crabbing in the bay, not that Lucius knows much about crabbing, having grown up east of the mountains where crab means white plastic stuff from Japan, but the boat guy is helpful, tells them how to bait the traps, where not to go so as to not float away forever.

Michael likes crabbing, crabmeat and butter, and laughing at his grandfather who isn't good at telling female crabs from male crabs and who drips butter down his shirt and says, "Fuck, excuse the language," as he wipes at his chest. And Lucius likes Michael, and if he is sorry about anything in life, it is not his own divorces, but the one that sent this grandson to live with the boy's mother in California and only two trips a year to check in with Gramps.

He should take a look at that tide table. Liz would know where to find one. He signals to her to go back to the car. They'll knock on doors of empty houses later.

26

Sunday Afternoon: Storm Warning
Joan

Joan finds the Nebraska phone number on Madge's cell phone. After ten or so rings, an aged voice answers. "Hello?"

Must be Roger's mother, Joan guesses, and she asks for Roger.

"He's not here," the woman answers. "He just came for a day or so and said he had to get home. We hardly had time to talk." Roger's mother is either sad or angry. Maybe it was the same thing when one is ninety.

"He's left? Already?" She shouldn't have said it that way. The slip seems to have pushed the mother's outrage to an even more intense whine.

"Yes, he has. I told him he might as well not come if he couldn't stay around a while and trim the bushes and clean the gutters. He doesn't realize I need him sometimes."

"I'm sure he'll be back soon, Mrs...." Joan glances at the cell phone directory, "Hickman. He speaks of you often."

Sounding mollified, Mrs. Hickman says she supposes so; he was a good son usually. Joan hangs up and turns to Lou and Jackie who are listening. "We may have an unexpected visitor soon. Roger seems to have figured things out."

27

Early Sunday Evening: Turning Tide
Lou

"You already know about my son-in-law divorcing me." Jackie is hunkered into the sofa, half of her lit by wavering strokes of candle flame, the other half in shadow. Lou is relieved when her long-legged friend shifts, brings her strong face into view. "Madge guessed right. My attorney is working out a settlement, despite a few last minute hitches, my fault. In a few months, I'll be free of that marriage, of that stepson, of the past miserable months. I'll only miss a sweet man who thinks I am his mother."

After they had skimmed each other's stories over an early risotto supper, Joan told them to get ready for a slumber party, and they have settled in front of the fire, wrapped in wool and chenille against the evening's chill. Lou lit the candles and set out the wine. Since she was in charge of the ceremony, she decided they would begin by reciting the Bible passage, *Whatsoever*, but only she could remember it all. Jackie mumbled like always and ended with a quiet "Shit." Then Lou told them to draw dune grass straws to see who will go first, and Jackie got the long one.

Joan is the only one wearing a nightgown, peach satin. Lou and Jackie's pajamas hold either gardens of flowers or cats. The glow from Jackie's candles, the soft robes swathing bodies, the wall of dark rubbing at the windows create a mythic scene. Lou smiles. They really are old crones whispering tales at midnight.

"No solrisinal, rising sun women in this room tonight," Lou hears Joan whisper as she resettles herself on the floor cushion, her back against the sofa. "Can I do this?" But it's Jackie's turn to talk.

Jackie speaks carefully, enunciating as if she's parting brambles with her words. "Madge knew that I was going on a retreat with Xavier, and she imagined that he would come to my cabin during the night. So did I." She glances up, and Lou encourages her with a nod. "And he did."

Lou can imagine it. The answer to Jackie's dreams, the priest at her feet, confessing his love in passion-ridden terms. Then, if Jackie stayed true to form, she would have had a moment of free-floating joy, followed by the bursting of the ecstasy balloon. Jackie loved the chase, not the capture. Except for the old man. Lou wonders if Jackie's recent show of courage is because of the balloon or the empty string.

Jackie puts down her glass. "And, you probably won't believe this, but I ran out of lust for my priest that very week. Really, I did, just like Madge said." *She's through the thicket, has found the path, thank God,* Lou thinks, sees Joan's tongue wiping her upper lip in agreement.

"I had been writing down my thoughts, in a journal, and making a list of things, like Madge said, only my list was about all the things I didn't like about Xavier, such as his smartass smirk when I tried to talk about god or goddesses, the way he lectured whether I was listening or not, even his eyebrows. I thought how I would tell him he was being unfair to me, this twisting and dangling when nothing could come from it, I didn't need it any more, I was growing up, all that shit. So when he came in that night, I was ready."

Jackie looks at her friends, raises her chin a little. "He started crying. At first I thought it was about us, and I felt sorry for him, he looked so miserable. I opened my mouth to say something, maybe different than I had planned, who knows? He looked so pathetic. Then he wiped his eyes and confessed he had just had sex with someone, a priest friend, and he felt bad about it. Like he wanted me to forgive him.

"'Goodbye, Xavier,' I said. 'Go pray or sublimate or something.'" Then Jackie grins, rolls her eyes, pulls a hand through her wild hair. "Actually, I also told him to fuck off, which he had kind of already done, of course, and it felt good. I wanted to go home. And I did. To a mess, but to two people who love me. I'm getting good at Nintendo."

Joan laughs out loud.

"Madge will like that ending," Lou says, as she reaches to pat Jackie's black mass of curls. "So do I."

28

Early Sunday Evening: Green Flash
Joan

Madge does like it, Joan is sure. She can feel Madge's quiet applause at Jackie's discovery of the two people who love her and whom she loves without expectations or conditions. She and Madge had talked about Jackie sometimes, wondering what would bring her to this next place. Fred, of course, began the process, adoring her, calling her Mother, awakening Jackie's sleeping capacity for caring which had gone unexamined in a haze of libido and alcohol. Xavier, this last week with him, offered the opportunity for Jackie to walk away from what was and move on to what will be. And Madge caught it all in her story.

Lou points an open palm toward her. Her turn.

Joan leans back, feels Lou's boney legs at her back. "Not yet. I'm going to take a moment here," she says, "to think about a story Madge didn't write. About Madge herself. Fill up your glasses while I do some quiet remembering."

"I always wanted to be perfect," Madge confessed that day years ago. "I cooked with *Joy of Cooking*, raised my sons on Brazelton and Spock, kept the Kama Sutra under the bed, and went through five copies of Strunk and White, writing my first two novels. I was an almost-perfect woman. Then Jerry killed himself, and I realized I had skipped the most important book of all, the one that would have taught me to listen, to be compassionate. I hadn't really heard anything he was trying to tell me."

A year after Jerry's death, Joan and Madge sat drinking coffee on a sunny restaurant patio in Palo Alto. Joan had driven from Clarkston to the Peninsula to settle her mother's small estate and, more important, to escape her fracturing family. Madge had just come from meeting her agent, a new book in the works. "I don't know if I'll ever finish it—it or any other book. My hands refuse to touch the keys of my word processor." She wasn't weeping. Just the opposite, really, her face white, eyes dry and cold in their stillness, her lips barely moving behind the whispered words. "Whenever I look at its blank screen, a vision of Jerry, his face still and reddened with fumes, gone, floats across it." She glanced away, touched her mouth with her napkin. A fragment of a smile collapsed into a moan. "I feel so guilty."

Joan did not speak. Madge's shoulders heaved, her hands brought the napkin to closed eyes, pale crumpled cheeks. This moment was a precious gift. Joan waited in silent gratitude.

Madge straightened her shoulders, lay the napkin aside, and said, her voice shaky but determined, "I guess I need to talk. Okay?" and Joan touched Madge's hand. They sat for an hour, Madge remembering, working to forgive herself, closing her eyes when the words were too painful. Finally, she lowered her shoulders, sat back, her eyes alive again, almost smiling, and said, "Thank you." She signaled the waiter for coffee refills. "Now, friend, it's your turn."

Joan wasn't sure what Madge meant.

"This can't be one-way, you know, this sharing. You have to give me something too. Otherwise it would just be me kvetching and both of us walking away empty." Madge moved her cup towards the server. "What's going on? Where's Tim?"

Joan looked at Madge and wondered if she had ever understood what friendship was. She felt for the Kleenex in her purse. And then she confessed her Clarkston life, Madge sad for her, each of them dabbing at eyes, not embarrassed at the scene they must be making, two middle-aged women holding each other in a long goodbye, whispering soft words, beginning a connection that lasted until this moment and beyond.

The tape recorder on the trunk whirls, unnoticed white noise under the surf outside, the crackling fire in front of them.

Joan shifts, glances at Lou, adjusts a pillow against the shinbones of her friend, begins, ready to give as well as receive, as Madge taught her at that afternoon and again this weekend.

"Madge guessed right in lots of ways in my story. I had lived a good San Francisco life, built on dreams that were dreamt long before I got to Lee and the Gamma Psi's, but college and finding a rich husband were part of them. Tim wasn't rich, but he could have been, as a doctor. I would have children, a life of art and music and the *NY Review of Books* and money enough to fill in all of the emptiness left over from my childhood. I've never talked about my family, on purpose. The past didn't fit the person I was attempting to be."

She is surprised. This confession is not as painful as she had imagined, actually a relief, like opening a tight belt. She can feel warm air filling her lungs, feeding her words. "I was miserably poor as a little kid; I envied children with fathers and mothers who went to PTA; as a teenager, my hands were stained red every fall from sloshing cherries in maraschino juice."

Lou interrupts. "Maraschino cherries?"

"I worked in the cannery. I bleached my hands for days before I came back to college in the fall."

"Damn. All that time I thought you were sitting around reading F. Scott Fitzgerald in smoky coffee houses." Lou sighs.

"That was the impression I wanted you to have, a dream. Tim and I divorced because I couldn't live with the life we had come up with. Tim knew it, and so did Madge. She also knew that I married Brian because he was the only piece missing from my new life, a rich well-known man. And that's why he married me, to fill in a gap in his life, although he was reluctant at first. Perhaps he knew all along that he could never change his philandering habits, or sexual compulsions, as I diagnose them now. But we needed each other to complete our vision of who we were. No, that's wrong. To complete the world's vision of who we were.

"I've always worried about how people, you two, in fact, see me. I think that's why I fabricated a new me, a different life." Joan pours a glass of wine and pauses. No need for her to go into the rest of the story. Madge told it as well as it could be told—until the man in the periwinkle pants wandered into it, uninvited and welcome. Joan brings the glass to her lips.

Joan had driven to Yachats and was a day away from Madge and the beach house. She was running away, she realized, but it felt more like she was heading towards something, the next place, whatever it might be. A rill of anticipation made her smile as she sat down for dinner in the restaurant. A man standing at the side of her table thought she was smiling at him.

"Are you traveling alone?" At her nod, he asked, "May I join you for dinner? I'm a little bored with myself after three weeks on the road." He was in his sixties, she guessed, firm-cheeked and bodied, laugh lines, freckles on his hands.

"I'd enjoy the company." This was true. She had eaten alone in Mendocino, feeling isolated in a sea of white table-cloths and vacationing couples at the inn. Tonight, someone to talk with would be a good antidote to the subtle alone-ness that had bloomed like a pale winter hellebore as she had driven north along the rainy Oregon coast that day.

He wore a yellow golfer's shirt and bright blue pants and looked as if he might burst into song at any moment, a yo-del perhaps, in celebration of the good day his grin indicated that he must have had. Joan couldn't help grinning back. A cheerful person across the table is almost as good for blow-ing away the blues as a Mercedes with the top down, she realized.

Bill, retired and on his maiden voyage as a true old fart, had been visiting children in southern Oregon and was head-ed for a mother in Oakland. Eight-eight, he said, and she was still going strong.

"Good genes," Joan commented. "You have a lot of voy-ages ahead of you, sounds like." She wondered if she sound-ed like a therapist. She hoped not.

"I try to take each day..."

"...as it comes." She didn't much like the cliché, but he seemed to be living it. "And today it was golf?"

"Every day it's golf, even in this Oregon mist. You have to have a purpose when you suddenly stop living one life and step into the next. So, for right now, it's playing golf.

Maybe next year it will be chain-sawing wooden bears."

"You'd have a lot of competition around here. Who do you suppose buys all of those creatures lined up along the road?"

He laughed. "I have one in the car right now. My mother will love it on her porch. You don't like them?

She wasn't sure if he were joking or not, but she liked his teeth. They were probably his, flashing whitely at the end of every sentence, signs of an open-heartedness, contagious, in fact, and she found herself teasing him and at one point, tapping his hand with her fork to make a point. She couldn't remember ever doing that before, except maybe once to reprimand a greedy son grabbing at a second cupcake. Childlike. That's what he was. Harmless.

Dinner over, he suggested they walk down to the ocean edge and watch the sunset since the clouds had moved on to the east. He took her hand as they stepped across the black rocks and found a perch at the water's edge.

"Have you ever seen the flash of green?" she asked.

"In Hawaii. Not here."

"I always make a wish at the last moment of sun."

"Tonight?

"Yes."

"Me, too," he said and his warm hand held her shoulder, touched her neck. Silent, they watched the orange disk flatten out, sink behind the darkening sea.

I can make a choice, Joan thought. *A left-hand detour off the highway.* His arm wrapped her like a warm scarf against the rising ocean breeze.

When he asked if he could walk her home, she said she would like that. She was glad she had taken off her wedding ring as she left San Francisco. Perhaps it had not been to keep the diamonds safe in the lockbox of the car as she traveled. And maybe he would not notice the white ghost of a marriage imprinted the skin of her fourth finger.

And he hadn't. Not until after they had made love, and he had taken her hand in his as they lay back against the pillows, their bodies still vibrating with the rhythms of sex. "Rings?' he asked.

"Maybe," she answered. Explanation was not necessary, perhaps not even possible.

"It's okay," he said. "Not my business. I've been a widower for five years. No more rules about anything, far as I am concerned. Take what comes and be glad is my theme song. And I'm very glad about you." He closed his eyes.

And I am glad about you, she wanted to answer. She had found out that she could enjoy sex with a stranger, and that he, her dear guinea pig, found her satisfactory. She also found out that breaking one's marriage vows, such as they were, was easy if one were angry enough, and that was what she had been for weeks. Like Brian, an angry person also, for his own reasons. *Not my fault.* As she fell asleep, she began to accept the truth of that idea.

Bill got up early the next morning to make a tee time. When he asked if he could see her again, she said that she needed to be on her way. She thanked him for the evening, and although he couldn't have known what the evening had really meant to her, he was pleased and said he hoped their paths would..."

"...cross again." She kissed him on his firm cheek. "You are wonderful medicine," she whispered as she led him to the door, glad that she had found her nightgown and that it covered her body now exposed to the cold light of day. His spotted hand touched her breast, brushed a nipple. She delighted at the surge she felt in her...loins? Do they say loins anymore? She felt a little crazy as she shut the door. She crawled back in under the blanket, tried to recapture the movement of his penis inside her, the weight of his gasp as he came, the kindness of his fingers that brought her to her own breathlessness moments later. A detour? An escape? Or, and she laughed aloud, a cul-de-sac. It didn't matter.

"I have left Brian. He doesn't know yet." Joan feels the cushion brush against her back as Lou leans towards her. "It's okay, Lou. This the best part of the story. I met a man on the way here, a sweet mirage of a man who liked me and golf. It is as simple as that. After a lifetime of believing I had to be something other than myself to be loved, this man liked me just as I was."

"Was?"

"Am. I hope. Talking about it is helping to clear up the details. Damn," Joan laughs. "I'm having an epiphany. Therapy must really work."

Jackie says "Shit" for no reason Joan can determine, and Lou sits back as Joan goes on. "The moment I accepted the fact that Brian was unfaithful, was even taping his dalliances, was lying to me, the dream of the perfect life fell away. It was as if I had hit the delete key and all that remained was a new, blank page. Bill, a man in the periwinkle pants, appeared and allowed me to experience for a few hours what an imperfect, joyful, unruly world could be like, how that blank page could be filled with a new dream."

"So," Lou asks, "perchance, you're taking up golf?"

"So, I'm going to try to bring back the girl with the maraschino cherry hands, wash her off, start her out again knowing she's okay despite her red fingertips." Joan glances at her lacquered nails. They might have to go, too. "Besides, I don't know Bill's last name or his address."

Behind her, Jackie laughs. "Joan, you remind me of the former me. Do I have to tell my painter stories again as a lesson to you? At least I knew his name, not that I can remember it now."

The idea of Jackie teaching her anything stuns Joan for a second. But she realizes it is true. Jackie has led the open, the humor-filled, risk-taking life that has eluded Joan forever. This woman lives every minute of the day. She has no secrets. She is her own person. Joan turns to face her. "You've been trying to teach me for years. I'm just a slow learner when it comes to freeing one's spirit. You graduated a long time ago, magna cum laude."

Jackie's cheeks are pink, her eyes glow with pleasure. "Thank you," she says, and she grins.

"Methinks thou art a little hard on thyself, Joan." Joan feels Lou lean forward, touch her shoulder, give it a lingering squeeze. The hand was warm, felt like a blessing, a moment Joan knew she would remember for a long time.

"Forsooth, let's drink to all the Bills in your future." Lou raises her empty glass and Jackie passes the bottle. The fire crackles and a log crashes into splinters of sparks. Somewhere on the beach a dog barks at the waves washing over her feet.

29

Early Sunday Evening: Clearing Skies
Lou

Lou sets her wine glass on the chest, enfolds herself in a
tight fuzzy hug. "Yesterday morning I hated myself for not
getting up when I heard her walking stick clicking on the
terrace, her soft steps gritty with sand. Only our promise to
her kept me paralyzed in my bed, crying, trying not to wake
you two up. Then I heard you, Joan, whisper goodbye from
your room, her side of the bed still warm, and I knew you
were crying too. And Jackie, you called out in your sleep,
somehow aware of her leaving.

"I waited, we all waited, until the sun rose and then we
got up, knew Madge was gone. It had not been a dream. For
an instant, I wanted to go out, capture, drag her back to us,

but instead we went for a walk away from her, as we had said we would."

"Seems like forever ago," Jackie says.

Lou unhunches her shoulders, loosens her wrap. "Then this morning I read the story she wrote for me, and I remembered again why I had made such a terrible promise. Madge helped me when I most needed her. I needed to return the favor."

"Yes," Joan says. "Me, too."

"She came up to the mountain and stayed for a while after I left Robert and my old home. She asked few questions; she listened as I babbled, not making sense even to myself, about loneliness in the midst of a life full of people, about the deep sadness that had settled in my bones making me heavy with a grief I didn't understand. She paid attention to my endless complaints about my husband and the dreariness of my days, and she said only, 'Your feelings are real. Don't doubt them.'

"We sat in that little cold cabin, bundled against the wind slipping through the chinks in the logs, and I talked until I was empty of words and we had run out of firewood. Then she asked, 'What will you do now?' and I knew. The cabin would become my home, the firs outside my companions, the mountain my solace. From then on, she visited every few months as I worked on the cabin and settled into my new life. We wrote often. I told her about my alpine garden, my new friend Susan. I didn't tell her everything."

Lou lifts her folder from the table, flips through the sheets to the end, takes out a pile of pages torn from a spiral notebook, the only paper she has brought with her. "Madge missed one part of my story, one I've never told anyone about, one I didn't let myself think about for forty years. It explains things. For me, maybe for you." Lou clears her throat. She hasn't read aloud since the boys were small. Before that, in literature classes with Dr. Elizabeth Wilton. Reading aloud is a matter of breathing evenly, tasting the words on one's tongue, her professor had instructed.

"My ending starts when Susan and I decide to take out the old red rhodie in front of the cabin." She tastes the words. *If There Be Any Virtue.*

"Okay, so we take it out and maybe transplant a wild one in the same spot. Some ferns, a little epimedium. Okay?" Susan is planning again, her eyes still closed.

I do not respond. This time the hydrangeas have carried me to 1956, to the drawing room of the Victorian house to which my professor, Dr. Elizabeth Wilton, had invited me for tea. Green and purple stained glass grapes shuddered under the rap of the doorknocker behind which the teacher's small shadow floated. In the entry, a Chinese pot held a tall stand of dried blue flowers, hydrangeas, remains of the past summer. Pink and white cakes teetered on tiered plates in the sitting room.

As Dr. Wilton took my coat and hung it on the mirrored hall tree, a soft trail of violins meandered in the quiet air. The scent of spiced tea and lemon and honey welcomed me as I settled into one of the winged chairs. Dr. Wilton poured, her hands sure, her cheeks rouged under a veil of powder that softened tiny lines, her skin that of a mature woman. My mother's age, I thought, were she alive.

The fingers that offered me a second cup of tea ended in nails so perfect they seemed to be tiny shells. White tips, pink, waxy centers, trimmed cuticle, half moons rising out of them. I, conscious of my own chewed stubs, curled my fingers into my palms and hesitated to bring my cup to my lips.

"I'm so glad you've come," Dr. Wilton said, "but please, here in my home, call me Elizabeth." At my nod, she continued. "I have admired your writing and your perceptions of the Romance writers. I especially enjoyed your Spencer paper and later the Yeats piece. Do you realize that you are an anomaly among college students today? You actually seem to enjoy mulling over the writing of dead men." She paused, sipped, her amused eyes watching me over the edge of her cup.

"I try to imagine their lives. I try to understand whatever it is within them that compels their writing. I love 'Songs of Innocence,' the very human person behind those ideas. Who wouldn't?"

"About 98% of my students, if I'm one to judge."

Elizabeth leaned over the serving dish, chose a tiny éclair and popped it into her mouth, a limber streak of pink. Fulsome, the solarium would describe it. Behind the tall window's lace curtains, the afternoon darkened, but we kept talking. After a moment in which we had shared bits of our childhoods, the professor turned, pulled a thin book from the shelves behind her and read a few lines of Coleridge. I listened, enthralled with the husky voice, the careful lips from which "A little child, a limber elf, singing, dancing to itself," sang out.

It didn't seem strange at all that at the end of the visit, a perfectly-manicured hand was laid on the small of my back, a set of peach lips pressed into my neck, a soft thank-you floating between us as we stood at the door. "Come back again, my dear," I heard as I walked down the path.

Of course, I went back many times that spring, no longer hesitant to call my teacher Elizabeth as we argued Shelley and Wordsworth, quoted underlined verses from Whitman and Blake to make our points, lolled under the huge oak in the side yard and read, interrupting each other with an occasional, "Listen to this." And finally, one sunny afternoon, in a quiet sitting room, tender fingers traced the slope from my cheek to my shoulder, meandered along the valleys of my rib cage. "Sweet one," Elizabeth murmured, "Are you ready?"

Nothing about this woman frightened me. Everything about her offered comfort and an intimate connection that I had only imagined as I tried to fall asleep in my narrow sorority cot. I lifted my face, and met that fulsome mouth with mine.

A tongue tip separated my lips, sought my tongue. It tasted of tea and desire.

I pulled away from the fingers that touched the buttons of my blouse. "I'm sorry," I said. "I can't." *Yet*, I wanted to say, but instead I stood, straightened my skirt. We did not speak as I took my jacket from the coat tree, opened and then closed the purple-graped door.

Three weeks later, Elizabeth Wilton, calm and professorial in her doctoral hood, thanked her senior scholar and wished her well in front of several hundred parents and friends assembled for graduation. In the years that followed, only occasionally, in the midst, say, of re-reading Tom Jones, or after a moment of ephemeral joy at rediscovering "Tigre, tigre burning bright," have I revisited the sadness of that goodbye.

I open my eyes. Susan's chair is empty, a swath of Doug fir shadow darkening the deck. I inhale a panicked gasp; then I hear the soft whistling of a gardener at work.

Susan kneels at the edge of the iris bed and tugs at yellowed spears. She clips away at spent blooms. A pile of limp debris lies at her side, and I get up and bend towards it, intending to add it to the compost barrel behind the alders.

"Look." Susan points to a white blossom peeking from under an iris. "We have a visitor. A globeflower. *Trollius laxlus*, something. The word must be out about our great B&B for wildflowers. Last month I discovered two trilliums, remember?" She looks up at me. "Who knows what will come next?"

I kneel next to my friend. I stroke each velvet petal, tell myself I am ready. I raise my hand, trace the curve of bone from Susan's ear to her cheek, as soft as the flower. Susan turns her eyes, her lips, toward me. "Who knows what will come next?" she says once more. Her hand touches mine as she leans forward to learn the answer to her question.

We will not live together. We each desire days of silence among the first growth trees, the still glow of dawn through a familiar window. We will be together, as we choose, when we choose.

So when I receive a blue envelope inviting me to a coming-together with my three college friends, the ones who still speak my patois, whose lives I have watched over the forty years since we dispersed into our next places, I ask if Susan will come with me, and Susan says she will not. She also has a past, like me, and the past is lived separately and is impossible to share. When I protest, say she will love these friends, Susan answers, "I love you. That's enough."

I will drive to the coast without her. I stop at Susan's house on my way down the mountain and leave in her roadside mailbox a dried spray of hydrangea, pressed flat, a bookmark between the pages of *A Journal of a Solitude*.

30

Sunday Evening: Calm Before
Lou

Lou folds the sheets of paper and looks at the silent women at either side of her. Joan, still leaning against a floor pillow, her head at Lou's knees, has closed her eyes, her hands in her lap. Jackie, at first slumping into the cushion of her chair, pulls herself upright.

"Cool," she says.

Joan's eyes blink open at Jackie's voice. Then she says in her soft, warm way, "Cool. Why didn't I think of that? To find love, that is indeed cool, my friend."

Lou is not sure whether she will cry or laugh, especially when Jackie moves next to her on the couch and starts playing with her hair. "It's standing straight up like in a comic book. Are you frightened? No bears around here."

She pats and pushes and Lou lets her for a minute. Then she swats at the patting hand and says, "Only when you fondle me."

Lou feels both Joan and Jackie pull away. Jackie gets up and lays a last piece of wood on the fire. Joan resettles on the other end of the sofa. The dim air swirls with uncertainty, and Lou regrets her awkward joke. What made her say it? To match Jackie's light-hearted acceptance of her confession? To back away from any further revelations? To end the discussion?

"I'm sorry," Lou manages to say. "I've embarrassed my best friends and myself." She starts to get up, but Jackie won't let her.

"No fair." She holds up a palm, points a "sit" finger. "I finally have a close lesbian friend and I have some questions."

"Jackie!" Joan protests. "My God! We're not in the solarium anymore."

"Feels a lot like it. And this information wasn't covered in your midnight readings, or anywhere else back then." Jackie looks at Lou. "Okay?"

Lou knows that Jackie is capable of outrageous questions. She's curious how she'll answer them. "Shoot."

"Dildo?"

"Carrot."

"Missionary?"

"If two female missionaries do it."

"Go down?

"All over."

"Orgasm?"

"Why not?" The inquisition goes on for another question or two, when Joan clears her throat, licks her lips, and asks, "Front to back?"

Lou frowns. "That still confuses me. Joan, bring the book next time we get together. We've got to review Dr. Van de Velde's list again."

The questions end when Jackie moans, "Damn, we were innocent, weren't we?" She has lain down on the floor, a pillow under her head. Lou coils in the corner of the couch, her arms around her narrow knees, feels her white hair springing up again as she sighs. Joan is chipping away at her red nails.

"Lambs to the slaughter," Lou says.

"That first night we met at the dorm at the cookie shine, you know how it felt, like the world was new and just out there waiting for us?" Jackie's voice is that of the young Jackie Lou remembers from that first meeting so long ago.

"We were all scared, I think. Stayed that way for a long time, maybe still are for different reasons." But not so much, Lou thinks. Not with Madge's stories to inspire us in this next place. "Madge was our center, wasn't she?"

Joan looks up from her nails. "Still is. Will be always." She might have gone on with that thought, might have also reminded them that the alarm was set for 4:30 a.m. and a few hours of sleep wouldn't hurt, but she also undoubtedly knows that memories of that Friday firelit evening will invade their dreams, cause their eyelids to refuse to close, their eyes to peer hopefully into the darkness, to search for Madge.

31

Friday Evening: Tsunami
Madge

That first night together, after the dishes have been cleared away but not the uneasiness that had flavored each forkful of Costco lasagna, Madge tells them to get comfortable. "You'll need more wine. This might be a long evening." She reaches for a folder lying on the table in front of her. "I need your help." Her glance, steady now, takes them all in as she pulls out its contents, places the papers in her lap. "To finish my latest book. I began writing it almost two years ago. I call it *Think on These Things*.

"This is the first of four stories about four old friends. Us. Your stories are not finished. However, this one will be, tomorrow." She pauses, picks up the pages in front of her, adjusts her glasses. "This is my story. Please forgive me if I stumble once in a while. You'll soon know why." She begins to read. A slow flow of words fills the air.

WHATSOEVER THINGS ARE OF GOOD REPORT: MADGE'S STORY

Roger has assured me that I am still good looking, that my dark hair, lit with streaks of blond to cover its creeping grayness, is as lovely as it's ever been, but sometimes I look into the mirror, search for my sixty-five-year-old cheeks, and what I see is a blurry double exposure. A young face veils the one I have now, expectant black eyes, big toothed grin, almost a beauty. A face that just missed being May queen by a couple of hundred votes, didn't become Sweetheart of Sigma Chi despite a boyfriend's ardent promotion of my best qualities, hair, I think, maybe breasts, although back then I'm told they called them jugs. I came in fourth for Homecoming queen.

"Handsome," Roger says. Handsome, in fact, is appropriate for a woman my age but not the accolade I sought in those days.

Those days. I return to those days often lately, stepping through a strange fissure that has developed between then and now. Escaping the now, perhaps.

"There, done. Shall we send them out today?" Roger looks at me. "The invitations to the Solarium Club. Isn't that what you used to call yourselves?"

I breathe, try to untangle myself from my thoughts. "Mark the weekend on the calendar. Maybe we can cross off the days as we get closer?" I smile at this man I adore and add, "Knowing what day it is, *is* helpful."

Roger's big-knuckled hand leaves a large X on a square on the calendar that is tacked to the wall in the kitchen. "This is today," he says. He circles a Friday several rows of squares below the X. "This is when you'll see your friends."

Good. I still have time. To try to think this through. To decide.

I sit in the nook, cutting up the peppers and those brown things while Roger fixes dinner. "What's this?" I ask.

"Mushrooms, Madge. You like them."

"I know I like them. I just don't have their name," I answer, and in front of steaming plates, I have discovered that smells trigger memories. At the moment, the beef is taking me to a Saturday evening a long time ago. Not with Roger. With another man, Jerry, my then-husband. The scene floats in the air between the nook's clicking forks.

"I'm in love with someone else."

Jerry and I are using our new steak knives, like butter, he has commented, cutting into the fillet mignon I splurged on that afternoon.

I am aware of the candlelight, the rifts of music in the air, the quaking of the deep fault line between us, a critical shift.

"Who?" I ask.

"It doesn't matter."

Somehow it doesn't.

"Ready?" Roger asks. "To go for a walk?"

"I think so."

We walk, my arm on his, without speaking. Amidst the quiet tickings of feet on pavement, another path appears.

A rain soaked trail to a football field, the young Madge says, "Ugh, I hate wallowing in muck."

One of the girls at my side snickers. "Anyone else would have said slipping in the mud."

I go around the puddles, walk slightly forward of the others, know I should keep my mouth shut. At sixteen I have more words than anyone I know. I have to be careful not to use them.

Ironic now. I squeeze Roger's arm. "Did you ever feel odd?" I ask as we leave the yard.

"I've always felt odd," he answers.

"And what do you did you do about it?"

"Nothing. It didn't bother me."

"You didn't care what other people thought of you?" I can still feel the twist in my stomach that signaled that step into the muck of unpopularity "I can't imagine not caring."

"Do you care now?"

"I don't know. Seems as though I should." We arrive at the post office and stand in line to buy stamps.

"I used to go to the same clerk every time I came here. She was my good luck charm and she always knew what I meant by 'Inside and outside postage, please.' I would close the envelopes with her wet sponge, and when she piled my manuscripts one on top of the other and toss them into the bin, she'd always say, 'Hang in there, girl.' She had red lips, a big blond, half glasses perched on the end of her nose. Her painted fingernails clattered like birds' feet against the desktop. Silver with rhinestone diamonds at Christmas; pale pink with purple swirls in the spring."

"And did she bring you luck?"

"I won my first writing contest after one of those 'Hang in there's.'" I glance down the row of windows. "I think she's been gone a long time."

We step up to the counter. When the pimpled clerk asks me if he can help me, his fiercely bitten nails distract me. My own hands are empty of a manila-wrapped manuscript. I look at Roger who pushes the blue stack of envelopes across the wood surface. "We need a book of stamps," he says, "and will you take these?"

The man's eyes do not look up from the screen at his right. He nods, points to the little electronic box that tells us what we owe him. In a moment we are walking away from the building, approaching a group of young people sitting at the tables on the sidewalk outside Coffee Time. "Something to drink?" Roger asks. "We odd ones will fit right in here."

"You don't have enough metal ...stuff...poking...into your body," I say as I sit down and push a rumpled newspaper to one side. It's getting worse. Two words lost in one sentence. A whole sentence gone at the place we have mailed the letters. If I start with A and work my way through the alphabet, I can sometime bring the word forward, but it's not often that reciting the alphabet fits in, time wise.

"Earrings, piercing." Roger says. Of course. Earrings. We ordered lattes, a word I have not lost. The unimportant words are disappearing first, not the ones I need to function—like "latte."

Months ago, we looked up Alzheimer's on the Internet, borrowed books from the AD Association. We went to homeopaths, ingested ginkgo, tried cross word puzzles. I cried, of course, and Roger held me, told me not to be afraid. Then one day I blackened the kitchen with a forgotten frying pan on high heat, and Roger took over most of the cooking. Now, when I try to follow recipes, I cross off each ingredient as I stir, or I will not remember where I am in the process. Roger and I have worked out a system of notes to remind me of the day's schedule, of the location of my phone, my purse (always at the end of the drain board), my keys, while I still feel comfortable driving. I can read, but my fingers have forgotten the keyboard. My mind drops words like cherry blossoms. This, of course, is the greatest tragedy.

A sip of coffee. A lovely room. Tea not coffee. A man smiling across from me hands me a folder. I open it. Read it. Sign a paper. Receive a check. Am suddenly very afraid.

"Sisters is just right," the man says. "The next one will be even better." Another person sits at our round table, nodding.

"Madge is the real thing," he says. My agent.

The two men grin at each other, then at me. I am crying, using a cloth napkin to blow my nose.

"Tell me again about *Sisters*," I say. Roger sighs. I know he has performed this favor before.

"What made you think of it?" he wonders.

I raise my cup. "The round table. My excitement, maybe. I'm looking forward to the beach party with my friends." Triggers. Perhaps I'll write a novel entitled *Triggers*. I will let my mind take me wherever it wants to go, free rein, see where I end up. If I go back far enough, I will be in utero, wordless. Almost like now.

"Your successful debut into mainstream women's novels. It made you almost famous." Roger reaches for my hand when he says this. "It was set in the early Fifties, a young woman goes off to college, poor and innocent and scared. She is asked to join a sorority, a kind of hardship case, and since she's never had more than one good friend at a time, a house full of sisters seems unbelievably right.

"And things are pretty idyllic for a couple of years. Then one of the sisters is found crying and bleeding in the housemother's bedroom, the housemother frantic. Lily has inserted a pom-pom stick into her vagina to try to dislodge the lump that is preventing her from getting the curse. The lump lives, as does the sister, although she's no longer a sister, having been unpinned and sent home. Five years later, our heroine meets the shamed woman by chance and discovers that she has more in common with her than she ever suspected. Her husband of two years, ex-student body president and recipient of a Fulbright grant, is the father of Sammy, the lump.

"Ah, now I remember," I say. "And she didn't have an abortion?"

"1950's," Roger explains.

"Of course," I answer, a glimmer of past conversations instructing me.

We talk, Jerry as close to tears as I am. He calls a friend to ask how to go about it, his pale skin stretched like a rubber mask across his cheekbones. "You could go to New York," he whispers to me.

"Ryan says that he knows a doctor. . ." Then he stops, settles the phone in its cradle, lowers his head into the bowl of his hands

"We need to get married, don't we?"

"Jerry and I were married a long time," I say.

"Eighteen years. Two sons, Jim and Grant," he adds, just in case.

I am tired of remembering. Besides, I need to get busy making plans for the party, the friends who will be visiting me soon. I push back my chair, stand. "Time to go," I say, and Roger laughs.

Madge stops reading, tried to clear away whatever it is that was closing her throat. A swallow of wine doesn't help. Perhaps this will be the most painful, impossible part of the plan, this baring of herself. Perhaps this was where it will all go awry, years of work stricken down by a voice that had dried up like an old well. The others watch, still, waiting. Then Joan reaches out, takes the folder from her hands, says, "It's okay, Madge. I'll finish for you." She reads.

Some days are better than others. Today I haven't had to follow the list of housecleaning chores as I moved from room to room. I've even set last fall's dried apples to soaking in order to turn them into the applesauce with cinnamon that Roger enjoys over his cottage cheese. Two people phone, and I let the answering service take the messages as I finish the vacuuming. My summer garden is exploding with coreopsis and zinnias and delphiniums and I pick an armload of stems to fill the entry hall vase. I know the flowers' names because Roger and I have labeled each mound, the copper frames of the cards so attractive that visitors to our garden have copied them.

Then I relax with a cup of coffee and listen to the messages. My agent, Harry Macken, is getting a little worried about the deadlines for *Think on These Things*, my next book. Bob has called him. Is something wrong?

Bob. I start with A, find his last name in the G's. Bob Gordon, my latest editor at Macmillan, my creaking mental Rolodex tells me. That's what I am supposed to be doing, not cleaning house. Finishing the four stories. I go to my desk, find the hard copy of what I've done so far. Damn, where is Roger?

Next message: Hi, this is Ruth. We are hoping you and Roger are still coming to dinner Saturday night, Madge. The group will be interesting and quite lively, especially if you guys are there. Please let me know.

Roger tells me that I do okay at this sort of gathering. I am cheerful and willing to listen to others, to nod and pat arms. "It's not important that you remember everything they tell you. Did you ever?" he asks, and I'm sure I did not, but there are moments when raised eyebrows inform me I have asked the same question more than once of the lovely red head in the jade green dress or the smiling husband of the hostess. However, I'm quite sure that few acquaintances have figured out just how out of order I am. Roger, my guardian angel, rescues me whenever he can.

Not your usual angel, of course. When I first met him as he lifted the metal gate off its hinges and settled it into the back of his pickup, I was a little frightened of him, of the kerchief banding his forehead, his dirty hands. The gate had warped, needed to be replaced. I found him in the Yellow Pages; European craftsmanship, he claimed, and while I wasn't sure what that meant, the new gate was lovely. He pointed out the smooth welds, the intricate scrolls of iron, the brass tips on the spears. "A perfect match," he said, looking over the sixty feet of iron fence his gate was joining. "Perfect for this house, too."

I'd bought the place on a whim after signing a three-novel contract. Spanish stucco, tile roof, iron casement windows that flung themselves out into the summer, a garden that beckoned, and a new kitchen with a gas stove and two sinks. I didn't need two sinks, or the three bedrooms, or the three bathrooms, because I lived alone, wrote every day, rarely entertained, but I could afford the place because my books were selling. I would have room for grandchildren, if my sons ever gave me any, and I just might be inspired by these lovely arches and dark floors to have a party or two, which, in fact, I did, to celebrate first, Jimmy's marriage and then, Grant's, to competent young women whose careers took them to other parts of the world.

A few years later, the gate rusted. Roger came to repair it. And he came back to work on the iron balconies outside the bedrooms, on the interior railings on the curved stairway. And he came back finally because I asked him to, and he stayed. He still wears his hair in a ponytail, gray now, pulled back from a high forehead, and he looks at me with intense brown eyes, a kind-faced man, six years younger than I. He uses his headband only when he is welding, and I am still amused by my friends' reaction to it. His hands are usually clean, now that he is living in my house.

I remember all this because, as we lay curled into each other each evening, Roger whispers this goodnight story until I sleep.

"Hello, Madge!" His voice seeks me. "It's almost time to go to the meeting."

"I'm washing up now." I look at my calendar, see by the marching X's that it is Tuesday, read "AD group," pat my hair and feel my stomach tighten.

Cookies and coffee wait on the paper-covered table to one side of the circle of chairs. Five or six people mill about the room, unwilling to sit down too early, to appear too anxious. At least this is how I feel as I pour myself a cup of decaf and watch Roger do the same. The group was his idea. "I don't see how sitting around moaning about our failing memories, our embarrassing moments, or crazinesses will be helpful to me," I had protested. "I don't want to talk about it!"

"You don't have to talk," he answers. "Just listen."

"I don't want to listen, either."

"Just once."

So I went, sitting beside Roger and inspecting the twelve people circled like a wagon train against the unknown. The sick ones were not distinguishable from the ones who were well. All carried an aura of sadness that blued their words. I did not speak. Nor had Roger.

Afterwards, the counselor, a gray-haired plump woman with soft hands that reached out to arms and shoulders, thanked us for coming, invited us to come again. The door opened, and I felt as if I were exiting an airless tunnel. I shook my head, took Roger's arm. We had walked a few steps away from the building, a church of some kind, when I felt a light tap on my arm. A woman, fifty-five, perhaps, one I had noticed in the group because of her tailored suit, gold earrings, polished shoes, said, "Try it again. It may not seem so now, but you will begin to find solace here. Trust me."

For a moment I wondered how the woman knew it was I and not Roger who was ill. Then Roger handed me his handkerchief, and I realized I was crying.

So we have returned, several times. I have begun to talk. So has Roger, and I understand that he needs the group more than I. It is difficult to listen to the stories because what I hear is my future, and I'm quite sure I will not be as brave or calm as these people seem to be.

"At work, they would tell me to do an assignment, and I would not be able to do it and not understand why. Every day, I would look at the top of the newspaper to see if it was a day to go to work."

"I just couldn't think of a word and the person I was talking to did this 'come on, come on' thing with his hands and it made me very angry."

"People don't look at me anymore, just at my husband."

"I'm using a tape recorder to take notes at meetings and use my Spell-check when I write. When I need to make a phone call, I write down what I want to say. I'm not sure how long I can do this. Katharine helps me."

Then I speak. "I'm learning to deal with my...forgetfulness, by changing the subject, or I answer questions with other questions. I find myself trying to disarm others by praising them."

"Oh," Roger turns to me. "Is that what you're doing? I was hoping you really do think I'm terribly good-looking."

The group laughs, not for the first time that evening, and even Phil, who is depressed enough to admit being treated for it, tells of looking in the mirror and seeing his son. "What a way to lose 25 years." Laughter again.

I can't help joining in again. "So how depressed should I be when my mother appears in my bathroom mirror?" Phil, on cue, reaches in his pocket, offers me a vial of pills.

"Damn! How can we laugh?" I ask Roger on our walk home.

"How can we not?"

I have not lost my libido. In fact, it seems to be blossoming, like a flower on a forgotten cactus, in an unlikely way for an old declining woman.

A barrel cactus, its yellow petals stretching toward the light filtering through the blinds, greets me as I open the door. I have not been in this

room for months, the length of time it has taken me to stop hating Jerry.

I am stunned by the flower and the chaos. Blueprints and drawings fan across the workroom floor. Cabinet doors hang crazily; inside, books are toppled, some ripped apart. The cactus, a souvenir of our trip to the Southwest the year before, is the only intact survivor of Jerry's last swing at the world.

I sit down at his desk, weep for my dead husband, for my marriage, for myself and then I begin to pick up papers, file them in the deep drawers lining the walls.

Cactus. Blossom. Myself. I retrace the sprawling trail of my thoughts. Ah, sex. Roger doesn't seem to mind me waking him at night, touching him, whispering *Please.* I haven't had the courage to mention this compulsion at the group meeting, and Roger and I have not talked about it, although once he patted my hand in a gentle warning as we sat in a restaurant, my fingers creeping towards his zipper. I wonder if this sexual itch is a secret kept by everyone with Alzheimer's. No one I know talks about sex.

Not like in college, when the sisters would stay up and tell jokes and get aroused. We called it getting hot. Once over a carrot suggestion, I remember. Even back then, however, no one admitted to actually doing it under the bushes in front of the sorority house, even though hands pushed up under cashmere sweaters, squeezed past waistbands of Pendleton plaid skirts, leaving strings of mucous dripping into a toilet bowl to be inspected, wiped away.

Nowadays women in novels call it getting wet, not hot. And even at my age, I get wet sometimes as I hold, stroke, Roger's penis. But I don't speak of it. Some truths refuse to become words. The truth, for instance, that I never loved Jerry, ever. The truth behind his death, discovered amidst the debris of his workroom, a note to a young, unattainable boy.

"I'm in love with someone else," he confesses at dinner.

"It doesn't matter," I answer, because the Someone Else doesn't matter. "Everyone has fantasies," I say, "even happily married architects with two years of contracts on his desk, with a somewhat successful novelist wife, two fine, straight-teethed, un-acne-ed boys." A life. The Someone Else

is a figment to be observed, not touched, I tell him, from a park bench or the stands of a high school gymnasium. I have guessed about the existence of other figments, as a storyteller might, and I am quite pleased with my tolerant acceptance of them.

This, at least, is what my journal tells me.

He did not deny their existence. However, this one looked back at his figmentor, (Is there such a word? I later wonder in the same journal) as he wiped his salty face with a white towel, picked up his racket and went on to win the set.

That look is the beginning of the end of Jerry. I know this from the letter I uncovered in his workroom that day I found the courage to enter it, a letter now tucked into the rumpled pages of an old journal, a confession both of love and of shame.

I can't continue this torture. I love you as I've never loved anyone, and you threaten to report my calls, my following you, to the police.

You laugh at me even as you hold someone else's cock in your hand, your tongue in his mouth. Tonight you asked for money to keep silent.

I am being played for a fool. I am a fool.

I have never written of Jerry's despair. Another truth that refused to become words, like the truth of the depth of the grief I feel at this moment for my own self, for Roger.

However, this is a good day. I find this year's journal and open to a new page. My pen moves slowly as I make my plans, try to find the words for what will happen. To remind myself, should I forget.

When the doorbell chimes, I glance at my watch, then at the calendar. It does not reveal an appointment. I rise and go to the door. When it opens, I see a familiar face.

"Hi, Mom. I had a layover in town so I decided to drop by."

My son. Jimmy. Who lives in...someplace on the east coast. I wrap my arms around his waist, pull him into the house. "I'm so glad!" I inspect the man who grins at me. His dark hair is his father's, his hooded eyes mine. He is and he is not the little boy who still lives in my memories. Then he laughs, asks if I have any cookies.

"Let's see." I go to the freezer and pull out a plastic container. Inside are the chocolate chip cookies I must have made a week or so ago, the recipe checked off at each ingredient. I pour a glass of milk, set them in front of my son at the kitchen table. "I knew I baked those cookies for a purpose," I say. So far everything is okay.

"So how are you, Mom?" he asks, "and Roger?"

"We're good." I answer his question with another. "But how are you? And the job? And everyone? You look wonderful."

Jim describes his work as an engineer, Jennie's work (ah, Jennie, that's right) at the magazine, the house they are thinking of buying in Bethel, not far away from where they live now, but more in the country. "You remember when we drove through it on the way to Vermont," he says,

I wonder if this is the time to tell him.

I practice silently. "Actually, I don't remember. I must be getting old, Jimmy. I'm having trouble with my memory." And he will laugh, "Everyone has trouble with their memories nowadays, Mom. We're all overloaded with information, need to kick back, relax." And he'll ask what I am doing for fun these days and when we are coming back east again. "New York is only four hours from Boston, you know. You could take in a few plays..." Boston. Of course.

No, I decide. It's not time yet.

The back door bangs open, and Roger pushes into the kitchen, his arms wrapped around two large grocery bags. "Whew!" he wheezes as he puts them on the counter and then he turns and sees Jim. "Oh, my God! What a surprise." He glances at me, back at my son. "How long are you here for?" When he hears, he says, "Too bad you can't stay longer. Can you reschedule?" He unloads the bags, puts away the groceries. "I've bought enough food to feed an army, and the guest room is ready and waiting.

The words seem innocent enough but Roger's smile is his troubled one, the one I've seen only a few times, in doctor's offices, in late night talks. He knows, of course, that Jim can't reschedule a plane flight. Why would he even suggest it? And why isn't Jim noticing the reversal of roles here, Roger the housewife, I, relaxed at the table biting into a half-frozen cookie? It's clear to me that Jim's visit is not a casual drop-by in between planes. He has come for a reason.

Roger seems to know this also. Tension wraps like yellow warning tape around his words. Caution, he is signaling. To whom?

Then Jim says, "I think I can do it. Let me check." He pulls out his cell phone and moves into the living room.

His voice murmurs softly as I stand, walk to Roger bending at the fridge, wait until he rises and say, "You asked him to come, didn't you?"

Roger reaches to me, places a hand on each of my shoulders. "Madge, they have to know."

"Of course, but I wanted to do it. Later. When it needed to be done. Why this charade?"

"I hoped to make this easy on you, to not worry you, just an unexpected family gathering. I should have known you would see through it." I flinch as he leans forward, kisses my cheek. "Grant is coming. Later tonight."

My sons. Tonight. "I hate you for this," I whisper as I pull myself away from his grip on my shoulder.

"I know."

When Jim comes back into the kitchen, Roger says, "Your mother has figured it out." And despite my stiff body, lowered eyes, my son takes me into his arms and holds me. His hand rubs the small of my back, in just the way I used to soothe him.

I have not forgiven Roger by the time the door chimes once more. I am sitting in my chair in my writing room, going through the alphabet bringing back Grant's wife's name, H - Heather. I am not sure I can go downstairs. It is too much like the other time that my sons came to me to learn of a tragedy. I do not need a journal to bring back that scene. Not yet.

Jerry slumps in his car, dead. The ambulance and the police arrive, his body is closeted somewhere else. His sons need to be told. I call each boy, catch one of them at a dorm party, the other's phone is answered by a girl who calls to him, "It's your mother."

One son comes home stoic and tight-lipped; the other weeps quietly in his room and at the service. The silent one finally says, "I never knew him when he was happy. Was he ever?" His brother asks, "Why? and I have no answer for either of them.

I push myself up from the chair, rub my eyes and go to greet this second son. When he sees me coming down the steps, he runs to meet me, takes my arm as if I am an invalid. "Grant," I say. "No crying tonight."

He squeezes my hand, manages to say, "Okay." He kisses my forehead. Already his eyes are moist.

Roger offers wine as he stir-fries our dinner. Jim mixes the salad; Grant sets the kitchen table with the familiar everyday dishes. I let them do these tasks, sipping my white wine, listening to the bravado of their cheerful voices, laughing when they do, the love in the room a poultice for the pain inside me. We sit down to eat and then the dishes are cleared, coffee poured, the last of the cookies on a plate between us.

I look at Roger, say, "This is your show. Get on with it."

Roger ignores my anger. "I love you, Madge. And I respect your sons and their connection with you. They deserve to know how your life is changing, that you trust them to understand. Shall I tell them or will you?" He speaks so slowly that I know he has rehearsed this preamble, that he abhors what is about to happen as much as I do.

It is not that I cannot find the words to tell my sons of my diagnosis or that I believe they will disintegrate upon hearing it. Sons, stoic or tearful, manage this sort of news and go on. The problem is that I am afraid I will disintegrate as the words leave my mouth, that I will burst like a rubber balloon at the prick of its skin, the truth let out to the world. Holding it in is what has kept me...what? Still believing I could stave off reality? The way I felt when my doctor handed me the prescription for a new drug, even as he said, "Not a cure; but it may slow it down." In denial, of course, of the fact that I will end up in diapers, as guileless as a babe, gleeful at the pretty flowers I am handed.

"At least she seems happy," they will say. "Always glad to see people even if she can't remember who they are."

And at the end, my sons will visit their mother in the locked wing that reverberates with the moans of my fellow sleeve-plucking patients. My boys will find me in front of a TV in the crafts room, and I will look up and say, "Who are you?" Jim's face will go stone still, and Grant will turn away.

Until then, Roger will cook, read to me, clean me, spend years of his life consoling me or what is left of me as I dissolve until I cannot remember how to swallow, to breathe.

I'll keep Roger the longest, I think. But what can I offer him in return? He will pour himself out to me until he is an empty vessel, as empty as I, and at the end, alone.

I raise my chin.

"Another glass of wine, please." The boys point at their own glasses as Roger pours. I begin. "I'm not sure how Roger got you both here; perhaps he's hinted at a disaster, and if so, it is. I have Alzheimer's Disease. I've been diagnosed by my doctor and several others. My symptoms are the usual. I am losing the names of things and people. I can read, but in the last month my writing has slowed down. My fingers are disconnected from my brain, from the keyboard. Sometimes I don't remember what I've written and have to start all over again. I also have trouble recalling what I have said or what people have said to me, especially when I am tense or worried. I make notes to remind myself how to clean the house, run the washing machine. More often, Roger makes the notes. I look about the same, but when you came to the door this afternoon, Jimmy, I could not think of your name for a moment, even though my heart told me I loved you dearly."

Roger takes my hand, rubs the knuckle he knows aches most days.

"The prognosis is that I will not recover, that I will lose everything, within a year or five years, or perhaps ten. This disease is not kind to its victim, nor to those who love her."

Jim's chair scrapes against the floor as he pushes back, says, "Mom, everyone forgets things. God, I'm thirty-five and I forget lots of things, my own phone number."

Roger steps in. "Not the same, Jim."

"There has to be a medicine for this. They've been working on it for years." Grant's voice quavers. He is not crying yet.

"Only a few experimental drugs to slow down the progress. Your mother is taking one of them."

Then they are silent, each seeking a place for his eyes to rest, give him time to absorb this news. I look at my three men, and know they love me, know I love them, know, especially, that I must not cause them any more pain than has been inflicted this evening.

Then they stand, and my sons come to my side and they tell me that I am a great mother, a strong and unmovable rock in their lives, that nothing, even this, will change their love for me. "Nothing," Grant repeats, choking on the words, reaching for a napkin to wipe his eyes. Jim takes my face in his hands. "I love you, Mom." and he kisses me on the lips. I don't remember either of my sons kissing me like that, the gesture so intimate it feels like giving birth. Then he straightens, befuddled perhaps, says, "Let's relax. Watch a little TV." Pull ourselves together he means. We wander into the living room, stunned, like survivors of a cataclysmic event.

Later, no one is willing to say goodnight even though the television is drained of watchable programs. Roger suggests we play a game of Pitch. Grant objects, says he can never remember the rules.

"Well, neither can I. We'll be even," I answer, and the first startled hah of laughter fills the air, followed by another. The game begins. We argue. We consult cheat sheets and at the end, I come in second, behind Jim. "Even a handicapped mother doesn't make you ease off, does it, my son?" I say. Again, a gasp, then a recovery, another joke. "You made me what I am, Mom," he answers. Grant is blinking, and it is time to end this.

I kiss my sons, go to my bedroom. A lullaby of murmuring voices lulls me towards sleep. I wish Roger were beside me now. I would like to touch him, feel his warmth.

The next day doesn't begin well. At breakfast I find myself again searching for the name of my agent as I talk about my novel, almost finished, I think. For a minute, I cannot even remember its title. At each hesitation, Roger fills in the words, Harry Macken, *Think on These Things*, so quietly that only those in on the secret would notice. My sons notice.

Boston. Heather, Jennie. I stand on the porch and wave them away in their taxis. Their faces look back to me, tell me that they are worried, afraid, sad for me and anxious to get on with their lives.

Roger settles himself next to me on the porch rocker.

"I'm glad you organized this clandestine sleepover. I guess it had to be done, and I couldn't have done it without you." I lean against his shoulder, let my hand wander.

Roger laughs and leads me indoors. Afterwards, I go to my desk and open my journal, pick up my pen, inscribe words I hope tell the truth.

We spend the next week going over the first rough chapters of *Think on These Things*. "I have become your amanuensis," he says. The word is stuck somewhere in a brain cell. A slave to a writer. I glance over my glasses at him. He grins back. "It's not a bad job," he says.

The novel will be four stories, each telling the life of a woman approaching seventy. "Older than crones," one of them says. "But wise, right?" another asks. They know each other intimately even though their lives intersect only occasionally. None of the stories is finished yet.

"Got a ways to go," Roger says.

Each evening, after our work time, he mixes us a drink, his scotch, mine vodka. "Sun over the yardarm," he says, as if that explains this new routine.

"What is a yardarm?" I ask, confused. "And why are we celebrating it?"

He hesitates, eyes me. "Are you worried about me?" he asks.

Yes, I want to answer, but this may not be as true as it was a few weeks ago. A memory blooms, my mother, in her eighties, after the death of her friend. "I can't cry anymore," she says. "All my juices have dried up." Dried up. That's how I'm beginning of feel. An essential spring is going dry. "A little," I say. "Let's have another small drink."

An email arrives from my editor. "We're waiting impatiently," it reads. "What are you working on? We hope it's the last page!"

I am working on remembering who you are, I would like to answer. Instead, Roger sends a noncommittal reply. Taking a break, he types. Will be in touch soon.

Another good day arrives. I wake up feeling almost whole. "Roger." I say after breakfast, picking up a pencil, wanting to get started, "what will we eat at the beach house?" We decide that each woman will make one meal, either a lunch or a dinner. Roger will plan the menu, buy the food. He will write out the directions for the meal I will cook. Just in case. On this good day, I don't think directions will be necessary.

When we've finished our lists, we pour fresh coffee, talk. And I get out my college yearbook and point to the Gamma Psi photo. Black and white grins beam under poufy hair, eager glints in wide eyes. I want him to know these sorority sisters, these friends who will visit at our beach house.

"That's the housemother Mrs.— I don't remember. Her one gift to us all was to teach us how to iron the sheets we were about to lie between as we all marched off to marriage."

I search the faded faces, find Joan's. "She was so...California. Cool. And lovely. She's still like that. This is Lou. I always thought she would end up a poet. I can remember her chain-smoking, reciting Beowulf at one in the morning. Her black hair is pure white now, has been for years." I trace a finger down the names at the side of the page. "Here's Jackie. She was one of our bad girls. And very funny. She's still funny."

"And this is me. By my prissy hair cut, I seem to be a goody two-shoes, right down to my Peter Pan collar, but I had another, not so sweet, side."

"You still do. That other side is what makes you a keen observer of human foibles, a writer." Roger says. "And a lover," he adds with a brush of his lips on my forehead. "What will happen when you get together next week?"

"I think we'll find out we are still the young women we were in these pictures. Deep inside."

32

Friday Evening: Overwash
Madge

"So now you know." Madge takes the folder from Joan. "Thank you for your lovely voice. Much easier on the ears than mine will be when I'm finally finished this evening." She is glad someone else has taken her place for a while, but she mustn't be distracted. She has much more to do. "I want you to help me with the end of my story, not only mine, but yours also." Her friends glance at one another. Unease makes them recross legs, raise empty glasses.

"It's okay, it really is." She wants to hold each of them, feel warm breasts and arms against hers, for just a moment or two. Instead she makes her mouth firm and fingers the sheets of paper in her lap that will guide her through the next step in her plan.

"In the past two years, once I knew I was never going to recover, I've been thinking about our stories. Not like the silly one with us in the rocking chairs getting our thighs massaged by young studs, although the idea continues to be intriguing. Instead, I've been experimenting with your lives, as I have known them, attempting to understand what truth is, exactly. I've come to the belief, and, I'm sorry, I have to look at my notes, words flying out now like midnight bats."

Madge likes that image; she must have used it before, artifacts rising to the surface. "I believe that truth is found in the threads of love that wind through each of our days, but not necessarily in the stories that contain these days.

"When you read your stories, don't be dismayed that I've dug into your pasts, into your dreams, re-arranged things to my own liking, like a child kneeling into the moist sand on a sunny day. The words you've given me, precious light-filled beach agates, support the slippery, unstable walls I've patted into sand castles. Quickly, before the tide comes in and wipes out our creations, help me finish this project. We need turrets, moats, flags, a sentinel to point towards what will come next, a moment to cheer what we have done."

Madge has not intended to be so obtuse. She has written this part without Roger's editing, unlike the four stories in *Think on These Things*. She feels her mouth go dry. Her friends averted their eyes, aren't looking at her. She has gotten off track. It is time to read the next sentences in her lap.

"You're asking us to help you, with the stories, with your story." Joan, as usual, is getting it, despite the castles.

Madge nods a thank you. She needs Joan, will continue to need her until this is finished. She touches the papers in front of her. She looks at the three solemn women who await her next words, realizes she will not use her notes, will not use a metaphor to soften her request.

"I am not going to be able to finish your stories. You'll have to do that yourselves." She sets the file on the table at her side. "And I want my story to end with my death. I want to die, quickly and without anguish to my family and to you. I will not follow Jerry's lead and allow myself to be found with a confessional note and a cortege of guilt-stricken family and friends, some of whom wield whips to their conscience-bent backs to this day. Nor will I remain alive to torture my loved ones as I lose myself and them cell by cell."

"Shit." Jackie, her eyes wide with dismay, shifts, glares at Madge. "Are you thinking we'll hold a pillow over your head until you stop kicking?"

"You aren't asking us to murder you, are you?" Joan asks, her voice quiet.

Madge is sorry to see that Lou is crying, that Jackie is angry. She understands her friends might be saddened at first by her request. She herself is finished with sadness and anger and denial, and she shakes her head. Death holds no threat anymore, an open door to whatever comes next, but her friends see that door as closed, locked by fear. They haven't come close enough to it yet. "I'm just asking you to lie a little, for a few days."

JO BARNEY

"Why?"

"Why you? Or why?" She has the answers to both questions.

"I can understand asking friends to lie when it's important. But why?" Joan leans toward Madge as if the answer might slip by without her catching it.

Madge hesitates, picks up the file, finds her words, words she wrote on a good day and is glad she saved for this moment. "I want my sons to mourn me because they have lost a mother, not because she killed herself, and they weren't there to help. I want Roger to mourn because he has lost a partner and not because he allowed me to try one more time to be on my own and should have known what I would do."

The cold ghost of Jerry passes through her, forces her to pause, take a breath, gather herself. "And, money plays a part in this decision," she continues, turning a page. The difficult next words were loosed. "Roger is the beneficiary of my insurance policy, a large sum, the premiums covered by my publisher. I can never repay him for the years he has devoted himself to me, my writing. I can give him a comfortable life after I've gone. But he cannot be involved in any way in my death. I have convinced him to take this time to visit his ailing mother in Nebraska for a few days. Since the policy has a suicide clause, it also can't look as if I've done myself in. That is where you come in."

The sheet of paper in front of her had reflected that day's afternoon sun, the pen had moved across it snail-like, left the tracks leading to this moment. Madge smiles. Yes, a good day.

"Shit."

"Jackie, stop it." Lou lifts her head, wipes away a lock of white hair falling across her wet eyes. "I'm so sorry you're sick, Madge. I can't imagine you dying, now or later. I can't imagine..." She swallows, lies back against the chair, her voice a shudder, "helping you die."

"Perhaps not. If you can't, I'll find some other way to leave." Madge folds the papers, needs to add one lingering thought. "I will not allow myself to descend into a mewling caricature of myself being spoon-fed by an overworked stranger and visited by people who tell me they are my sons. I will not."

Suddenly, she is very tired. She's done all she can, has come to the end of the lines of words on the script in her lap. With her friends' help, tomorrow morning she will go through a door, walking stick in hand, mussel bag tied to her waist, and head towards whatever is next. She can't think of what she will do if they say no. She stretches her legs, closes her eyes. She hears the others get up, the shushing of parkas being slipped on.

"We're going for a walk. We'll be back." Joan touches Madge's cheek as she passes behind her. Her hand said yes.

After the door clicks shut, Madge gets up and reaches for the walking stick lying on the mantel. This tough branch of oak has guided her through many miles, along magnificent trails. She and it have one more mile to go, the last mile. She rubs her fingers over its leather grip, tells it, "Only a few more hours, friend."

33

Friday Evening: Whirlpool
Jackie

The three women leave Madge and walk for a mile or so without speaking. The tide is coming in and at first, they concentrate on finding footing on smooth rocks being lapped by wavelets. Then Lou stops and looks out into the gray, unfolding ocean and says, "I'm in."

Jackie can't believe it. "What?"

And Lou repeats herself, not looking at them, calling into the muffled roar. "Dammit! I'm in. I owe it to her." Then she covers her eyes with her hands and sways, her knees sinking.

Joan steps to her side. "Good." The two of them wrap nylon-clad arms around each other and bury their faces in each other's collars.

Jackie doesn't get it. Why in? What did they owe Madge? They were friends, of course, but friends don't kill each other, did they? They might stand by a friend in trouble, sympathize, rub a little almond oil on the sore spots, so to speak, but...It was the almond oil thought that made her hesitate for a moment. Then she knew. "I can't help someone to die," she says as she pushes through the cobweb of doubt that for a moment had clouded her resolve. "It isn't right, you know. Not right." Her argument has nothing to do with Xavier's religious view of suicide. It is about the way life just is. Life begins and it ends without our control. That is the way it has always been. "What if Madge was your sister or mother? Would you be able to do it, whatever the 'it' is?"

Joan and Lou loosen their holds on each other and turn towards Jackie, their cheeks red with cold and tears. Lou's lips barely move as she whispers, "I have no sister. My mother died as she wished, in the arms of her God. Madge is a friend asking for help. I want to help her."

"My God, isn't there another way to help? Like making her see that being surrounded by people who love her is the best way to go? For everyone? Or couldn't she do Death with Dignity or something, like I've read about? Xavier calls it playing God, but Madge doesn't have any religious reason for not asking her doctor to help, does she?"

JO BARNEY

Joan shakes her head, looks away. "Doesn't work that way. You need a deadline, a diagnosis of imminent death to schedule your death like that. Madge could live for years."

Jackie blinks against the sudden sting in her eyes, and she understands she is not talking only about Madge. She was also talking about a stolen man with no deadline, an empty room, a ragged wound where she had once felt his love as she had changed his diapers, as he said thank you, Mother. She walks away from the two women, against the wind, her shoes sinking into the wet sand, filling with icy ocean. No, everyone has deadlines, she thinks. We just don't know when they are. What if everybody messed with the plan, played God like Xavier said, changed the plan, then what?

When Jackie gets back to the beach house an hour later, the others are talking softly, and they stop as she pours herself a glass of wine and sits down in a chair by the fireplace. The only sound in the house is the dim rumble of the ocean outside. She gives the pile of cooling coals at her feet a prod with the toe of her shoe as she says, "I think I should leave." She wonders if they can hear her voice, the words caught like small sharp rocks in her throat. She brings the wine glass to her mouth, swallows against the pile up. "I can't help you, Madge."

When she manages to raise her eyes, she sees that Madge is smiling. "It's okay. You've already had your share of death and dying." She puts down her book and hands Jackie a folder from several stacked on the table in front of her. "Do take this with you. It's a gift, my story about you."

Jackie looks at Joan and Lou at that moment, and a surge of anger stops her breath. Hasn't it always been this way? Purposefully left out of conversations between the two of them? Like she somehow won't get the picture, anyway, whatever that picture was? Like she doesn't matter. Even in the solarium. She had provided laughs, but when things got serious, they whispered, left her abandoned in the smoky drifts of their cigarettes.

Always. She remembers the way their eyes had widened when she first confessed to her crush on Xavier, and she knows they had talked and laughed about it after she'd gone to bed or gotten wine-stricken and fallen asleep on the couch. And when she married Fred. Same looks, same poor Jackie, there-she-goes-again smirks exchanged like she is blind or unconscious or stupid.

And now even Madge, who's always listened as if she is intrigued with Jackie's life. "I wish I had the guts to jump out a window and run away for a while," she'd said forty-whatever years ago as she put ice on Jackie's cast and brought her coffee. "So what did you do?" she asked, pulling her feet up on the cot, eager to hear the details of Jackie's escapade. Now, even from her, a dismissing *You've had your share of death and dying.* Like everybody has a portion of grief ladled out by some equal-opportunity hand of fate and that Jackie'd used hers all up with Fred and Xavier, and she won't be getting any more, in fact, can leave right now since she is running on empty. Can't one of them even say she wishes Jackie will change her mind?

She tosses Madge's folder back onto the table and goes into the bedroom to pack. When loop of wool from her gray sweater catches on her wedding ring, she stops throwing her clothes into her bag and tries to untangle it before the snag tears a hole. She twists the ring, uses a thumb to ease its hold on the yarn. The thread has slipped under a prong, won't move, and she is tempted to bite it in two, hurry the damage, get on with packing. She tugs once more, realizes she cannot see what she is doing because her eyes are filled with tears. She stills her fingers, sits down, the sweater piled in her lap, and considered her situation.

Fred used to pull at her like this, not meaning to, not understanding the damage his needs could cause, the connection between them created by the hand of fate or a goddess, maybe, and she, while trying to protect herself from his tugs on her being, could not let go of him. Then his son Ron cut them loose of each other, and now both she and Fred were less than whole.

She takes off the ring, lets it rest against the soft web of wool, sets the sweater aside and lies back, tries to think what the new Jackie she'd discovered at the retreat would do to untangle the threads.

No, she is not the same person she once was, even if her friends cannot see it yet. She has let go of the fantasizer, and the risk taker in her has been temporarily quelled also. She stirs, asks herself, *What if Madge were Fred?* What if he had asked her, in a moment of clarity, to help him die, had looked at her with sad eyes, had called her Mother one more time, what then? She knew what she would have done, risky as it was, scared as she felt.

They look up in surprise when she comes through the doorway without her suitcase. She leans over the arm of Madge's chair, kisses the top of her friend's head, smells strawberries. "If Fred could have asked, I would have said yes. So how can I say no to someone who has never judged me no matter what kind of trouble I'm in, who trusts me now to help her." Jackie covers Madge's quiet hand with her own gnarly one, small still bones pressing against her palm, the secret handshake. "So tell me what we're going to do."

34

Friday Evening: The Chart
Madge

Late into the night, the wine flows and the fire burns steadily as Madge holds her notes and explains her plan to them.

"The low tide is the key," she says. "I wrote a description of this part of the coast a few years ago for magazine article. I'll read part of it so you'll understand.

'The beach meanders for three or more miles to the south, ending finally in a small harbor dedicated to crab and oyster seekers and a rustic hut of an inn for those who prefer their crustaceans on a plate. To the north, a triangular jut of rock interrupts the ocean's rhythm and creates slanted anxious waves that peel away shards of granite from its cliffs. The stone falls with thuds that sometimes awaken people in the nearby beach houses.'"

Madge looks up at them, offers them a promise. "You've never been here when it's possible to see what's on the other side of the head. You will be overwhelmed with the beauty you'll find."

She returns to her manuscript, describing the cove as if she were waiting at its entrance. "'Beyond the head lies a pristine curve of sand, guarded by five huge monoliths rising from the ocean, approachable only at the lowest of tides. When the tide table forecasts a minus 2.5 tide, the locals carry burlap bags and baskets and slip past the pointed rocky head to raise iron crowbars and screwdrivers against the beards of the wild mussels massed below the water line.

"'When low tide of this measure comes in the early morning, however, even the most avid devotees of mussels stay in bed, for access to the cove will last only one dark hour before the watery gates flow shut again.'"

Madge lays the papers on the end table. "That article never did get published. Ironic, isn't it, that you three will be its only audience? I knew I wrote it for a reason." She picks up the tide table on her lap, one line highlighted. "I will go for a walk," she says, no need for a written page to guide her words now, "because I can't sleep. I will wander past the entrance to the hidden cove, be welcomed by the spires and monoliths looming in the pale sky. I'll not return."

"We wait, look, call for help. When?" Joan asked.

"Tomorrow morning. You'll guess that perhaps a sneaker wave got me as I walked the waterline. You'll find my walking stick."

"That's too soon, Madge. We have to get used to the idea." Lou moans, does not continue.

Madge must be firm now, despite the pain she hears in Lou's voice. She shakes her head. "I can't wait. The next - 2.5 tide is a month away. A month is a long time for me."

"It may be days before you are found. Are you sure?"

Madge gives her friend a long look. "You'll be here to find me." Then she smiles. "Are you sure? That is the same question I asked you a few years ago, Lou. 'Are you sure you want to begin your life all over?' When you said yes, do you remember what I said?"

Lou meets Madge's gaze. "I'll never forget it. You said, 'Well, then, you must do it.'" Lou's voice quavers with her next words. "But the question then was about a beginning, not an ending. I felt strong, free, as I chose to live a new life."

One more time, each time the words are easier to say. "And I feel the same, making this choice to die."

"Then you must do it."

Jackie stands up. "The pact has been made, no turning back, right? Like jumping out a window. You can't turn back after you've let go of the ledge. At least that's what I've been telling myself for the past hour or so. A little wine will help, won't it?" She fills their glasses, spilling a little and not bothering to wipe it up.

"To us," they toast and they sip without saying more until Jackie's "Hah!" makes them look at her. "Remember the time the pervert was jerking off in front of our basement window during chapter meeting, and Madge screamed and everyone told her to be quiet so they could watch?"

Lou chokes on an almost-laugh. "It was my first and only penis for five years, a precious moment."

"Then there was the time Joan came in from a date and her cashmere was on backwards."

"I said that's how we wore them in San Mateo."

"'And inside out?' someone asked you. 'Of course,' you answered." Jackie is on a roll now, small chuckles encouraging her. "And you took it off, stepped into its arms and pulled it up and cinched it around your waist with your wide belt." Jackie stands up, pretends to hitch up a sweater, buckle a belt. "'Upside-down, too,' you said. 'The neck is for easy access to one's netherparts.'" She demonstrates. "You were so cool, Joan."

Jackie collapses onto her chair, reaches for her wine. "And Madge, what did you do with all the notes you took during Joan's evening classes in how to fuck?"

"Our girl jester," Madge hears Lou whisper to Joan.

Madge squints her eyes in thought. "I can truly say I don't remember." Then they laugh again.

Madge had hoped for this laughter, this resurrection of memories on this night. It seems strangely right that they will spend their last hours together meandering through the years, as if they have limitless time to poke into crevices, discover almost forgotten moments, share them like glowing agates held in palms. Ex-husbands are exhumed, wild and ungrateful children shaken again in exasperation, the solarium air swirling in the smoke of old memories.

Then they are quiet. They can no longer avoid the approach of dawn. Lou blows out the candles, and one by one they take Madge in their arms, hold her, leave her shoulders damp with their tears.

"I'll always love you."

"You are magnificent, the bravest person I'll ever know."

"I am honored to be your friend."

And Madge kisses each of them. "Thank you." She can think of nothing more she needs to say.

Minutes later, as she and Joan rustle against their pillows, she hears a quiet intake of breath, a murmur, "Oh, God, Madge, what will I do without you?" Madge touches a wet cheek, answers, "You'll do fine, dear friend. As always. Let's talk a little more. Perhaps you'll sleep."

35

Sunday Evening: Storm Surge
Lou

A knock. Lou reaches the door first. A tall figure, a man, stands on the porch. He steps forward. "Hello, Lou," he says, his quiet voice husky, tired.

Joan stands behind her, says, "Come in, Roger. We've been expecting you." Lou holds the door as he comes in, takes off his stocking cap, holds it a moment as he glances around, then tucks it into his pocket. A graying ponytail curls down the back of his wool jacket. He blinks as if he has just crawled out of a dark hole.

When Joan suggests that metaphor, he shakes his head. "Just Nebraska." Then his mouth softens, and he asks, looking at each of them. "How are you doing?"

"Shit," Jackie says. "He does know."

Lou reaches up to take his jacket. He holds up a hand, steps back. "I'm not sure I'm staying. I shouldn't be here. Madge made that clear."

"She told you?"

"No. She hid her last notes from me. She couldn't find them when she was packing to come here, and she had to ask me to help her. I found them, read what she was going to ask of you." Roger, still in his jacket, has moved towards the sofa. Lou can see, in the light of the fire, the deep lines, the gray shadows of fatigue on his face.

"You have to sit down, rest," she says, and this time he lets her take his coat, and he sinks into the cushions. She has seen a face like that a long time ago, the face of her father as he touched the fingers of his dead wife, and tears no longer offered solace. Jackie brings in a glass of wine for him, Joan offers her chenille throw, Lou takes his hand for moment, then gives it back to him, and they wait for him to speak.

"My car is outside. It shouldn't be here until tomorrow."

"Of course." Lou reaches for his jacket, riffles pockets, finds the keys. "I'll do it," she says to Jackie who is about to follow her. "I'll park it in someone's driveway, someone not here this week. We need to stay in the cabin as much as we can. Lucius may be out looking around, could drop by."

Lou glances at Joan who is standing by the window, watching something moving below her.

"Lucius, in fact, is coming this way, going house to house as we advised him to, flashlight in hand." Joan gives Lou an

uncertain glance. "Are you sure?" Lou doesn't answer as she
ties her robe closed, looks for her slippers. "Just be careful.
Park it in a driveway or something. I'll take care of Roger
and Lucius, when he gets here."

Joan takes Roger by the arm, is standing him up, leading
him out of the room. Roger follows her without a sound. She
calls out as she closes the bedroom door, "Jackie, look like
you're sloshed."

Outside, Lou starts the car and slides it out of the driveway. Lucius will be suspicious of a rental car parked in front
of a vacant house. She knows just the place, moves up the
dark road in the opposite direction of Lucius and his flashlight. She tries not to let the idea of two hundred feet of
sheer drop on her left take over as she turns into a sharp
right and continues up towards the woods at the top of the
hill. The other thing to remember is the ditch along the
road. Right side or left? Doesn't matter. She just needs to
find the driveway of the old house at the edge of the stand
of cedars that line the ridge.

It is grassy, hardly a driveway at all, just an old track
left when the house was abandoned by the family who had
lived there until part of the roof blew off. Madge had led
them on a walk up there the last time they were here, and
they had picked huckleberries and turned their tongues blue
as they sat on the old porch. Should be right about here, she
thinks, slowing, almost stopping. Then she does stop. Nothing is familiar. The heavy green trees have disappeared. The
moon is rising over scrub brush and stumps, and over a huge
structure, a house perhaps.

She edges forward, squints at what she realizes is a garage door set into a two-story wall of windows. The white stickers on the glass panes reflect the faint flare of light the moon is offering, a house so new no one has moved in yet. Lou gets out of the car. An unfinished house might not have an automatic opener on its garage door. She yanks on the handle and with a whiny groan, the door goes up. Inside, piles of lumber and debris line the walls and floor. She goes back to the car, turns into the driveway, and edges slowly into the garage. The stuff she is driving over crunches and bangs, and finally she can't go any further. She gets out, pulls down on the half-opened door, and it closes, all but about a foot.

Mission accomplished, Lou thinks, scuttling down the road, trying to keep her slippers from sliding off. If she meets with Lucius she can say she needed to get some exercise or something. She'll have to put off feeling bad about the desecrated trees for another day.

36

Sunday Evening: Flood Tide
Jackie

Jackie isn't pretending to be sloshed. She is. The evening of
revelations, the stress of telling her own true story, the
shock of Roger walking in, and of course, the glasses of wine
that accompanied all this activity have affected both her
vision and her ability to walk across the room, which she is
working on at the moment. Someone is knocking. All she
knows is that Lou and Joan have rushed out somewhere,
leaving her to act as if she's drunk, for some reason. Not a
difficult assignment, she thinks, as she runs her hand along
the wall for guidance and heads for the door. "Hang on, I'm
coming," she calls reaching for the knob.

Lucius stands there, his baseball cap in hand. "Sorry it's so late. I saw that the lights were on and decided to stop by." He waits to be invited in, and Jackie can't think of a reason not to.

"I was, ah, taking a nap, Sheriff. But come in and I'll try to get myself together." She pats her hair and pulls her robe around her. "I'm not sure where the others are. I mean, they are somewhere here." When Lucius steps in, she closes the door and leans on it for a moment. Where are they? She flings an arm in the direction of the couch and says she'll be right back.

In the bedroom, Joan is applying lipstick and is frowning at her in the mirror. "I said act like, not be, Jackie." Joan turns. "You are needed here. When Lou gets back, you are to— Are you listening? You are to say that the tension of the day has caused you to drink a little too much and you are going to be sick. Leave the room. Make sick sounds and then call out good night. But don't go to bed. Go out on the deck and sit in the farthest chair from the window. Stay there."

"I can do that. Being sick. But why?"

"Because Roger is in your bed, pretending to be you. It's the only place I could think of—in case Lucius wants to look around, for evidence or something." Jackie is relieved that Joan leads her into the living room and sets her in a chair.

"Jackie said you were here, Lucius." She yawns. "We're thinking we should get some sleep, if we can. Tomorrow will be a stressful day—both of Madge's sons are coming in. Roger, too, if the message got through to him. His mother was a little vague on the phone. Anyway, do you have some news? Is that why you're here?"

Lucius looks around. "Is Lou still up?" He looks at Jackie, who looks at Joan, who smiles at him.

"She's out for a little air." Then she sits beside the sheriff, and Jackie knows exactly what Joan is going to do. She'll lick her lips and put her hand on his body, arm probably, maybe knee. Then she'll look into his confused eyes and tell him he is the most virile man she's come across lately. Well, no, she won't do that, but he'll feel like that is what she's saying. He won't have any strength to doubt whatever she is about to say. She's so good at this.

Jackie has always envied this talent, and at first she felt a surge of smugness at the news of California girl's latest marriage fiasco. Even perfect teeth didn't always guarantee success, but there is something special about her mouth. Jackie runs her tongue over her lips, tastes sour wine, and then a bubble churns its way up into her throat. She will have to leave the room soon, for real. She looks at Lucius, who is smiling at Joan, who is saying, "We're so appreciative of your taking this so seriously, Lucius. So what is happening?"

Lucius seems about to tell her when Lou, white hair in a frightening flurry, bursts through the front door, her robe open and flapping over her cat pajamas. When she sees Lucius, she stops, says, "Oh," and wads a dangling belt into a knot at her waist. Jackie, from her fuzzy viewpoint, thinks Lou looks as if she's just escaped from an asylum, but Lou pulls herself together and says, "It's a perfect night for a little run, and I really needed the air." She shuffles a bit as she comes into the living room. "It's been a long day, this waiting, you know." She sits down and looks at Lucius, who is staring at her running slippers.

Lou coughs with a half-giggle. "We're all a little crazy, you know."

That is Jackie's cue, and just in time. "I'm sorry. I have to—I'm going to be sick. All this tension..." She stands up and goes to the bathroom door. "Please go ahead without me."

37

Sunday Evening: Backshore
Lucius

Lucius definitely smells a rat. Running in the middle of the night, in her slippers? One of them drunk, throwing up at this moment in the bathroom, the other one in fresh lipstick despite her bathrobe, putting the make on him? They are trying to distract him. Either that or they are all crazy, like Lou said. Maybe both. He plows ahead.

"We've knocked on most of the doors, and only a few people responded. None of them have seen Madge Slocum, although a couple of them know of her, her writing. And no single men here that we could determine. So if she went with someone, she really went somewhere."

Both women frown, and Lou, still panting, says that wasn't like Madge. She might create a little storm, but she wouldn't abandon ship.

Lucius glances at the dividing wall next to the kitchen and sees that the tide table is no longer lying on it. Liz has gotten one for him, but he needs to know which line had been highlighted to test a theory he's been mulling over, especially with these women acting so weird, guilty actually, not that he suspects they are murderers, or anything, but stranger things have happened. "I'm thinking that the only area we haven't looked yet is in the cove on the other side of the point. I've never seen it, but my assistant tells me that you can't get around except when the tide is very low. Do you know about that?"

Joan shrugs. "I haven't been there either. We never visited at the right time, I guess. Lou, where is that tide table we had around here?"

"Junk drawer, I think." Lou goes into the kitchen after sending a look at Joan that Lucius catches also. After some rattling and slamming, Lou returns with a small gray book in her hand. "This is it, I think." She hands it to Lucius, who finds the June page and the highlighted line: -2.5. Yesterday morning, the morning Madge Slocum disappeared.

"What?" Joan has moved in next to him again.

"She could've walked north instead of south, gone to this cove."

"Why would she do that? And why didn't she invite us, if it's such a special place?" Lou leans over them, squinting at the orange line.

"What time?" Joan is warming his thigh with hers.

"5:21 a.m., it says here. Or," he hesitates in order to give himself time to pull back, to get Joan in focus, "I hate to think it, but somebody could have gone with her to the cove."

For a second, Joan's blue eyes flicker with surprise. "You mean you think someone has hurt her, maybe left her there?" She gathers her lips, thinking about something, Lucius sees, not quite about the horror of the speculation, more like should she go along with it. He recognizes that look. Calculating. Second wife, again.

"I can't bear to think of anything like that." Lou straightens, skinny hand to forehead. "No one would ever hurt Madge, would they, Joan?"

Joan shakes her head. She's decided. "No, of course not. But the cove is the only place we haven't looked. How low does the tide have to be to get around the point?"

"Liz would know." Lucius' finger follows the line of numbers down the page. "No other -2.5 all month; only this -2.0 tomorrow morning." He reaches into his pocket and pulls out a cell phone. "She should be back home by now. I'll ask her." When it doesn't connect, he goes to the phone on the kitchen wall.

Liz, her voice muffled as if she is still under the covers where her father has probably awakened her, tells him that a -2.0 is iffy, would probably involve getting wet, and they'd have less than an hour in which they could get around and then back. The waves come at diagonals from both sides and are dangerous to fool around with, she adds. "I can remember one time when me and a bunch of kids…" Lucius interrupts with a thank-you and hangs up. He repeats this information to the women.

They don't need to discuss it. "We're going around the point in the morning," Joan says. Lou adds, "The three of us."

Lucius understands that they'll go whether he's with them or not. The tide book is the only lead he has, and it points to the cove. "Okay, but only if I can find a couple of other guys to help. We'll use a rope or something to keep us together in the surf." He's on the phone again when the door to the deck rolls open, and Jackie steps in, her face white with cold and maybe with wine.

"Sorry, Joan, I had to come in. I was freezing my butt off, and I think I'm going to throw up again." She swoops across the room, her blanket catching on corners of chairs. "Excuse me," she says when she steps on Lucius' shoes. "I'm no good at this."

"None of us are," Joan tells her as she captures the shivering shroud and heads her toward a bedroom. "Here's your bed, all warm and waiting for you." Lucius hears the bedsprings creak, and then Joan comes back, her fingers at her throat. "We are cracking up," she says. "What in the hell was she doing on the deck?"

"Looking for Madge, in her Jackie way," Lou answers. "And we'll all be ready at 5:00 a.m. to continue the search, Sheriff."

Once again, Lucius knows he's being dismissed. The women walk him to the door, and as he makes his way down the road to his car, he notices that he has the tide table in his hand. If it is a clue to this mystery, the possible perpetrators have handed it over without a twitch of hesitation.

38

Early Monday Morning: Sneaker Wave
Joan

As the door closes, Joan smiles at Lou. "Worthy of Mamet, with a little bit of Coward mixed in. A comedy of errors, or is it manners? I never get those terms straight. We make quite a team." She's not surprised any more, Lou pulling through like that, her tears dried up, at least for a while.

"Jackie helped too. But we need to sober her up. And find a place for Roger until tomorrow afternoon. And move the car back." Lou begins to unknot the belt of her robe. "Methinks this little drama isn't over yet."

"Any coffee?" Roger, leaning against the doorframe, looks even worse than ever, hanks of long graying hair escaping the rubber band and snaking across his lined cheeks. Joan starts the pot as he takes off his jacket again and follows her into the kitchen. So far, Roger's arriving a day early is the only hitch. Joan's annoyed. If he knew about the plan, why is he here to upset it? "Tomorrow's going to be tough. Did you hear us talking?"

"I want to go around the point with you."

Lou is tucking her pajama top into a pair of old lady jean, and Joan hears her murmur, "Shit," a good word, Joan realizes for a lot of situations, even when Jackie isn't around. "I can't think how, Roger. Madge was very clear. You are to be left out of this."

Roger takes the cup of coffee and stands in front of the cold fireplace. "I should never have allowed her to come here, involve you."

Joan kneels at Roger's feet, wads up some newspaper for the fire, piles kindling on it, strikes a match, watches as the flames take hold. "So why did you?" She knows the answer.

"For the same reason you three have agreed to go along with her plan. I owe it to her. She saved my life."

He has his own story to tell, apparently. Did Madge plan this, too? This unwritten tale? Joan places two small split logs on the fire and stands up. "Let's talk." Lou is already curled on the couch, waiting.

Roger takes Joan's usual spot on the pillow on the floor and for a moment, his hair falls loose as he pulls off the band and combs it with his fingers. He looks like Gabriel the Archangel, the glow from the fire behind him a golden halo. Good looking in a gritty sort of way, Joan decides, as if angels sometimes need baths.

His hair recaptured, Roger sips on his coffee. "I was a heroin addict when I met her. She gave me a reason to stop using. She went through a month of hell with me, brought me food, listened when I raved, locked the bedroom door and stood with her back to it when I tried to break it down. I walked out a shaky but new person, and she asked me to live with her, help her manage the details in her life so that she could write. She also asked me to be her lover. I agreed to everything. But she didn't ask me to help her die."

"You know why, of course. So why did you come here now, instead of tomorrow or maybe never?" Lou's voice is a tense, a non-Lou growl. *Fucking up the plan*, Joan imagines her thinking. Jackie would have said it out loud.

Roger puts his coffee down, the cup rattling under the tremor of his fingers. "I have to be there when she is found. I have to finish this, say goodbye." His words escape between small heaving sobs.

Now what? Lou signals with her eyebrows and Joan shakes her head. The flames have become waning yellow darts, and Roger is no longer an angel. "Forget the car for now. We need to get some sleep. Maybe it will come to us, what to do." Joan is so exhausted she cannot force herself to think about the final step in the plan, the wading into freezing ocean swells, approaching the great stones, the looking for Madge among them. She only wants to close her eyes for a bit. She lays her head back against the chair. Then, except for the shower running in the bathroom, the house is silent.

The fire is completely out when she awakes, the dark sky outside the window paling into gray. Sometime while she was asleep, she has realized that Roger is a stranger to the sheriff; that, in fact, Roger looks like a stranger to anyone who sees him the first time, the long hair, the knit cap, the old wool coat.

She pulls herself out of the chair, finds him in her bed, eyes open, unfocused. "I can smell her," he murmurs.

"Strawberry. I know." She touches his shoulder. "Roger. Listen. Did anyone see you when you brought Madge here to help her set things up, the notes and stuff?"

Roger turns toward her, thinks. "She had me drive her car. It was dark when we got here, and she asked me to leave early in the morning, in case one of you arrived unexpectedly. She said she didn't want to worry you by having me around. I went along with it. I pretended I didn't know what she was going to do." He blinks, about to fall apart again.

"Does anyone else around here know you, some other time you came with Madge to this place?"

"We came here so that Madge could write. We only met one or two of the summer people. August folks. No, no one knows me." He pulls up the quilt, rolls toward the wall.

Joan yanks the quilt back, takes his startled face in her hands. "Good. Get some clothes on. We haven't much time." Then she says the same thing to Jackie and Lou in the next room, neither of them asleep. "What did I miss?" Jackie asks, feeling for her robe.

When the three women approach the beach though the dunes two hours later, the sky is white, and the sand stretches out in a smooth wet mat almost to the edge of the point. Lucius stands below them, as do two men carrying loops of ropes on their arms. Larry and Steve, volunteer firemen, Lucius explains. They demonstrate how the rope will work, how each of them will grasp it with one hand, balance with the other, a line that reminds Joan of pre-schoolers walking in tandem. She whispers that Lou should stay behind Jackie, to make sure she's hanging on, her hands, you know. Joan will stick close to Lucius.

Neither of them says anything about the mussel-gatherer in the yellow slicker and rain hat in front of them, an empty bag flung over his shoulder. If Lucius notices, Joan will say that they've seen him crossing the dunes in years past, from the deck of the beach house. He's a regular; probably taking more than the limit of mussels every time he ventures into the cove and selling them at the fish store in town. Madge figures that he's so desperate-looking people let him get away with it, like transients and Dumpster divers in the city.

39

Early Monday Morning: Spring Tide
Lou

Lou wraps a hand around a knot and pulls to test her grip. Jackie does the same, and Lou can see that her fingers manage to curl around the rope. As they move forward, the cliffs in front of them appear to be growing out of the receding surf. Lou wonders if anyone else has noticed the hazy figure stepping into the rockbound ocean edge. At that moment, the waves splash against his body and he uses a walking stick to keep himself upright. She glances back at Larry sloshing behind her. When she looks up again, the man is gone, and Lucius is pointing at the black rock behind which the man has disappeared, and Joan is talking and gesturing, the noise of the waves drowning out her words.

Lucius stops and calls back over his shoulder, "Are you guys sure?" Lou is sure. *Then you must do it*, Madge whispers somewhere close. Ahead, Jackie flexes her gripping fingers. Even in the dawn's light, her knobby knuckles show themselves below her cuffs. "It's okay," Jackie says. The crisp air seems to revive her and she grins. "This reminds me of the time I climbed Mt. Hood, only it's water instead of snow, and flat instead of up, and I was young instead of old. Let's go."

"Shit," she says steps later, shaking a foot as icy water flows into her Nikes.

Behind Lou, Larry laughs.

Five minutes later, Lou leans into the face of the rock wall, the balancing hand reaching for holds, the other attached to the bobbing rope, her feet senseless. She slides into a hole slippery with anemones and bangs a shin into a sharp mound covered with seaweed. Her hand stings as she grabs at clusters of tiny barnacles. She goes down on one knee and sees her pants leg darken with blood.

"Almost around," Lucius yells. Then a wall of water, a sleeper wave they'll call it later, plows into Jackie and lays her flat against the pile of riprap at the base of the head. Lou goes down next to her, swallows salty brine as Larry pulls her, then Jackie, to their feet. Jackie has lost her wool cap, seems to be looking for it, is tugged over the last hump of rock before she can find it. She pulls the dripping hat over her hair as all six of them step onto soft wet sand.

Lou coughs, seawater filling her mouth, and takes Jackie's arm to steady herself as she spits. Her feet have sunk to the ankles in quicksand. Joan stands next to her, about to say something, when Lucius swears. Everyone turns to see what he's seeing. Tangled in morning fog, huge dark rocks pierce through the mist. Birds guard their peaks, calling out warnings; the ocean, mysterious, smooth as glass, has slunk away leaving behind a glistening landscape. Just as Madge had described.

"I'll be damned. We're on Venus." Lucius still hasn't moved.

Maybe, Lou thinks, if Venus is dark gray, its sky, starless, deep blue, if its arched windows lead to an endless sea, if its inhabitants, feathered, anxious, speaking in shrieks, flit about, panic-stricken, as they poke in to the sand, or soar above the water looking, looking, never resting. Always in a hurry, seeking. The six intruders on their planet are not in a hurry. Lou feels the rope drag from her fingers, as it drops to the sand when Jackie and Joan let go of it. She can't lift her eyes from the rocks lined up like mourners at the edge of the still, low tide. Somewhere...does she sees movement? Her heart quickens. Maybe...?

"That guy's found something. Let's go." Lucius has stopped winding up the rope, is pointing to a small black outcropping fifty yards down the beach.

A man in a yellow slicker, Roger of course, stands at the base of the rock and beckons to them. They are close enough for Lou to see the mussels armoring the rock, protecting a secret. Lou begins to run, the others following, stumbling, wildly pushing their bodies towards it, shrieking with the birds.

Then they drop to their knees, their tears an ocean of grief. Lou reaches out to Madge, wedged under an overhang, her beautiful face the wrong color, her eyes clouded with salt water, her smile a trail of wet sand flowing from her mouth. She wears a necklace and bracelet of green seaweed. The cuffs of her pants are caught round her knees, her stiff legs and arched feet make her seem as if she's about to leap up and out of this hellhole. One hand clutches the bag strapped on her chest, her gift to them.

"She came back here for mussels," Lou moans. "For us." She's remembered her lines. Madge has reminded her.

Lucius tells them to not touch her yet. Larry pulls a camera from his parka pocket, takes pictures, the flash offering details they have missed, the abraded forehead, torn nails, the tire iron piercing a shoulder of the rain jacket, its blunt end lodged against the ledge of rock above, pinning her body like a butterfly to the sand.

"Okay," he says.

The women pull at the iron pressing into the rock, holding her down, and when it is loosened, they crawl under the ledge so that they can close her eyes, brush the sand from her face. Their fingers close her eyes, brush away grit from her lips. Lou unlatches the backpack and the mussels fall out onto the sand at her knees. She can't bear to look at them as she begins to gather them up, pile them into the front of her parka. Joan takes Madge's hand, rubs warmth into stiff fingers, Jackie closes the hole in the shoulder of the jacket and pulls the collar up to protect a cold neck, and Lou stands, mussels dripping through her jacket, and remembers Madge's last warning.

"Lucius, we need to get her back," she forces her frozen lips to call. "The tide..." The water has come alive, the birds are skittering frantically away from the new waves, the roar of tide and gulls is rising.

Lucius motions to the men; the young one, Steve, bends and picks her up. "Over my shoulder," he says. The two men lift Madge and drape her across his back, and Lou sees him shudder as water drains down his spine. She tries to speak, but she cannot.

She can only follow the others, step in their steps, wrap her fingers around the one cold mussel shell she has managed to slip into her pocket.

"Almost there," Jackie yells. Lou sees Lucius reach for Steve's belt as he stumbles and yank the young man up. Madge is shifting on Steve's shoulder, her dark hair swirling against and catching against his wet Levis. The fireman groans as he sets her down on the sand.

Lou and Jackie wait, not wanting to leave Madge, as Joan asks, "What now?" California Girl has folded her trembling arms inside her jacket, and her empty wet sleeves move on their own accord in the sea breeze.

Lucius removes his cell phone from its plastic bag and holds it to his ear. "Damn." He looks at Steve. "Can you carry her to the car? We'll take her to town, to the hospital. We need a death certificate," he explains, apparently lip-reading the question on Joan's quivering lips.

Joan shuffles to Lou and Jackie. "We have almost done it," she whispers, and she points toward the cabin, and they glance one more time at Madge and then they turn toward the dunes.

Joan looks at Lucius, manages to make the words emerge. "We expect Madge's sons sometime today, and Roger. Please let us know where she is and what to do next. The family will make any decisions." A massive tremor rattles her last words. "You're as cold as I, I'm sure, Lucius. Get going before you get pneumonia." Her lips twitch into a frozen facsimile of her terrific smile, and she adds, "Thank you. You've been wonderful."

Lou, looking back at that moment, knows that if her arms hadn't been inside her jacket, wrapped around her ribs, Joan would have reached out and touched him.

40

Monday Morning: Shoal
Lou

By the time Lou and Jackie drag in, Roger has showered and is wrapped in the terry cloth robe that hung from the hook in the bathroom. His eyes are red-rimmed, but his gray ponytail is orderly, his face pale but clean. "Go ahead, Jackie," Lou calls as she pulls off her wet shoes and jacket. "See what you can do with your hair, and the rest of you. I have to retrieve the car." When Roger stirs to protest, she adds, "I have to do it. Only an old white-haired lady can get away with this if I get caught."

The front door blows open as Lou reaches for the knob. Joan, blond hair in dripping wads, her arms struggling to get out from under the grasp of her jacket, hisses a "Stop!"

when she sees Lou. "Don't go anywhere." A hand escapes and grabs Lou's elbow. "We have to get the car back."

Lou notes the wave of pleasure she feels at the sight of California Girl's hair sticking out like a molting Medusa, blue eyes wider than ever. Deranged, maybe, or at least one cog off. Vulnerable. California girl looks better than ever. Lou finds the zipper's pull, tugs, and opens Joan's jacket, and when she steps away from it, Lou wraps her arms around the shivering body and says, "It's okay, Joan. I'm taking care of it."

Joan doesn't move for a moment, maybe taking in the warmth of the hug, then she jerks away. A little manic. Lou thinks.

"Listen, this is important. We need it back to explain Roger. I'll do it. I just have to get out of these wet clothes."

Joan's fingers twitch as she works at the buttons on her jeans. After a moment, she pauses, wipes a wrist across a wet cheek, says, "Shit, I give." She leans on the kitchen divide, says, "You do it."

Joan has handed the problem over to her. The cold and a row of Levi buttons, and maybe the scene at the foot of the huge rocks, maybe the whole weekend, have allowed this woman to finally trust her. Another first.

The dry wool mountain socks wick away the cold in her feet as Lou hurries up the road to the house. Her nose isn't doing as well, but in ten minutes, she'll be in the shower, nose thawing. She rounds the last curve, sees the roof of the house against the bare sky. The clear cut is even more ghastly in the daylight. One tree has been left on the hillside, the one she supposes they tied the machinery to, to keep it from rolling down into the valley below. A witness tree observing the devastation greed can cause. The thought catches her in midstep, and she pauses.

Then she sees that the garage door is open, the car still inside, nestled in debris. A man in a painter's cap and sweatshirt stands in the driveway, arms akimbo, looking at it.

Lou takes a deep breath. Noel Coward, not Mamet, she thinks. "Thank God! I found it!" She runs up to the man, grabs his arm. "How did it get here? Oh, God, I thought I was going crazy!" Lou is channeling Jackie and surprises herself at how well she can babble. "I went out this morning, and there was no car! I knew I had driven it to my cabin yesterday, nobody drove me here like last time, but it wasn't there! I'm so relieved! How did it get here?"

By now the man has pulled his arm away from her and is scratching his head. "Yours?"

"Yes, mine! It must have been stolen, hot lined, I think they call it, teenagers out for a joy ride, scaring me to death!" She steps into the garage, jumps over teetering piles of drywall debris. "Thank you, thank you!"

She has the keys in one hand, the other on the door handle, when the man says, "No. No," and moves toward her. "No take. Boss come."

Lou opens the door, slides in and starts the motor. *"No problemo,"* she says, grinning through the window as she puts the car in reverse. "I tell him. *Yo esta esposa."* She doesn't know how to say grandmother, a more likely relationship, in Spanish. She rolls her hand from her mouth to him as if words will soon flow to her husband, the boss, and backs the car out, crunching her way to the driveway and then to the road. *"Adios,"* she calls as she pulls away.

A pickup truck passes her along the way down, and she decides this isn't time to stop and investigate what she is dragging under the car. She's pretty sure it isn't the worker. Too tinny.

41

Monday Morning: Ebb Tide
Jackie

Jackie can't decide what to do with her hair, what's left of it. She can feel three ugly stubs along the base of her hair-line in back, and despite what Joan says, they show when she bends her neck down, like she's into punk, old-woman style. "Joan, come in here!"

Joan has returned her well-ordered blond self, at least on the outside. Hard telling about the rest of her, or any of them, at this point. Roger is quiet on the deck; Lou is using up the last of the hot water in the shower. None of them has said anything about this morning, about Madge. Maybe they've said it all by now. Or perhaps the scene beyond the point will be what they talk about next time they meet. Time heals, like they say.

"Joan, you've got to do something with my hair."

Joan takes the brush and begins on Jackie's head. "It'll grow out." She lifts the top layer in back, touches the bristles underneath. "Maybe. You gave your all, my dear. You deserve a medal. Or a wig." She pulls what's left of the curly black hair back into a soft low bun, turns Jackie's head so she can see it. "Hardly shows. You just need a big clip to hold it there."

Jackie hardly recognizes herself in the mirror. The wild black cloud of hair she has had for years is tamed. She likes the face, the chin especially, that has emerged. Her hands may be bad, but her neck has survived the years. Better than Joan's new one, in fact. She hadn't noticed with all that hair. She'll keep it mostly black, though, to go along with the great neck. Contributing black hairpieces to a mussel collector in need of a disguise may have worked out okay for everyone.

"You'll never have to feel bad about your neck," Joan says. "Or any other part of your body." Once again, Joan is mind-reading like good friends do.

"None of us has to feel bad about anything." Lou has come out of the shower wrapped in a towel. "What's next, Joan?"

"The boys are coming this afternoon. I imagine Lucius will be by, too, to tie things up. We need to tidy up, get rid of the pile of hair in the bathroom basket, for one thing.

Unless you want it back for a keepsake, Jackie? And maybe cook something for dinner? Pasta?"

Jackie chooses to clean up rather than cook, and says goodbye to three rubberbanded hanks of hair as she dumps the basket into a plastic bag. A bit drastic, she thinks, but Lucius will never connect the hairy mussel collector with the sleek man on the deck, a slightly balding, gray-haired fellow who has just arrived in the rental car outside, the car with the strip of drywall metal still dangling from its undersides, according to Lou who was too exhausted to do anything about it.

Jackie goes out with the garbage and lies down on the driveway. She forces her fingers to bend around the aluminum strip and in a moment, has it loose in her hand. She tosses it with the plastic bag into the can. When she finishes vacuuming, she'll offer Roger a drink. Then they'll sit on the deck and be quiet together.

42

Monday Afternoon: Doldums
Lou

Lou finds chicken breasts in the freezer and half a dozen tomatoes in the bowl on the counter. She chops on an onion and decides to throw in a carrot and what's left of the celery too. Garlic. Onion. Her thoughts are elsewhere, on the mountain, with Susan, wandering through the forest cabin, remembering her sons sitting under the firs. "Are you scared?" they asked. She had answered no. But she had been. Until Susan, first, then this week, when the love she thought she'd never have came rushing towards her with such spectacular results—Susan who cared for her despite or because of her aloneness, a set of friends who chose to tell the truth to each other and to lie for each other.

Esposa, indeed. She can hardly wait to tell Susan that story. The chopping done, the chicken and tomatoes cooked, the water heating, she pours a glass of wine and joins the silent Jackie and Roger outside. The sun is finally out. Lou leans back. A line of pelicans skims the waves below her. Waves have swept away the day's footsteps.

43

Monday Afternoon: Swells
Joan

Joan, looking things over, finds the walking stick next to
the door and replaces it on the mantel. The tide must have
brought it in, she'll say. What else will she need to explain?
The guesses about a lover? In case it comes up while the
sons are here? Stress, of course. No one wanted to believe
the truth; they were all grabbing at straws. What if Jim or
Grant mentions the Alzheimer's to Lucius? Well, she had
her good and her bad days. They knew, but she was herself,
more than herself, sharing her writing, in a good mood, the
mood they had mentioned to him before, the day they had
arrived. Madge had apparently felt so good she was going to

surprise them with mussel stew. A recipe for it lay on top of the fridge. Anything else?

She lies down but cannot close her eyes. Where will they all sleep tonight? Perhaps the one B&B in the village has room—or the motel in the town. Is that her problem? She decides it is, and she gets up to call the number Madge has listed in her phone book. The B&B has two rooms. Someone can sleep on the couch. Joan goes back to the bedroom, sinks into a pillow, and wonders what else she has forgotten.

Joan knows what's happening. She's obsessing about details in order avoid thinking about her return to her life in San Francisco. Abruptly, something blue-panted-Bill said, one of his aphorisms spoken in jest about himself and his golf, pops into her head. Pride goeth before the fall. The fall. Her fall. The pride part she can accept, but she can't let herself imagine how far the fall will be, how her life will change. Damn that cheerful fountain of platitudes, she thinks, with an angry twitch that sends an earring clattering to the floor. He's set her up for a psychic break. A knock at the door delivers her from this dismal thought. The others can't hear it, so she slips on her shoes and goes to answer it.

Monday Afternoon: Detritus
Lucius

Lucius holds the plastic bag in the crook of his arm, as if he is protecting its contents. He isn't, of course. The wet, torn clothes need no special treatment unless one considers that they are the last things to touch their wearer before she drowned and thus are sacred. Which, of course, they might be to the women to whom he's delivering them. He knocks again.

The door is opened by Joan, as he knew it would be. Joan is the leader, even now, maybe especially now. Lou is the thinker, the one who watches. Jackie is the clown, making them laugh even when she's crying. Despite everything, especially his suspicion of women in general, Lucius has decided he likes them. They are plucky, a word he's never found a use for until now. Strong, loyal, good liars when they have to be. Madge, too, he's pretty sure. Maybe he'll find out the reason for the lies today. Maybe he doesn't want to know. He steps in, hands the bag to Joan.

"Madge's clothes, right?" She takes the bag and sets it beside the door. We'll wash them and put them with her other things for her sons." At his look, she adds, "This afternoon. Roger's already here." She gestures towards the deck and Lucius sees two women and a man through the glass doors. "Do you want to meet him?"

Lucius does. As he walks through the living room he notices the walking stick on the mantel and goes to it. "A real keepsake," he says. It is damp under his fingers.

"Yes. We're glad it washed up for us to find. A little like a message in a bottle, an hello, a miracle, really, considering all of the places it could have wound up."

Joan leads him to the deck. "Take this chair. I'll get one from inside."

The man, Roger, opens his eyes and frowns a little as if he's trying to figure out who Lucius might be. His eyelids are heavy, his face lined and pale. As he sits up, Roger turns his head, and Lucius sees that his graying hair is pulled back into a soft tail. Lucius isn't against ponytails, but this guy seems a little old for one. At least it isn't a mullet. Lucius reminds himself that he once wore a mullet, back in his hockey days. No need to be judgmental. Besides, Roger may be of assistance in clearing up a couple of things.

"When did you get in?"

"This morning...while you were out at the point."

"Didn't think there was a local flight from the city in the morning."

"There wasn't. I rented a car and drove after I got off the redeye from Lincoln. I came as fast as I could after Joan called. But not soon enough." Roger looks out to the water, does not go on.

"I'm sorry. I have a couple of questions I have to ask." Lucius leans forward, wonders if the man is listening. "What was Madge Slocum's state of mind the last time you saw her?"

Joan answers instead. "She was fine, happy, looking forward to seeing us, to a holiday. Why are you asking?" Her unsmiling gaze warns him that he's going too far. Roger resumes his survey of the ocean's movement.

Lucius shrugs, turns back to Joan. She's not about to reach out, touch his arm. "Routine. An accidental death has to be confirmed, just like any other kind. Most of the facts point towards an accidental drowning. A few don't"

Jackie pushes up her sunglasses. "Like what?"

Lucius hesitates, decides to say it, despite Joan's dark frown. "Like the abrasions on her face. The coroner will determine if they happened before or after death. And, I'm sorry to have to mention this, the metal stake through the jacket. If she hadn't been wedged under the rock, her body might have never been found, or it could have come up miles away. Mysteries, you know?"

"You're still considering the possibility she was murdered, aren't you?" Joan's question crackles with anger.

Murder or something else, Lucius wants to say. He isn't going to show his hand yet, but these folks are covering up something, even Roger in his shut-down condition. Why is one of his hands all beat up, scraped and raw? You don't get that kind of treatment on the redeye.

Lucius glances at Lou, silent, horizon-focused as usual. "Did she mention the low tide she marked in the book, like she was going to go around the point?" He won't get a straight answer, but whatever one he gets might help.

Lou turns to look at him, seems to be considering how to respond. "I've thought about this a lot, and I feel so guilty. When I got here I looked at the menus she had organized, and I said I had hoped that we'd be having mussels in the wine broth like she'd made once before. She got out the tide book and said that there would be a low tide the next morning, very early." Lou's face closes up, and Lucius can barely make out what she is saying over the surf's roar below them. "She said she was sorry, she just wasn't up to going out that early. It would be too cold." Lou shakes her head. "But she did."

Roger emerges from his torpor and reaches for Lou's hand. "No one blames you, Lou. No one."

"You jerk." Jackie again. She has planted herself between the sun and Lucius; she's frightening in her huge blackness. Squinting, he waits for a swinging fist. Her face moves in close. "We're just trying to get through this day, and here you are, insinuating things, making us feel even crappier, playing detective-God to make yourself important instead of the sheriff of a backwater town where the crime of choice is fucking cows. You need to leave."

She has a grip on his arm and has one side of him lifted when she grimaces. "Shit," she says, and drops him. He sees why. It's a wonder she can hang onto her pocket book with that hand. Her mouth still works. "Get out," she yells.

Lucius has learned one more thing about these women. They work well together. He lets himself out after telling Joan he will need to come back with papers for the sons. She says this evening would be good. The women will be leaving in the morning.

As he drives away, he goes over the evidence. A woman who knows the tides gets caught behind a rock in a cove and is unable to escape, in fact, is pinned down behind a rock, and on top of that, is weighed down by an illegal number of mussels in a pack she carries on the front of her body. The woman has not told anyone where she is going at 5:00 a.m., and no one hears her go. Her friends find her walking stick on the beach but do not report her absence until late that day. They say she might have a lover, might be somewhere close, but retract that idea a few hours later because she would never let them worry. They insist on a search party, which turns up nothing.

And then there's the walking stick, he tells himself, as he pulls up in front of his office.

Last night, when he remarked on the tide book and said they should go behind the point in the morning, it was as if the women had already decided to go and were waiting for him to suggest it. They go; they find their dead friend. So does a mussel hunter who makes it around the point before they do. A guy with a tall walking stick, a lot like the one that now lies on the mantel, wet.

Lucius pulls in front of his office, not willing to get out of the car until he completes the thought. Suppose the man with the bruised hands, this Roger, helped the women kill their friend. That would explain the strange vibes he receives every time he sees them. Motivation? Maybe money. Maybe she left her money to them. Shouldn't be hard to find out.

"My mom says everything's about money. Her and my dad watch Perry Mason every noon and it's always money." Liz has listened to his conjectures with the bright eyes of a paperback mystery lover. He probably shouldn't have told her his suspicions, at least before they got to be somewhat more substantiated, but who else was there? Times like this he misses his first wife, who at least pretended she was listening, among other things. However, in the telling, he begins to get the feeling that his ideas are all wet. None of those women would murder a friend, even if the friend isn't really a friend. He'd bet his retirement on that, once he tries to imagine Lou and Jackie and Joan sitting down and planning it like Madge's menus. Even for money. Especially for money, despite what Liz's mother says.

Maybe the sons will shed some light on this. Lucius tells Liz to close up the office and heads to the practice range. A bucket of balls will settle his stomach if not his doubts. On the way out, he picks up a pink telephone message Liz has left in the IN basket. Jack Marshall, the guy building the McMansion up on the hill, wants him to know that an old lady is using the garage. Does he have to post a security guard or what?

Liz has not indicated what tone of voice the Or What was delivered in. He wads the paper and tosses it toward the wastebasket.

45

Monday Afternoon: Blowout
Lou

"So far, so good." Jackie's little diatribe seemed to impress Lucius, and all that remains now is to tell Jim and Grant today's sad story. At least one version of it, the one Madge wanted her sons to hear. This may be the hardest part. Lou looks through the window at the devastated man in the lounge chair and realizes that it is his to tell. Madge would have thought it a bit ironic. She hopes Roger can do it. She moves through the sliding door and sits down beside him.

When Jim and Grant arrive an hour later, Lou answers the door, and they look at her and know. She brings them into the living room where the others wait, and Roger rises to meet them, extending a hand, then collapsing against each of them in turn. "Tell us," the sons say. The women are silent as Roger describes how he arrived early, went to the point ahead of the sheriff and the others because he knew in his heart what he would find, and he wanted to be the one to find her. He tells of the full mussel bag, the tire iron that held her under the rock so that she had been found, the carrying of her body out of the cove and then to the hospital.

Lou can hardly stand to hear his words, to know what he is not saying, to realize the courage it is taking to tell this story. She turns away, wipes her eyes on her sweatshirt, sees Jackie reach for a cocktail napkin.

"A terrible accident," Roger says. "Your mother was taken by the sea she loved. We'll never know if she lost track of time, fell, or was overwhelmed by a sneaker wave. We'll never know."

The sons do not ask questions as he speaks. Tears wet Grant's cheeks. Jim looks toward the ocean, unmoving.

Lou bends to light a fire. Her own sons will weep when she dies, like these two sons, despite what they will know about her as time goes by. Sons are quick to forgive their mothers. These sons have forgiven theirs for becoming ill. They will also forgive her for dying and disrupting the rhythm of their lives.

Grant speaks. "You said she was okay the day she disappeared. Was she, Lou?"

She doesn't have to lie. Yes, Madge was okay. She knew exactly what she was about. She was looking forward to the next few days. Lou does not say that Madge's words lay in her lap that first night, were read in hesitant phrases, pages turning softly. They do not need to know any of that. Or how Madge burned those pages early the next morning, the warm ashes fluttering and sinking in the coals as the others woke up, found her gone. She does not tell them of the walk the three of them had taken along Madge's ocean, grieving as the ashes cooled.

The sons go out on the beach, their strides in counterpoint across the rough dunes, shoulders brushing, jarring missteps. When they reach the hard wet sand, their legs find a rhythm, the slow beat of a mourning drum, perhaps. Lou, watching from the window above them, believes she sees their hands touching as their bodies blend into one moving entity below her. She turns, feeling a breath on her neck, and finds Jackie and Joan standing behind her, also watching. "We're like them, aren't we?" Jackie says. "In this together."

"Yep," Joan answers, "and we're not quite finished."

46

Monday Late Afternoon: Seventh Wave
Lucius

What old lady? Lucius has just shot a ball two hundred and fifty yards toward the back fence and in the midst of a flood of heady satisfaction, the question floats to the surface. When he and Liz scoured the village, they found very few old ladies with the exception of the three at Madge's beach house.

A phone call later, he discovers that the Hispanic worker has the license number of the car in his pocket. A drive past the Madge's beach house confirms it is the same as that of the car parked in the driveway when he came by this morning. Another car, also a rental, is parked next to it. The sons have arrived. Lucius pulls up behind them. A few months ago, he and his grandson found out that at some point, a person has to dig fast with both hands bring up a razor clam. A lot like now. He'll have to meet the sons first, though, before he starts digging.

Jackie answers the door. Despite her sad eyes, she looks good, her wild hair tamed against her neck, her lips red and curved in welcome. "Come in, Lucius," she says. "I was about to have a glass of wine. Will you join me?" Lucius says yes and looks around. A pot on the kitchen stove is bubbling a little, Italian, he guesses from the smell of garlic. Jackie watches him glancing at the emptiness of the living room and says, "They're all out on the beach. Jim and Grant are taking their mother's death very hard." She hands him a glass of red wine. "Roger, too. We're all screwed up." She leads him to the couch. "Sorry I yelled at you this morning. Joan reminded me later that you were just doing your job."

She's pretty calm, Lucius thinks, *for a woman who was screaming like a banshee three hours earlier.* This probably isn't her first drink of the day, the way she's leaning back against a pillow like she is in total control of herself, of everything. He watches as she drains her glass and sets it on the trunk in front of them.

"You seemed uncomfortable with things this morning, like there is something..." she pauses, raises her eyes, "wrong with Madge's death, not that it wasn't wrong to begin with." She blinks away the wetness gathering on her eyelashes. "I mean, suspicious. Right?"

In different circumstances, Lucius might believe that now it is Jackie who was coming on to him, but she is so still against her pillow, so sad, he wonders if it's maybe meds, not him, she's experiencing. Maybe she really is cracking up, as he guessed she might the first day he met her.

A good time to start the digging, maybe. He settles his wine glass next to hers, their knees almost touching.

"I hate this part of my job," he says. "Dotting all the *i*'s before I can close the file. I do have a couple more questions."

Before he can begin, Jackie asks him to bring out the bottle of zin from the kitchen. She'd like a little more. So would he, she says. And she'll answer as truthfully as she can.

He pours them both another glass, takes a swallow, and plunges in. "Why was Roger here a day before you said he had come?"

Jackie hesitates, fingers brushing her lips as if to grant them forgiveness for what they are about to say. "He loved her. So much that he disobeyed her instructions, took the risk of being caught. He had to be a part of it all."

"Caught?"

"In the know, about the plan. No one was supposed to know. Except us three, of course." Jackie shook her head, looked into her glass. "I knew it couldn't work, right from the beginning. Even if Madge had planned everything down to the last detail. The others wouldn't listen to me."

"Madge planned her death?"

"Of course."

"Why all the—"

"Because of the insurance. Roger can't be involved in any way. Her sons will get her estate, her books, the houses, but the insurance is for Roger. But only part of it if they know she's killed herself." Tears wander down her strong jaw and drop to her breast. Lucius wishes he had a handkerchief to hand her.

"And her sons. Madge didn't want them to know."

Lucius doesn't get it. "Know what? They had to know that she died. Dead is dead. What difference would it make, how?"

Of course, it would make a difference, Lucius realizes. Which would be easier to accept, a mother who drowned or a mother who abandoned them? Even he, having experienced some abandonment himself, knows the answer to that question.

His hand finds its way to Jackie's knee. She wipes away the trail of tears on her chin with a sleeve and looks down at his fingers, silent.

"I'm sorry," he says. "The question should be, 'Why?'"

Her leg moves under his hand as she turns toward him. "She couldn't write any more. She was losing all her words. She was losing all of her people, even the boys. She was losing her world. If she had to lose all this, she wanted to lose it on her own terms." Jackie's brown eyes rise to his, unblinking, steady. She is asking something of him.

Yes, plucky, loyal, good liars, except that these women are even more courageous when they tell the truth. Lucius understands they are daring him to be as brave, to join the plot, finish Madge's story the way she had planned. He considers the idea for a moment, and he can't think why he shouldn't. Like he said, dead is dead. He squeezes her knee in answer. He likes the smile she gives him, likes that it is his hand on her, not the reverse.

"Must have been a sneaker wave," he says, "like you all guessed."

Monday Evening: Moonlit Ripple
Joan

Jim and Grant have gone off to the B&B to sleep, perhaps, and to meet with Lucius and the doctor in the morning to make the arrangements for Madge. They will also deal with journalists creating their obituaries for a writer no one anticipated would die mid-novel and nowhere near the end of a successful run. Roger, sleeping at the moment in the back bedroom, will talk with Madge's publisher, her agent, other literary hangers-on.

Her three friends will pack and leave. But not quite yet. In the morning. At the moment, they are lounging in front of the fire, the dark windows reflecting flickers of soft faces, a moving chiaroscuro scene, Joan thinks.

"Jackie, we love you. No one else could have done it. Really. A confession from a woman who a few hours before wanted to duke it out with him. His suspicions confirmed. His ego plumped up to overflowing. His hand on your knee." Joan is feeling the wine, but she knows the truth of what she says. She tips her glass at the other two, and Lou adds, "You betchum, Red Rider." She also has had a couple drinks and has put aside the medieval English for the moment.

"Lucius isn't a bad guy, you know." Jackie's eyes have lit up at Joan's compliment, and she is spreading the credit around. "You were right, Joan. I didn't have to get hysterical or anything, like you said. He understood right away."

Lou grins. "I loved the way you just let his hand be there, silently connecting the two of you."

"Knee cap Morse code. Joan taught me."

"A handy skill." Joan is lying on the couch and tries not to spill her wine as she lifts it to her lips. Impossible. She sits up. "I couldn't do it; he was getting gun-shy around me, antsy, like he wasn't sure what I'd touch next. We needed a surprise attack. You, Jackie, who couldn't ever stay in the same room with Lucius without getting mad or sick." Joan empties her glass and reaches for the bottle. "And we need to drink to our Mexican buddy who ratted on us, and to a still-damp piece of wood which gave it all away, and to our dear friend Madge who inspired us to rise above our mundane ambitions and become story tellers of the highest ilk."

"Hear, hear," Lou says. "And to you, Joan, who realized in time that we were in deep shit, story-telling wise."

"What's ilk?" Jackie asks.

"Doesn't matter," Joan answers.

Jackie pouts. "You're doing it again."

"And you enjoy it."

"I'll miss her."

Lou nods. "But she left us a lot to remember her by. Including her versions of our lives in *Think on These Things.*"

Joan lets an idea flit through her, cause her heart to quicken. "I recorded what we said last night, for no good reason. Maybe we could finish her book somehow. Our goodbye gift?"

"A new take on closure? I hate that word."

Joan knows it's not the word Lou hates, of course, it's the reason the word exists. "And I hate goodbye, too. How about a project to keep Madge alive and part of us?"

"We could dedicate the book to our friendship, to solariums, to..."

"Finding things of good report. For women like us who might be wondering if such things exist. Madge would like that."

"Don't look at me," Jackie says. "My talent lies in impressing sheriffs. I majored in P.E., remember?"

"But Roger could put Madge's book together." Lou's bare feet hit the floor as she sits up, wine splashing onto her toes. "He's been reading and editing her books for a long time. What do you think, Joan? Only please hold up publication until I talk to my sons?" She sighs. "They're in for a surprise."

"You've got a year at least. By then they'll know, and it'll be okay." Joan realizes this last Madge project is possible, runs her tongue over her upper lip. "I've only a day or two before I will finish up my story." She nods at Jackie. "Maybe just a 'Fuck off and go pray somewhere.' Only with Brian it will be, 'Go stray somewhere.'" She'll have time to practice on the drive to San Francisco. It'll be a short sweet speech, attached to a short sweet plan for dividing their goods, for renewing one season opera ticket, not two, for dumping a dream, learning to live free.

"We're about done here, aren't we?" Jackie looks exhausted by her success, their success. And Joan knows, by the flood of sadness filling this flame-flickered room, a sadness that no amount of wine and laughter can hold back.

Lou closes her eyes. "I'm not sure I'm through crying."

"We won't ever be, do you think?" Joan murmurs.

Jackie yawns, perhaps too drained to think about that sad idea. "Madge would say that old ladies need their sleep."

"And that tomorrow's another day." Joan hears his wise voice, the man in the periwinkle golf pants again.

"Whatever that means. Like is that hopeful?"

Lou sits up. "It's the best we've got, Jackie. Madge taught us that, didn't she?" She pulls her cat pajama leg over a skinny shin, shifts to get up.

Jackie yawns again. "A little like jumping out window, I think."

California Girl takes over. "We have to move Roger to the couch. Or the three of us could sleep on it like in college, falling into each other's bony legs and hips."

"Waking up with cramps."

"Spilling cold black coffee down our robes."

"Talking about sex."

"Instead of doing it."

"Speak for yourself."

"Don't brag, Jackie."

"I still can't get over how Lucius knew what we wanted him to do. He just gave my knee a squeeze, said, 'Okay. Probably a sneaker wave.' And then he and got up and left. We should probably thank him."

Lou sighs one more time, stands, makes her way to the kitchen with the wine bottle and the glasses. "Methinks you'll find a way, friend. Let's move Roger. We're way too old for the couch."

ABOUT THE AUTHOR

After graduating from Willamette University, Jo spent the
most of next thirty years teaching, counseling, mothering,
wifing, and of course, writing.

Her writing first appeared in small literary magazines and
professional publications. Since retirement, she has had time
to write four novels and two screenplays.

Her stories and essays, as well as the novels, reflect her
observations of women's lives and the people who inhabit
them: the children, husbands, parents, friends, and strangers
who happen by and change everything.

Do you love the Penner Publishing book you've just finished?

Great books deserve great readers.

Please review this book on your favorite retailer, bookish site, blog or on your own social media.

Penner Publishing is a boutique publisher specializing in women driven fiction. We love our romance heroines saucy or sweet. We also love a great story even when there isn't a hot hero involved. It's all about the woman's journey.

Be sure to visit us at:
www.pennerpublishing.com/readers-club
Facebook.com/pennerpub
Twitter.com/pennerpub

CPSIA information can be obtained
at www.ICGtesting.com
Printed in the USA
FSOW01n1334310716
23279FS